Protected

Atlanta's Finest Series

Sharon C. Cooper

Amaris Publishing LLC

PROTECTED
By
Sharon C. Cooper

Prologue

Maverick "Wolf" Farron glanced out the window of the black Escalade as his driver, Thomas, pulled to a stop in front of one of the well-hidden warehouses. As the leader of Diego Kingz, the most feared organized crime syndicate in Southern California, Wolf often had to make an example of people. Like today. Today he would show his crew what happened to those who betrayed him. A lasting reminder of how important loyalty was in their business.

Thomas parked in front of the warehouse, then opened the back door of the vehicle. Wolf stepped out and gave the industrial area a cursory glance. Despite it being the middle of August, unlike other parts of the country this time of summer, locals enjoyed the breezy seventy-eight degrees. Birds chirped, and Wolf soaked up the sounds of nature as he released a long breath.

He had purchased the property, three hundred acres outside of San Diego, almost twenty years ago. Now it was valued in the millions, and it was just one of a few good business decisions he'd made.

1

To anyone looking in from the outside, the land was used by a construction company. The factory, heavy equipment, and a few other buildings could be seen from the street. No one could see this warehouse tucked away from the road with mountains as its backdrop.

Elder, Wolf's head lieutenant and one of Wolf's oldest friends, exited the building. "Hey, Boss."

"Is everything set up?" Wolf asked and rolled up the sleeves of his white dress shirt that was a stark contrast against his dark skin.

Elder nodded. "Yes. Just waiting for you."

Wolf's heart hardened as he and Elder strolled toward the rollup door. There'd been a time when he trusted his crew above all else, but now that they'd discovered a traitor in his inner circle, there were changes to be made.

Wolf should've known this could happen again. He'd made that mistake of trusting the wrong person once before, and the Kingz ended up in a gang war with the Euclid Disciples, one of their rivals. It hadn't ended well for either side. After losing several of his men in brutal deaths, Wolf had found out that his own flesh and blood—his son—had been the one to betray him.

Never again. Never would his son be able to double-cross him again.

Thinking about that time in his life sent fury coursing through Wolf's veins. The duplicity had cut deep and was unforgivable, but Wolf had made sure it would never happen again. Killing his son had been his only choice and one of the hardest things he'd ever had to do. But he'd had to use his death as an example to the others who thought they could deceive him and get away with it.

Now, here he was again showing the Kingz that he wouldn't tolerate disloyalty.

Wolf stopped inside the building and removed his

sunglasses, tucking them into the pocket of his shirt. While Slick, one of their captains, pulled down the overhead door, locking them inside and keeping the outside world outdoors, Elder filled Wolf in on the latest.

"It didn't take long to find Franz. He was holed up in some woman's basement," Elder, whose real name was Roger Thompson, said close to Wolf's ear.

His friend was tall and formidable. They'd grown up together in Lincoln Heights, one of Los Angeles's roughest neighborhoods. Products of drug-addicted parents, they couldn't wait to be on their own and both had left home at sixteen.

Living on the streets at that age had been hard as hell, but they'd survived, thanks to an OG who had taken them under his wing. He'd introduced them to gang life, a community of brotherhood. Now, over forty years later, Wolf was known in these parts as one of the meanest, most badass leaders around.

"Once word got to the woman that we were looking for Franz, she wanted him out of her house. Long story short, we picked him up, and he's hanging in the back."

They moved further into the dimly-lit space. A few light fixtures hung from the rafters, but the windows near the ceiling were the main source of sunlight. The space imitated an auto garage with ten bays that hosted several vehicles in various states of repair. Auto parts and miscellaneous supplies added to the desired effect of making the garage look legit.

Moments later, they entered the torture chamber, a well-hidden room at the back of the building. As twisted as it might seem, peace settled over Wolf. His gaze took in twenty of his most trusted soldiers, standing at attention in a semi-circle. All heights, sizes, and builds, they looked lethal standing before him with their arms behind them and their feet spread shoulder width apart.

Yeah, these were the men who he knew had his back. The ones who he could count on for anything, even murder. And today they'd get a firsthand lesson on what happened when they betrayed him.

Wolf's gaze landed on the man in the middle of the space with thick plastic on the floor beneath him. He hung from the rafters with chains wrapped around his wrists. No doubt Franz's arms felt as if they were going to fall off since his feet were dangling several inches off the ground. He'd been hanging there for a while.

Slick handed Wolf a pair of white, waterproof overalls to slip into over his clothes. These interrogations tended to get a little messy, and this one would be worse. Normally, he brought people into this room to force answers out of them, but Wolf already had his answers. Franz had thought it was okay to start a side hustle using some of the Kingz's product. His stupid ass should've known he wouldn't get away with it.

"Just shoot me," Franz said, his breaths coming in short spurts. His head was cocked to the side as sweat and blood dripped from his battered face.

Wolf chuckled as he slipped on a pair of thick gloves. "And give you an easy death? What would be the fun in that? Besides, you wouldn't want to deprive me of the opportunity to torture you, right?"

All humor left Wolf's tone as he approached a rolling cart that held chains, hand tools, power tools, and a torch. He grabbed a thick chain and wrapped it around his right hand, covering his knuckles.

"Wolf, please! Don't! I gave Slick the money that I made," Franz cried. "Please! I'm sorry. It won't happen again."

"You're damn right it won't happen again!" Wolf roared, startling a few who looked on.

4

He allowed his gaze to lock onto everyone standing around to witness what was about to take place.

"Let this be a lesson to all of you. If you *ever* think about betraying me or the Kingz, remember this day. You don't get to steal from me, and if any of you try the same shit that Franz tried, this will only be a *taste* of what I'll do to you."

Wolf punched Franz in his left side, and the chain punctured the skin there, and blood trickled out. He was also sure that he had broken a rib or two if the man's screams were any indication. He put all his six-feet-two inches and two hundred and forty pounds behind his next punch. Then Wolf followed that up with another one-two jab to Franz's torso as if he was getting a workout in on a punching bag.

It would've been bad enough if he'd just used his fists, but the thick chain added a hundred percent more pain. A few members of their crew flinched with each punch. Maybe they were empaths and could physically feel the hits themselves. Others cursed under their breaths.

Wolf didn't let up. This felt good. It felt too damn good to work off some of his fury that had been building since finding out what Franz had done. He didn't have to kill the guy, a good ass-whooping would suffice, but he had to follow through with his plan. He had to teach everyone present a lesson that they'd never forget.

When Franz's screams quieted, his head hung awkwardly to the side as he fell in and out of consciousness. His breaths were ragged, and it was safe to say at least his broken ribs had punctured one of his lungs.

Wolf nodded to Elder and Slick to unhook the man. They set him in a nearby chair, then wrapped a rope around him to keep him upright.

"Please...no more," Franz barely managed to say, his voice hoarse and nasal as he struggled to breathe.

5

Wolf had no sympathy for people who weren't loyal to him. He tossed his chain on the rolling cart of tools and grabbed the blowtorch. Some of the Kingz watching looked as if they were going to be sick.

Good. The lesson was going over better than expected.

"Almost done," Wolf soothed as he lit the torch. "Almost done."

Chapter One

"Do I stay, or do I go?" Parker Wilcox mumbled into the quietness of his vehicle.

He leaned his head against the headrest of his SUV and stared out the truck's windshield at the numerous vehicles in the parking lot. It was his day off, yet he was at Supreme Security, where he worked, trying to decide if he should move forward with his plan.

Resign.

Relocate.

Restart.

It wasn't an easy decision. He didn't want to go. Yet, his life, and everyone's around him, could be in danger. It was bad enough he was taking the chance with his own well-being. He couldn't continue doing that with the people he'd come to care about.

Parker's mind drifted to the conversation he'd had with his boss, Mason Bennett, four months ago.

. . .

"You're going to have to lay low for a while," Mason said, and woke up his laptop by moving the mouse.

"Okaaaaay," Parker said slowly. "What happened?"

Mason turned his computer around so Parker could see the screen with a photo that had showed up on national news and the internet.

"Aw, hell," he growled. He turned and punched the air before linking his fingers behind his head. "I wasn't thinking. Damn, I should've been more careful."

One of the cameramen outside the courthouse had managed to get a photo of Journey, and Parker was partially in the frame. His head was slightly turned, but despite the cosmetic surgery he'd undergone many years ago, anyone who knew him before then might still be able to recognize him.

"I'm sorry, man," Mason said. "Had I known Journey would be bombarded by the media, there's no way I would've let you be on her detail. We should've known that this could happen one day."

"No apology necessary. If it weren't for you giving me a chance at a normal life, I don't know what I would've done. Hell, I don't even know if I'd still be alive. I'll lay low, but if my father or his people happen to see that photo, it won't take long for them to find out who I work for or where."

"Yeah, we'll cross that bridge when we get to it, but your dad doesn't want to go to war with us. Because that's exactly what will happen if he or his crew come knocking. Parker, you're family, and we take care of family."

"What do you want me to do? Leave town? Leave the country?"

"No, I want you to stay close so we can have your back," Mason said. "You can work the front desk for a few weeks...or months. Who knows, maybe we'll get lucky, and your father and his crew will still believe that you're dead."

. . .

Parker closed his eyes and released a noisy breath as thoughts bombarded his mind.

As far as he knew, his father, Maverick "Wolf" Farron, had no idea he was alive. Still, there was always a chance he'd find out. As the leader of Diego Kingz, an organized crime syndicate out of San Diego, the mean son of a bitch's reach was long. Maybe Wolf would never find out, but what if he did?

Parker's eyes snapped open, and he straightened. "I can't take that chance."

But the last thing he wanted to do was leave his team at Supreme Security. Or, as Mason referred to them—Atlanta's Finest. The team was made up of former military and ex-law enforcement personnel from every branch of government who traded in their badges to become personal security specialists. They provided protection for the rich and famous, and they were the best of the best. They had also become Parker's family. His *only* family.

And then there was Chelsey. Chelsey Bailey, the woman he was crazy in love with.

"Dammit!" He pounded his fist against the steering wheel and ignored the pain that shot up his arm. Thinking about her made his heart hurt. "How the hell am I going to leave town and leave her behind?"

Yes, he had broken things off with her months ago after his and Mason's talk, but he still loved her. However, knowing there was a chance that his father would come after him, he couldn't risk Chelsey's life any more than he already had.

Parker knew what he had to do and with that thought, he climbed out of the vehicle. Locking his SUV, he pocketed his keys and made his way to the back door of the converted warehouse. Years ago, Mason had fitted the building with state-of-the-art everything, and that included the security system.

Jogging up the few concrete stairs, Parker stopped in front of the call box and placed his hand against the sophisticated palm reader. Within seconds, the back door clicked open. Even though there were cameras everywhere, and someone monitoring who entered and exited the building, he hoped he didn't run into anyone. He wanted to get in and out without stopping to talk.

He headed for the back stairs to the executive floor where the bosses' offices were located. The area was, for the most part, quiet, except for a few voices that could be heard behind closed doors.

Good. No one in sight. Not even Egypt.

Egypt Durand-Bailey was the office manager and practically ran the company. Parker and the guys called her the queen of Supreme Security because she knew everything about everything. Mason and Hamilton Crosby might've been the bosses, but she was the person running shit.

Parker approached Mason's office door, hoping he was still available. The man was as busy as the president of the United States and could've easily been called away.

Parker knocked and Mason responded immediately. "Come in."

He pushed the door open and glanced across the room. "Still got time to talk?"

"Yeah."

Mason, a former Marine, sat behind his desk. He was a big man at over six feet tall with a bald head, chiseled, dark features, and a muscular build. Even sitting, he was an imposing figure.

Parker moved further into the office, his black motorcycle boots quiet against the plush carpet. The space was huge with beige walls graced with paintings, oversized masculine furniture, and photos of his family on several flat surfaces. Two, upholstered chairs sat in front of the desk, and Parker gripped the back of one of them as he glanced at his boss.

Mason eyed him for a couple of seconds and then tossed his ink pen onto the desk. "I'm surprised you wanted a meeting on your day off. What's happened?"

That was code for—*Have you heard from your father?*

Parker hadn't seen Wolf in at least fifteen years, and he planned to keep it that way. Yet, that photo, the one with Parker in it that the media had captured, could surface. It didn't matter that Cameron "Wiz" Miller, one of the company's owners and a tech guru scrubbed the internet in hopes of making the picture disappear, there was always a chance it was still out there.

"Everything's fine, except I'm leaving Supreme and Atlanta." The words tasted bitter on Parker's tongue because leaving his Atlanta's Finest team was akin to cutting off his right arm.

Still, he had no choice. He should've left a long time ago, instead of risking everyone's life.

Mason rocked back in his desk chair and sighed. Interlocking his fingers on top of his head, he stared at Parker. The man could be intimidating as hell even when he wasn't trying to be, but especially when he was staring you down.

In his late forties, Mason always carried himself professionally, and though he dressed like he worked in corporate America, there was still an air of danger about him. His facial hair was perfectly groomed, and the dark suit he wore made him appear larger than life. He looked like a boss man in more ways than one.

But he was more than Parker's boss. He was his mentor, his friend, his big brother. Fifteen years ago, he was also the guy who had found Parker, barely alive, lying face down in what could have easily become his grave.

Parker owed the man his life, and not once had Mason asked anything of him, except for him to never return to organized crime.

I should be dead. The words bounced around inside his head, but he pushed them to the back of his mind.

"I refuse to continue risking the lives of the guys here," Parker said. "As long as I stay, that's exactly what I'm doing. It's been four months, Mase, and even though nothing has happened as it relates to my father and the Diego Kingz, we can't take any more chances."

They'd had this conversation more than once, but Parker had finally made peace with the idea that he needed to move on. Or at least he was trying to. It was time to disappear—just in case.

"Is this about you being tied to the front desk for the last few months?" Mason asked.

"Seriously, Mase?"

Out of all that Parker had said, that's what the guy was coming back with?

Yes, Parker hated working the front desk. All the security team did. It was a mindless job, but someone had to do it. Years ago, after a threat on Egypt's life, a new rule had been implemented. There were to be armed security working the front desk 24/7. Prior to that, it had always been receptionists who monitored the entrances and the guests who entered the building.

But Parker wasn't cut out for desk work every day. He had moved to Atlanta from Chicago after spending years as a SWAT officer and a weapons specialist. A job he loved. The adrenaline rush, the energy, the danger. All of it. He had come here at Mason's request to join his Atlanta's Finest team. It ended up being the best decision Parker had ever made.

"I agree that having you monitor the front desk is a waste of your skills," Mason said. "However, it's the safest place for you right now."

Mason's cell phone, sitting face down on the desk, beeped, and he sighed as he glanced at the screen.

"I hate when Egypt's away from her desk. She hired a few new people and she's in the process of orientating them. She told me that I'm on my own for the rest of the afternoon. Meaning I need to take care of this."

Parker released a silent sigh. So much for getting in and out. "All right. I can—"

"You can stay right where you are. We aren't done." Mason headed for the door but stopped and glanced over his shoulder. "When I return, we'll talk about how you're *not* going anywhere. You don't get to walk away from us, Parker," he said, his tone hard and unwavering like the boss he was. "We're family and we stick together. You're protected. I wish Wolf's ass would show up here, because if he comes for you, he'll be coming for all of us. We both know that's a fight that won't end well for him. Now sit your ass down until I come back."

Stunned, Parker stood as he watched the man who he admired more than anyone in the world walk out the door and close it behind him.

Well, damn. I guess he told me.

Chapter Two

Parker dropped down into one of the guest chairs. Considering he had walked in there confident about his decision to leave Atlanta, now he wasn't so sure. If he was honest with himself, he didn't want to leave. He just thought it was the best decision to make sure he kept his *family* safe.

He rubbed his chin and glanced out the window that was behind the desk. Maybe there was nothing to worry about. Maybe he was freaking out for no reason. He had carried the burden of his past around for years, and it hadn't stopped him from living the life he desired. He had moved around the country for a while before settling on Chicago. He loved the city, and he had enjoyed being a SWAT officer.

Now that he resided in Atlanta, he felt like he was finally home. Even still, he was always alert, careful, and on guard. Yet, somehow, he'd managed to end up in a photo. Granted, he'd been on a high-profile case and they'd been ambushed by the media, but still, he should've been aware of the cameras.

Parker shook his head. Continuing to stay in Atlanta would

be a risk, but it wouldn't be the first risk he'd ever taken. Hell, he usually lived his life on the edge. This would be no different.

But what about Chelsey?

If he was staying, Parker had to make things right with her. His stupid ass shouldn't have broken things off in the first place. At least not without telling her why. At the time, he honestly thought he'd been doing the right thing. The less she knew about his past, the better. He also thought he would've left town by now, but no matter what he told himself, he wouldn't have been able to leave without her.

So if he did end up staying, he needed to come clean with her, and the guys he worked with. The guys who were more like brothers than co-workers.

Noise outside the office had Parker turning toward the closed door.

"Chelsey, I know what I said, and you did an excellent job on that assignment we gave you last weekend, but you still need more experience," he heard Mason say.

"Come on, Mase. The best way for me to get experience is by joining the security team and you giving me more field work. If I did such a good job at that party last week, why not hire me as a security specialist instead of an office assistant? Besides, you said yourself that you could use more women on the team."

Parker stiffened at hearing Chelsey's melodic, breathy voice. It was as if his thoughts had conjured her up.

A moment later, the door opened, and Mason strolled in, giving Parker a head nod as he continued to his desk.

Chelsey stomped into the room behind him. "You know I'm right. I..." Her words trailed off and she pulled up short just inside the doorway.

It was as if everything around them faded to black and they were the only ones left in the space. Parker had seen her from a distance, but this was the first time in weeks that he was close enough to breathe the same air as her.

His gaze slid slowly over her, and his body responded immediately. Increased heart rate. Pulse pounding in his ears. Sweaty palms. She was the most beautiful woman he knew. Her naturally curly hair was pulled back from her gorgeous face with a bedazzled headband, and the rest of her puffy curls hung free to her shoulders.

He liked when she wore her hair like that. It gave him a clear view of her smooth mocha skin, high cheekbones, and her bow-shaped lips.

Parker skimmed the rest of her body, from her low-cut red blouse to her dark pants that hugged her hips and covered her long legs. At five-feet-eight, she was the tallest woman he'd dated, and *dated* was being used loosely. Actually, she was the only woman he'd ever gotten serious with. The others were just women he hung out with.

Parker's eyes met her dark ones, and his heart kicked inside his chest at the vulnerability he saw in them.

Then she nibbled on her lower lip, and damned if his dick didn't twitch. He wanted to be the one nibbling on her gorgeous lips and other parts of her. In that moment, he wanted her more than his next breath. Of course, his body was on full alert and energized by every move she made.

All he could do was stare at Chelsey Bailey—the woman who held his heart in the palm of her hands and probably didn't even know it. But he was fairly sure she hated him, and rightfully so.

* * *

Crap! I knew I should've gone straight to work, Chelsey thought as she stared at the stupid bastard who had dumped her a few

16

months ago. She could call Parker a bastard now, but she'd once thought he'd be the man she would spend the rest of her life with.

Wrong.

Instead, he was the man who had broken her heart; not once, but twice. Actually, *bastard* was too good of a name for him. Asshole was much better.

But man...asshole or not, he still made her heart flutter at the sight of him.

How was that even possible? How could her body spark to life just by sharing the same airspace with him, especially when she was so pissed?

Her gaze swept the length of him, and though he looked fine as hell, Chelsey could tell that he had lost some weight. His face was thinner, and his strong jaw was more pronounced. It also looked as if he hadn't been sleeping well, if the bags under his eyes were any indication.

Nonetheless, that didn't detract from his good looks. His penetrating, whiskey-colored eyes bored into her as if he could see deep inside her soul.

God, she'd missed him. Missed their easy conversations. Not only was he easy to talk to, but he was a great listener. He also made her laugh, something they used to do all the time. More than anything, though, she missed his sweet kisses and being in his arms. What she wouldn't give for one of his bear hugs right now. They always made her feel as if all was well in the world.

Six feet tall with a muscular runner's build, he looked like a wet dream in the black Harley-Davidson T-shirt that molded over his chiseled chest and torso. And the medium wash jeans that weren't tight, but tight enough to show off his firm thighs and long legs, made her body stir with need.

She hadn't been with a man intimately since she and

Parker had broken up. Well, except for that slipup she'd had with him six weeks ago, but Chelsey was trying to forget that huge mistake. Still, seeing him had her horny. Which only pissed her off more. She didn't want to like Parker Wilcox, and she sure as hell didn't want to still be attracted to him.

Chelsey didn't know how long they stood there staring at each other without speaking, but it wasn't until Mason cleared his throat did she snap out of whatever trance she'd been under.

"Am I missing something here?" Mason asked. Chelsey jerked her attention to him as he looked from her to Parker and back again. "Do you two need me to leave so you can—"

"No!" They both said in unison, and Mason quirked an eyebrow.

"O-kay," he said slowly. "Then what the hell is going on?"

"Nothing, I was just leaving," Chelsey said and turned for the door, but glanced at Mason over her shoulder. "This isn't over, Mase. I'm not done pleading my case. You need more security specialists, and you and Egypt are wasting my talents by hiring me to work in the office. I'm just sayin'."

His chuckle followed her out of the office.

Chelsey unintentionally slammed the door behind her and hurried to the hallway that would lead her to the elevator. *Damn Parker for looking so good.*

Why'd he have to be there, today of all days? She'd been planning her visits to Supreme perfectly in an effort to not see him. Today was supposed to be his day off, and yes, she had checked. If her body betrayed her every time she saw him, what the heck was she going to do when she started working there full-time?

She shook her head. That was a question for another day, but one she'd have to think about.

When her sister-in-law, Egypt, suggested Chelsey apply for the office assistant position, she'd said no. But when Egypt mentioned that it might be a good way for Chelsey to get her foot in the door of Supreme, she reconsidered.

For years, after finishing her degree in criminal justice, she had been trying to get on at Supreme. Not only because the pay was outstanding, but also because she wanted the challenge. However, Mason was hard to impress. Supreme was known for hiring the best, and she considered herself the best. No, she didn't have experience with the FBI, CIA, DEA and any of the other agencies like most of the people on their team, but she'd been a cop for years, and now a parole officer. She knew she could do the job.

"Chelsey!"

She cursed under her breath at the sound of Parker's voice and kept walking. She'd take the stairs instead. No way would she get on an elevator and risk being in close quarters with his sexy ass.

"Chels, come on. Wait up."

"Go away, Parker," she said, but he caught her before she reached the doors to the stairs.

"I need to talk to you," he said quietly while glancing around. They had both agreed to keep their relationship a secret until they were ready, and when they were finally ready to go public, Parker dumped her.

Remembering that was like adding gasoline to a fire. Her anger sparked, and a barely contained growl rumbled inside of her chest.

"We don't have anything to talk about," she said through gritted teeth. "Now get out of my way unless you want to be walking funny for the rest of the day."

He flinched and took a step back, knowing that her ability to knee him in the balls came from practice. She had taken several self-defense classes over the years, some led by her brother, Kenton Bailey, a former FBI agent, and she could easily take down a man twice her size.

"Chelsey, please, baby. Let's go somewhere and talk. There's something I need to tell you."

She stepped forward, decreasing the distance between them. "The last time you wanted to talk to me, you talked me into your bed. Wait, no, that's not right. You talked me into a bed in one of the crash rooms."

Saying it out loud made her feel even stupider than she'd felt after their steaming rendezvous. She had stopped by Supreme one night when she knew Parker was on duty. Most of the guys didn't think much of seeing her since her brother and sister-in-law worked for the company. But Chelsey had been glad that she hadn't really known the new guy who was on duty with him, and Parker had been getting ready to take a break.

After their breakup, she had struggled to move on. She thought that if they talked, and he made her understand why he had broken things off with her so abruptly, that she could move on. The breakup hadn't made sense. No matter how she looked at it, no matter what he said, she couldn't come to terms with it.

Which was why she had needed to talk to him that night. But one thing led to another, and before she realized what she was doing, they were going hot and heavy in one of the crash rooms. Those rooms were usually for the guys who had back-to-back assignments and no time to go home. The small suites were located on one of the top floors and contained a bed, sitting area, and attached bathroom. And she and Parker had used one that night for a quick tryst.

Parker extended his hand to her. "Just come with me so we can talk."

Chelsey glanced down at his long, tapered fingers attached

to a strong hand that had brought her more pleasure than she could've imagined. But she couldn't go backward. She couldn't get caught up with this man only to have her heart broken yet again.

Twice was enough.

After their little tryst six weeks ago, she foolishly thought that meant they were going to give their relationship another try. *Wrong.* While they'd been pulling their clothes back on, Parker had told her that what they'd done had been a mistake. That it shouldn't have happened. Granted, he had looked contrite, as if saying the words were ripping him apart.

Still, that hadn't stopped her from slapping him, then punching him in the stomach before she ran out of the building.

Fueled by a renewed anger, Chelsey shoved his hand away, and then he made the mistake of blocking her path to the stairs. She needed to make a few things clear once and for all, because soon she'd be working for Supreme full-time. That meant they'd see each other daily.

They were standing inches apart, close enough for her to get a whiff of his intoxicating cologne. She had to be firm. She had to be strong. No way could she show weakness.

In a low, lethal voice, she said, "You blew any chance you had with me. So you can stand there and risk me kicking your ass, or you can get out of my way. I suggest you stay the hell away from me before you see how I deal with jerks."

Her threat was almost laughable. The guy had the ability to kill a man with his bare hands. Her threat to him was akin to throwing a water balloon on a forest fire—useless and pointless.

Parker huffed out a ragged sigh. "Dammit, Chelsey. We need to talk. It's important," he said, but still backed up. "At some point, you're going to have to—"

"You're dead to me, Parker," she said with more bravado

than she felt before shoving the door opened and running down the back stairs like her butt was on fire.

She was proud of herself. She didn't fall for his handsome face, pretty eyes, and that irresistible body that could make a grown woman beg for just a taste of him.

Nope, she was over him.

Never again. I will never let him get near my heart again.

Chapter Three

The moment the door closed behind Chelsey, Parker turned and punched the air with so much force, it was a wonder he didn't throw out his shoulder. Dammit! This situation with Chelsey was worse than he thought. It was going to take some serious groveling to get back into her good graces, and even that might not be enough.

His cell phone buzzed and for a second, he thought it might be her calling him. He pulled the device from his pants pocket and disappointment settled in. It wasn't her, but why the heck would he think it would be? She was the most stubborn woman in the world. No way would she be calling him for any reason anytime soon.

"Yeah," Parker growled into the phone, unable to keep the anger from his voice.

"You all right, man? I can stop Chelsey from leaving the building if you want," Laz, his friend and coworker, said. Parker's frustration spiked. "Or are you afraid she might actually kick your ass? I could totally see that."

Parker hung up the phone and then approached the closest

23

camera in the hallway, which was to his right, less than four feet away hanging near the ceiling. He lifted his middle finger and knew his buddy was falling out laughing. No doubt the jerk had listened to most, if not all, of the conversation.

Lazarus Dimas, who they all called Laz, was a former Atlanta PD detective who often skated on the line between right and wrong. He was also one of Parker's best friends who didn't miss anything. Though Parker hadn't been forthcoming about his relationship with Chelsey, Laz somehow found out. All he'd said was—*Kenton's going to kick your ass if or when he finds out, but I've got your back.*

Parker rubbed the back of his neck. What the hell had he been thinking confronting her in a hallway at Supreme? There were cameras everywhere. Thankfully, it was Laz who was monitoring them today and not one of the new guys or worse—Kenton, Chelsey's brother and one of Parker's best friends and coworker.

At some point, Parker would talk to him, but first he had to win Chelsey back.

Damn, I should've waited to talk to her.

Now he'd made a bad situation worse. He could've waited, gone by her house, and begged her to listen to him.

He growled under his breath, and when he glanced down the hall, Mason was standing near his suite of offices with his hands on his hips.

Ahh hell. This day just keeps getting better.

"In my office. Now!" Mason snapped before disappearing.

As Parker walked back, he debated on how much to tell his boss. Then again, maybe he wouldn't have to say anything about Chelsey. Maybe Mason hadn't noticed the tension vibrating between them.

Yeah right. The guys of Supreme weren't the best of the

best for no reason. Not much got by them. Whether they chose to acknowledge a situation was another story.

Parker reentered the office, surprised to see Hamilton Crosby sitting in one of the guest chairs. Dressed in a double-breasted suit, he always looked as if he was heading to a meeting. Which he probably was.

Hamilton, or as most of them referred to him, Ham, was a managing partner, and he and Mason shared some of the same duties. He was normally over the hiring of the security specialist, as well as interviewing potential clients. Lately, though, with how fast the company was growing, he, Mason, and Egypt had been sharing various roles.

"Close the door," Mason ordered. Parker did as he was told and had barely taken a step before Mason said, "What's up with you and Chelsey?"

Parker dropped into the seat. "It's complicated," he said after a few minutes.

"Well, un-complicate it," Hamilton said, "Because in two weeks she'll be working here full-time. We're not saying you have to confirm or deny that you two are in a relationship. We don't want any drama around here."

Parker didn't either. All he wanted was Chelsey back in his life, and he'd do whatever necessary to make that a reality. If he got her back...no, *when* he got her back, he wanted them to take their relationship public. For various reasons, not many knew they'd been seeing each other.

Hamilton stood with a file folder in hand. "I only stopped in here to get a signature from Mason, but I couldn't help but notice that you and Chelsey were in a heated discussion. We don't have a non-fraternizing rule here, and I'd like to keep it that way. But if you two bring drama here, we're going to have a problem."

"Understood," Parker said, glad that he nor Mason pressed for details on his relationship with Chelsey.

After Hamilton said his goodbyes and left, Mason said, "Now, let's discuss you getting back out in the field."

"Good. When can I start?" Parker asked, glad for the change of subject and more than ready to get back to field work.

This morning, he'd been prepared to walk away from the life he had created over the last four years. Not anymore. He was staying and planning to fight to get Chelsey back, while also getting back to the job he loved. He was born to protect people, and Supreme gave him the opportunity to work alongside some great guys. Parker knew he couldn't walk away from that.

"I want you, Laz, and Ashton to provide security for Jeff Hawkins. I'm not sure if you've heard of him, but he's the CEO of an international ecommerce company. He's hired Supreme to provide personal security while he attends a fundraiser."

"Did he say why he needs security?"

"Yeah, he's received a few threats due to approving the layoff of over 7000 employees a few months ago. He doesn't expect any trouble Saturday night, but he wants to be on the safe side."

Parker had heard of the guy shortly after moving to Atlanta. Hawkins had been considered one of Atlanta's most eligible bachelors, but in recent months, he'd had quite a bit of bad press. A serial dater, it sounded like he was the love-them-and-leave-them type, and women around the world were dragging his name through the mud.

"Hamilton and Egypt vetted him," Mason continued, "but Ham said the guy is a pompous know-it-all and might not follow protocols. Just so you know, he's been warned that you guys will leave him to fend for himself if he does anything to put either of you in danger."

Parker nodded. It always amazed him that people wanted protection, but they weren't always willing to do what they were told. Not even if it was for their own good.

They talked a few minutes longer with Mason giving him the details about the job. At the moment, Parker didn't care what assignment he got, he was just glad to get off of desk duty.

Now, if only he could fix the mess with Chelsey. Then his life would be back on track.

He'd think of something. He always did.

Chapter Four

Chelsey rocked back in her uncomfortable desk chair and watched as Gwen Andrews, one of her favorite parolees, completed some paperwork. One thing she wasn't going to miss when she left this job was her dingy, uninspiring office that was the size of a tuna can.

Okay, maybe that was an exaggeration. For the last three years, she'd had to come to the depressing space and try to encourage and help her parolees get their lives back on track. It hadn't always been easy, but for the most part, she enjoyed her role in their lives.

She never saw herself becoming a parole officer. Yet, she had decided a few years ago that being a cop wasn't for her. That's when she considered working in a different division of law enforcement. Chelsey had found the job opening the day after responding to a triple homicide call. The gruesome sight including a toddler's dead body positioned partly under a twin-size bed had sickened her.

She wasn't normally squeamish and could handle seeing

lifeless bodies, but that day Chelsey had known that being a cop was no longer for her. She hadn't wasted anytime applying for the parole officer position. It gave her the chance to stay in law enforcement but in a role where she could better help and support people.

Now, here she was again, preparing for another change in her career. She hoped working at Supreme would fulfill her in a way that law enforcement hadn't. Or at least help her narrow down exactly what she wanted to do with the rest of her life. One thing she knew for sure, being a part of Supreme would challenge her in a way that her current job didn't.

Chelsey sat forward and propped her forearms on the worn, oak desk. "I'm really proud of you, Gwen. You have accomplished almost everything you set out to do when you first got paroled. Including joining the peer support group."

"It has helped a lot. Glad you suggested it." Pride radiated in her eyes, and there was an independence about her that hadn't been there when they'd started working together. "I couldn't have accomplished anything without your help and belief in me. Chelsey, I'll never be able to thank you enough for your constant encouragement."

At thirty-six, the five-foot-four, hundred-and twenty-pound mother of two had served five of a six-year prison sentence for involuntary manslaughter. With olive skin, hazel eyes, and a timid smile, she didn't look like a former criminal. She looked more like a college student. Not a woman who'd been in an abusive marriage before accidentally killing the father of her children.

According to Gwen, her ex-husband had been drunk. When he backhanded their youngest daughter, Gwen lost it. It had been bad enough that he thought it okay to knock her around in front of their kids. But she drew the line at him laying a hand on her girls. She hadn't meant to kill him when she struck him on the back of the head with a baseball bat. No, Gwen had only been trying to get him away from her daughter. Still, she ended up serving time for the act.

Gwen was the type of client who Chelsey wished she could work with all the time. All things considered, the woman was thriving. The first time they'd met, Chelsey knew Gwen wanted to get her life back on track and was prepared to put in the work. She had vowed to do whatever necessary to create a better life for her and her daughters.

"I hate that I'm being reassigned to a new parole officer, but I'm glad you were my first," Gwen said on a chuckle, and Chelsey smiled. "I wish you could stay until my parole is up, but I understand the need to move on to bigger and better things."

Chelsey was confident that the move to Supreme Security would be better. Even working in the office with Egypt, the pay would be more than she was currently making. But it wasn't just about the money. She was also looking for the variety the job would bring. More than anything, though, she was confident that she'd soon become one of few women security specialist at the company.

"We'll meet one more time before you leave this place behind, right?"

"Yes, same time next week." Chelsey decided to do something she'd never done. She jotted her personal telephone number on a slip of paper and slid it across the desk. "Keep that in a safe place and stay in touch. Let me know when you're off parole and how the new job is going."

"I will, and thanks again for the job referral. The people at the printing company are great, especially my supervisor. Did you know that he worked my schedule so that I can drop my girls off at school and pick them up? On top of that, with what they're paying me, I'm able to save a little money. Hopefully we'll be able to move to a better neighborhood within the next six months."

"I have no doubt you'll make it happen." And Chelsey planned to make some inquiries with people she knew who owned rental properties. Any assistance she could give this woman to help her get ahead, she'd do it.

Chelsey dealt with all types of parolees. Her favorites were those trying to become a better person and create a new life for themselves, like Gwen.

But she also had to deal with those who didn't give a damn. From gang members to murderers, she'd had to work with them all, but the position shined a spotlight on something she hadn't considered. Many of her clients were products of the environment they grew up in. Some had grown up with drug-addicted parents or in foster care, and some had even lived on the streets, raising themselves.

So when Chelsey worked with parolees trying to help them get back acclimated into society, she kept that in mind. When she was a cop, there were many days when she felt like she didn't make a difference. At least in her parole officer position, she felt like she did.

She and Gwen talked a few minutes longer about the woman's current living situation, her kids, and the new job. Gwen spoke animatedly about all of it, her happiness pouring through her words. Before her husband died, she'd been a stay-at-home wife and mother. Now she was getting a chance to try new things and figure out what she wanted to do with the rest of her life.

Chelsey and Gwen were standing in the center of the office when the door flew open.

"Chelsey, I was thinking..." Victor McGill, her coworker and another parole officer, said before pulling up short inside the door.

"Haven't you heard of knocking before you enter someone's private office?" she snapped. He was one of her least favorite people and a person she wouldn't miss even a little when she left.

Victor didn't respond; his attention was solely on Gwen. From the top of her curly reddish-brown hair to the flats she wore on her feet, he didn't miss anything as his gaze strolled back up her body.

He moved forward and extended his hand. "Hi, I'm Victor McGill, and you are?"

Gwen didn't move nor did she respond. Still leery of some men, especially the slick talkers who could be spotted a mile away, she just looked at Victor's hand.

Chelsey stepped between them, forcing Victor to move back. "It's none of your business who she is." Thankfully, Gwen scurried out of the office without introducing herself but promising to see Chelsey soon.

"What is your problem?" Victor bit out the moment Gwen left the room. "I was only introducing myself."

Yeah, that's how it would start, but then he'd flash his attractive smile highlighted with twin dimples. He would then pour on the charm. The charm he had mastered and used on unsuspected women.

Chelsey couldn't deny he was a good-looking man despite being a tad bit overweight. At forty years old, his short hair was mostly black with a little graying near the temples. Average height at around five-foot-ten, he had at least fifty pounds on her. Still, Victor could probably turn a few heads. At least until he opened his mouth and started talking.

Considering how inappropriate he could be around the office, the man-whore should've been fired years ago for being a narcissistic, misogynistic jerk. Chelsey would be surprised if he didn't have at least a couple of warnings in his personnel file. His behavior and some of the things he'd said to coworkers, as well as clients, was often inappropriate. Most women around the office ignored him, or waved him off as a flirt.

In Chelsey's eyes, he was a predator.

Weeks after she had become a parole officer, he had found her in the staff lounge. She wasn't positive, but she was fairly sure he'd been high on something that day. Not high enough to be overtly noticeable, but high enough to step to her the wrong way.

She'd been reaching in one of the upper cabinets for sugar when he thought it was okay to grind against her ass. Out of reflex, she jammed her elbow back as hard as she could, catching him in his ribs. Then she punched him in the jaw, sending him sprawling to the floor where he had laid stunned.

"If you ever put your hands on me again, I'll beat your ass, and then I'll report you," she had said to him.

When he finally got his bearings, he apologized, claiming he had read her wrong. He thought she was interested in him. It had been a load of crap, but before they left the room, she set him straight. She made it clear that she wasn't interested, never would be, and if he stayed away from her, they wouldn't have a problem.

"Why are you here?" she asked, her patience dwindling as she headed back to her desk.

"I'm here to ask you out. I figured since your time around here is coming to an end, that you'll finally quit playing hard to get. How about you get dolled up and let me take you out for dinner on your last day here? At least with you not working

33

here anymore, we won't have to worry about mixing business with pleasure. So, how about it?"

Chelsey was about to log into her laptop but stopped and stared at him, waiting for him to say—*just kidding*. He didn't, and she snorted a laugh.

"We both know that's *never* going to happen. I don't even know why you bothered asking. What do you really want?"

She didn't have time for this foolishness. Not only did she need to finish some paperwork before she left for the day, but she had to think about what she'd wear on her date tonight. She had plans for dinner with a man she'd gone out with a couple of times so far. He wasn't the most exciting guy, but at least she wouldn't be at home thinking about Parker.

"Penny mentioned that you'll be transferring some of your client files to the rest of us. She said she's leaving it up to you on who gets what."

"Is there a question in there?" Chelsey asked, wondering where this was going.

If she could at all help it, she wouldn't be transferring any of her female clients to him. Their supervisor, Penny, knew Victor was a predator. Yet, he was still employed. Which made Chelsey wonder if something was going on between the two of them. Or maybe Chelsey's dislike of the guy was clouding her judgment about him.

Then again, she really didn't care. She was leaving and not looking back, and if she had any pull with Penny, Vic the jerk wouldn't get any of her clients. Even the ones who didn't give a damn about getting their lives together.

Victor moved closer to the desk and placed his palms on top of it. "I was wondering how many more cases I'd have to be responsible for."

"I won't know that until..." Chelsey sat back when she realized he was looking down her red V-neck blouse. *Pervert.* "If I hand off any cases to you, you'll have them a few days before I leave. That way we can go through them in case you have any questions."

"Okay, that works," he said, straightening. "So, are you saying no to me taking you out because of that motorcycle guy?"

Chelsey cringed inside. She'd gone a whole hour without thinking about her conversation with Parker earlier in the day. Now Victor had to ruin it by bringing him up. Granted, he didn't know Parker, but he had seen him a few times after work. Of course, Parker noticed him and each time made a big show of kissing her. According to him, it was to make sure Victor knew she was taken.

Yet, here she was, single again. If only he would've...

Nope. Not going there. Parker and I are over. Chelsey didn't know how many times she'd have to remind herself, but she would until it sunk in.

"I figured since I haven't seen him pick you up in a while that—"

"Victor, my personal life is none of your business. Now get out of my office and close the door behind you."

He chuckled as he walked backward toward the door. "I guess that means he dumped your fine, prickly ass," he mumbled under his breath, but it was loud enough for her to hear him.

She wanted to lob a retort, but she didn't. What could she say? Parker had dumped her, and technically more than once. Everything had been perfect between them...until it wasn't, and she'd been blindsided by his need to break things off.

It's done. We're over. Let him go. A task easier said than done.

Parker's words came to mind. *"Chelsey, please, baby. Let's go somewhere and talk. There's something I need to tell you."*

Even if she wanted to know what was going on with him, she feared he'd hurt her again. Whatever he had to say, he could've said the day he broke her heart.

I have to stay strong. No going back.

Still, she wondered what he'd wanted to tell her.

Chapter Five

I *hate dating,* Chelsey thought as she stared across the candlelit table at her date. They'd gone out twice before tonight, and she had hoped the third time would improve her opinion of him.

Nope. She still felt nothing for the guy.

She convinced herself that maybe dinner again with Terrance would be different. That maybe he wouldn't talk about himself all night. And just maybe a powerful spark would ignite between them, and she'd fall madly in lust with him. Then she could forget about Parker and start new with someone else.

Ha! Wishful thinking.

She wanted so badly to like Terrance Burton III. Not only because she was trying to move on from Parker, but also because... Okay, maybe it was about moving on from Parker.

Still, why'd this guy have to be so boring? She should've listened to herself earlier when she had considered canceling, but she hadn't because she didn't want to sit at home thinking about her ex. Now she couldn't wait to get home and curl up on her overstuffed sofa while devouring a pint of Ben & Jerry's. That chocolate fudge brownie ice cream was calling her name.

Chelsey lifted her glass of Chardonnay and took a sip as she glanced at Terrance. The dull man was still talking about his new car. At least they were at one of her favorite steakhouses near Midtown Atlanta. The dimly lit space was romantic with soft jazz flowing through the speakers, and the hum of patrons talking and laughing helped create a relaxing environment. Also, the food was as amazing as usual, and the blackened salmon practically melted in her mouth. So the date wasn't all bad.

"Every day I learn something new about my Acura," Terrance said. "I didn't realize I had adaptive cruise control. It blows my mind how the car can slow itself down to match the speed of the car in front of it. Then go right back to cruising."

What a waste of a handsome face, Chelsey thought as he droned on and on. The man was good-looking with smooth reddish-brown skin, an incredible body, and a swag that gave him a bad-boy vibe. She had always had a thing for bad boys, loving their edginess, self-confidence, and even their fearlessness.

Terrance had all of that with a bit of arrogance. He also had a good job as a data analyst for an international company, and he was taking night classes to finish his master's degree in computer science. He should've been a great catch—but deep down, Chelsey felt that something was off. She couldn't quite pinpoint what that was, besides him being boring, but there was definitely something about him that didn't add up. It was almost like he was too perfect.

Her brother always told her to trust her instincts, but when it came to men and dating, her instincts weren't the best. Just once she wished she could choose the perfect man. Instead, she had chosen this one. A man who was making her feel as if she was sitting in on a mind-numbing lecture waiting for it to end. More than that, being with Terrence only made her miss Parker more.

Chelsey sighed as she used her fork to push jasmine rice around on her plate. She actually didn't think she chose wrong with Parker. He was a wonderful man who cared about people and was committed to those who mattered to him. Even though they were no longer dating, she knew she could call him if she ever needed him.

God, she missed him. He had become such an important part of her life, and then *poof*, he was gone. She would always love him despite how mad she still was at the way he'd ended things between them.

I need to talk to you.

There's something I need to tell you.

His words played through her mind. What was so important that he'd wanted to tell her? Maybe in another day or two, once she knew she could control herself around him, she'd hear him out. That wouldn't be anytime soon, though. Lately, she waffled between wanting to punch him and wanting to make love to him.

How messed up was that?

"So how was work today?" Terrance suddenly asked, shocking the heck out of Chelsey. "I don't think I ever asked you, but how do you like being a parole officer?"

Nope he never asked because he spent the last two dates and several phone calls, talking about his work and what a great basketball player he was. Granted, occasionally he'd ask her a question about herself, but somehow the conversation always went back to him and the high opinion he had of himself.

"Today was okay. Made a few home visits, saw a couple of clients, and did a lot of paperwork. So it was a fairly routine day."

"You actually call them clients?" he asked, a deep frown on his face.

"No, actually I call them by their names, and they are my clients." *Asshole*. What did he expect her to call them? Thief? Murderer? Or something else crazy like that?

"I don't like the idea of you being around criminals all day," Terrance said as if she cared about what he liked or didn't like. "They might be trying to reform, but they are still criminals. I remember this one time when I walked in on a store robbery..."

And once again the conversation is about him.

It was almost laughable. Well, at least he didn't ask her more questions about work. Some people wanted to know everything about her job and her clients. Especially those clients who had committed murder.

It was amazing how her dreams had changed over the years. In college, she had majored in criminal justice. Her intention was to become a criminal investigator for a US government agency. After doing an internship with the FBI, she quickly lost interest. Then after Kenton, who used to be an FBI agent, became a security specialist at Supreme Security, Chelsey had decided that's what she wanted to do, too. Unfortunately, Mason was still insisting she needed more experience, but she would show him that she was ready.

"Chelsey?" Terrance said, waving his hand back and forth in front of her face.

"Oh, I'm sorry." Sitting up straighter, she was surprised to see their server standing next to the table. "What did you say?"

"I was asking if either of you would like dessert."

"Oh no. I'm good. Actually, I'm finished eating," Chelsey said and slid her mostly empty plate toward the server.

"What about you, sir? Would you like anything else?"

"No thank you. You can bring the check."

"Will do."

Even as they left the restaurant, the enticing aromas followed them out. Though the date had been just okay, everything else about the evening was wonderful. Good food, beautiful night, and despite the ninety-five degrees earlier, the temperature and humidity had dropped. It was still hot, but the light breeze kissed Chelsey's warm skin and had her breathing a sigh of relief.

"You look absolutely beautiful tonight," Terrance said.

"Thank you."

Chelsey had to keep herself from laughing. Of course he hadn't said anything, he'd been too caught up in talking about himself to probably even notice. But that was okay, the date was almost over, and if she was honest, she'd had worse.

"I like you in short dresses and high heels," Terrance continued.

The floral print sundress, with spaghetti crisscross straps in the back, molded over her size six figure perfectly. She'd worn the outfit to give herself that extra bit of confidence. After the day she'd had, she needed something to make her feel good inside while showcasing her assets. This dress, combined with the deep-red high-heeled sandals, had done that.

She walked a short distance in front of Terrance and sensed his gaze on her backside. A glance over her shoulder confirmed he was still checking her out, and she slowed to let him catch up.

"And those long, shapely legs..." he said, shaking his head in appreciation.

He didn't finish the sentence, but he was such a guy and was probably imagining them wrapped around his waist. Something that would never happen. She was positive they weren't going out again.

Chelsey didn't hold the legs comment against him. It wasn't the first time someone admired her legs. Running track in middle school, high school, and then getting a full scholarship to run track in college, had a lot to do with that. With the success of her track experience, she had dreams of working her way up to Olympic status. Unfortunately, after back-to-back injuries to her hamstring, as well as several calf strains, she let the dream fall away. Despite that disappointment, she still made it a point to jog every day, determined to stay in shape.

As they made their way to the parking structure next door, Terrance linked his fingers with hers. Though she was a hand-holder, it was weird holding his hand. Out of all the men she had ever dated, Parker had been the only touchy-feely one. Public displays of affection were his thing, except around their family and friends. Both, for their individual reasons, agreed that they'd wanted to wait to go public with their relationship. Now that they were done, that decision had been a good one.

Twenty minutes later, Terrance pulled up to the townhome she was renting and parked in front of the one-car garage.

Chelsea glanced at the porch, realizing she hadn't turned on the outside light. Good thing a nearby streetlamp and the single bulb over the garage emitted enough light to see the stairs but not much else.

Now came the awkward part of the evening—trying to get away without having to kiss him goodnight. That was something else he wasn't that good at—kissing.

Terrance climbed out of the car and hurried around, opened her door and helped her out. One thing she couldn't complain about—he was always a perfect gentleman.

"Thank you," she said and headed up the walkway with Terrance close by her side.

The darkness had her taking her time up the stairs to keep from falling. When they made it to her front door, Chelsey stuck her key into the lock but didn't push open the door.

"Terrance, thanks for a lovely evening," she said, trying to sound chipper as she turned to face him. "The restaurant and food were great."

"What? You're not going to invite me in?" he asked, closing the distance between them. "I was thinking that maybe we could have a nightcap, and then see where that leads."

Chelsey placed her hand on his chest to stop him from getting any closer. "Not tonight. It's been a long week, but thanks for dinner."

He flashed her a smile and slid his hand to her waist, drawing her closer. She didn't protest, figuring she'd give him a quick kiss good night before sending him on his way.

"I enjoy spending time with you," he said, and lowered his head and moved in to kiss her.

But a noise and sudden movement to her right made Chelsey freeze. Then she gasped when the muzzle of a 9mm gun came into view and pressed against Terrance's temple.

Heart practically pounding out of her chest, she didn't move, but she tried to weigh her options. Could she disarm the person without Terrence getting shot?

"Put your mouth on any part of her body, and it will be the last thing you do." The growly voice was low and lethal.

Chelsey's initial panic was quickly replaced with anger when she realized it was Parker. How the hell had he snuck up on them without her seeing him? Then again, with the light out, there was a blind spot in the corner where he could've been positioned without being spotted.

Her gaze darted to Terrance, and she cringed at the fear she saw in his huge eyes. His hands were slightly raised in surrender.

"Dammit! Put the gun away," she spat, and glared toward where Parker stood, though he was still partially hidden in the shadow. "What the hell is wrong with you?"

Her pulse pounded loudly in her ear as she forced her heart

rate to drop down to normal. This man had clearly lost his mind. What pissed her off even more was that he didn't lower his weapon.

"Pa..." she started to say his name but stopped herself. Though Terrance had a right to know who held a gun on him, he wouldn't get that information from her. "Would you please lower your weapon?" she said.

Instead of doing what she asked, Parker said, "How well do you know Mr. Terrance Burton?"

Chapter Six

Dread coursed through Chelsey as a multitude of emotions wreaked havoc inside her.

Parker wouldn't be there holding a gun on this guy if he didn't have a good reason. His question sparked several of her own. Like, why was he there? How'd he know her date's name? And what crime had Terrance done to warrant a gun to his head?

"I know him well enough," Chelsey snapped as that sinking feeling in the pit of her stomach sunk lower.

"Did he tell you that he lives with his longtime girlfriend? A woman he's been with for the last three years. Did he tell you that last week they celebrated his two-year old's birthday?"

Shock rocked Chelsey, but she didn't respond. She had done a preliminary background check on him to make sure he didn't have any warrants. Nothing more than that, though.

"By your silence, I assume you didn't know any of that. Which means you're probably not aware that his baby's mama is seven months pregnant," Parker said dryly, then added, "Oh, and congratulations Terrance, you're having a boy."

Chelsey could feel steam coming from her ears as she glared between Parker and Terrance. Parker because he probably only added that last comment for good measure, but Terrance...

"Is this true?" she whispered and studied her date who looked as if he was about to soil his pants. She was the biggest fool on the planet. Her man-picking skills were worse than she originally thought.

Whether Terrance responded or not, Chelsey already knew every word of it was true. Like the rest of his Atlanta's Finest team, Parker was one of the most resourceful people she knew. How he found all of this out didn't matter at the moment. What mattered was that she hadn't known any of it.

"Go home to your baby's momma, and stay the hell away from my woman," Parker said, and still didn't lower his weapon.

"Was anything you told me true?" she asked Terrance—but really, did it matter? "Never mind, I don't need to know. I suggest you leave before I let this idiot shoot you." When he didn't move, she stepped closer. "He's an impatient asshole, but he's an excellent shot. Now get lost and lose my damn number!"

Terrence slowly lowered his hands and slowly moved away from Parker as if fearing the gun might go off if he moved too quickly. Parker knew everything about every gun, and he was a master at using them. There was no doubt in her mind that the gun's safety was on, but still, accidents did happen.

When Terrance had put some distance between them, his bravery must have returned and he said "Chelsey, I'm sorry. I—l never meant..."

Turning, Chelsey gave him her back and she also ignored Parker who hadn't moved. She was so pissed at him. It was best they didn't talk right now. She pushed open her front door and started to enter when Parker touched her arm.

On reflex, Chelsey jerked away and swung at him, but he caught her wrist seconds before her fist connected with his handsome face. Thanks to boxing, his reflexes were lightning-quick.

She yanked out of his hold. "Don't touch me," she ground out, anger and embarrassment charging through her body like a live wire. "What you did was way out of line."

When tears suddenly filled her eyes, she lowered her gaze. *Dammit.* No way was she going to cry, but she was furious; she could barely keep her emotions in check.

"Sweetheart..."

She lifted her hand and glanced at him. "Don't," she croaked out. "You hurt me when you broke things off, but I guess that wasn't enough for you. You had to embarrass me too, huh? Because what you just did—"

"Sweetie, I am so sorry. If you give me a chance to—"

"No. We're done, Parker. Now get the hell off my porch!"

He started to say something else, but Chelsey slammed the door in his face.

How is this my life?

Once inside the house, she flipped on the light for the foyer and locked the door before leaning against it. A few rogue tears slipped down her cheeks, but Chelsey quickly wiped them away.

No way was she going to cry because of a stupid man. Or *two* stupid men.

"Ugh!"

Maybe they weren't the stupid ones. She'd been a cop, for goodness sakes. How had she read Terrance so wrong? How did she not know he was hiding so much baggage? She had asked if he was married and if he had kids. He'd said no to both, but she never thought to ask if he was in a long-term relationship or screwing some woman. Had she been stupid enough to have sex with him and then found out this information, Parker would've had to pull her off that asshole.

Parker... *Gawd!*

She pushed away from the door and headed to the stairs that would take her to the second floor. "I hate the male species. I hate them. I hate them. I hate them," she shouted with each step she took until she reached the primary bedroom.

Chelsey had moved into the townhouse a month ago. Though it was a little older than she had preferred, she loved the Midtown Atlanta location. She figured she'd live there a year before she bought her own place.

When she strolled into her bedroom, she flipped on the light and her perfume, Miss Dior, lingered in the air. She released a long, cleansing breath as the floral and woodsy scent surrounded her. It felt good to be home. It was going to feel even better to get out of her dress and high-heeled sandals and change into lounging pajamas.

Feeling more like herself, Chelsey padded barefoot down the carpeted stairs and to the bright-yellow kitchen. Forget the ice cream that she'd been thinking about all evening. She needed something more decadent to wash the blues away.

After pouring a glass of milk, she grabbed the container of red velvet chocolate chip cookies and took them into the living room. She set the items on the end table next to her, dropped down on the sofa, and picked up the television remote. She ran through a few channels before settling on HGTV, her favorite station.

"Should've done this in the first place," she mumbled and grabbed her cookies and the milk. Dunking the first one, she bit into the gooey goodness and moaned. "Yep, definitely should've stayed home with my cookies instead of going out with that loser."

After a few bites, Chelsey pulled her cell phone from her lounging pants pocket and called her best friend.

"Don't tell me the date is over already," India said by way of a greeting. "It's not even nine o'clock. Let me guess, he talked about how wonderful he is and how you're lucky that he took time to grace you with his presence."

Chelsey laughed. "Almost."

She told her friend about the boring date, and her ability to pick the biggest losers in Atlanta. As she replayed the dinner and the conversation her mood lightened even more. She couldn't have made up the events of the evening if she tried.

"Oh but let me tell you the best part. Parker was here when we arrived."

"What? My man Parker showed up to claim his woman? *Girrrl*, you should've started with that. Tell me everything, and don't leave anything out!"

"*Pu-lease*, you got it all wrong," Chelsey said and recounted Parker's surprise visit.

India howled with laughter as if Chelsey was telling a joke. It wasn't funny at the moment, but now that she was replaying the events verbally, it sounded crazy as hell. She could understand why her friend was laughing, because it was so over the top, even for Parker.

"That man of yours sure knows how to—"

"He's not my man, remember?" Chelsey grumbled.

"I would've paid money to see that," her friend said, still laughing and acting like she didn't just hear what Chelsey said. "I know you hate him, but I still love him for you. He's gorgeous, smart, witty, sexy as hell, and protective." India sighed wistfully, and Chelsey rolled her eyes. "If only I could land a man like that."

"Whatever. Have you forgotten he dumped me, *twice?*"

"I haven't forgotten, but we both know you're not over him,

49

and it's safe to say the feeling is mutual. Otherwise, he wouldn't be going to such lengths to talk to you. You always did attract the passionate bad boys. It sounds like Parker was living up to what you like in a man."

Chelsey didn't respond.

Parker was everything she wanted in a man, no matter how she tried to deny it. Her body and her mind missed him, longed for him, and craved him. How and why would she want to be with someone who was insane enough to hold a gun to a man's head the way he had? What did that say about her and the men she chose to spend time with?

"Let's go back to Terrance," India said. "I'm surprised you didn't sense something was up with him. Was he that good of a liar?"

"My spidey senses started tingling during the second date, but I went out with him again anyway. I knew there would never be anything between us, but you know how we women do. We try to give a guy a chance, even knowing deep down they aren't the one for us.

"What angers me, though, is the fact that Parker was the one who dug deep into Terrance's life. I'm so embarrassed. Now I have even more reasons why I don't want to see Parker anytime soon."

Chelsey's phone beeped, signaling another call. She glanced at the screen, surprised to see her sister-in-law, Egypt's, name.

"India, hold on a sec." Chelsey clicked over. "Hey, Sis, what's up?"

"Hey yourself. Sorry to call this late, but you're about to get your wish. I hope you're free tomorrow, because you're needed to provide security tomorrow night."

Chelsey dropped her sock-covered feet to the floor and sat forward.

"Yes!" she bellowed, feeling like she did whenever she placed first after running a hundred-yard dash in college. Like she had accomplished something she'd been working so hard toward. The powers that be at Supreme Security were finally giving her another chance to prove that she belonged on the Atlanta's Finest team.

"Count me in!" It didn't matter the job—she just wanted a chance.

"I'll text you details in the morning. For now, I can tell you that it's a fundraiser. I'm not sure how you'll feel about this, but the client, a CEO of an ecommerce company, needs a woman on his detail. You'll be going as his date."

Chelsey's mouth dropped open. "What?"

"Not a real date," Egypt hurried to say. "His actual date backed out, and after a short conversation, I suggested that we have one of our female security specialists pose as his date. Since he wants three people on his detail, you'll be one of them. Oh, and he knows that you'll be there to provide security and nothing else. Are you game?"

Egypt could've gotten someone else for the assignment, but this was Chelsey's chance to show them that she was ready to provide personal protection.

"I'm game."

"Be at the office tomorrow night by eight. Oh, and you won't need to wear a black suit," she said of the security specialist's usual uniform. "The attire is formal. Since this is for the job, you'll receive a generous spending allowance to buy an evening gown. Unless you already have one. If that's the case, you can keep the allowance as a bonus."

Chelsey chuckled. "Nice! Talk about perks."

"I know, right? But it's the least Supreme can do for you, especially on such short notice. Just make sure whatever you

51

wear, you can move easily in the garment. You'll get more information tomorrow."

"Thanks, Sis. I appreciate the opportunity."

"My pleasure."

Giddiness bubbled inside of Chelsey as she disconnected that call and clicked back over to the call with India. Suddenly the night was looking up.

"India, your girl got an assignment for tomorrow night."

As Chelsey told her friend about the job, her excitement grew. All she needed was a chance to prove to Mason and Hamilton that she could handle herself. There was no doubt in her mind that she was ready and if all went well, she'd be a shoo-in for one of the open security specialist's positions.

"Okay, so you know I'm saving to buy a house," Chelsey said. "How about you loan me one of your evening gowns, and then I can pocket the bonus from Supreme."

India laughed. "Girl, as much as you've talked about wanting to do security, the least I can do is loan you a dress. I have a feeling I already know which one you're going to choose."

Chelsey grinned. Her friend was an entertainment agent and was always attending formal events. Her massive closet had more clothes than the woman could wear in a lifetime and yes, Chelsey had the perfect evening gown in mind.

"I'm going to prove to Mason and Hamilton that they need more women and that I can handle the job."

"Well, be careful what you wish for. Hopefully the guy you'll be guarding doesn't turn out to be a jerk."

Chelsey wasn't worried. If the guy ended up being a creep, dealing with him would be good practice for future assignments.

"Now, let's get back to Parker," India said. "You need to swallow your stubborn pride and talk to him. Or if nothing else, you need to listen to whatever he has to say. You always said that the breakup didn't make sense. It sounds like he might've had a good reason."

"India, I'm not ready to talk to him, especially not after tonight. I felt like an idiot when he told me about Terrance."

"How did he know you've been going out with Terrance?"

"After our first date, Terrance and I had just pulled into my driveway when I saw Parker climbing out of his vehicle across the street. When Terrance got out to open the door for me, Parker climbed back into his truck.

"Terrance didn't notice him, and I made it look like I hadn't seen him. He took off as we approached the porch. I wouldn't be surprised if he got Terrance's license plate before leaving. Or knowing him, he might've waited down the street and followed the poor guy home. Who knows?"

"God, you sure know how to pick them. If I didn't believe in the girl-code, I'd make a play for your ex."

Chelsey smiled. When they were in high school, they'd heard about the dating code that India started calling the girl-code: *never date your friend's ex or your ex's friend.*

"You can have him," Chelsey said half-heartedly. "I can't go backward."

"Reuniting with Parker would not be going backward. It would be you hooking back up with the man who owns your heart. There's a difference."

"Yeah, if you say so."

"Okay, enough talk about Mr. Man. Let's talk about the event tomorrow night. Even if you'll be pretending to be this guy's date, you can check out any single men who'll be in attendance. Who knows, since you claim you're done with Parker, you might catch some millionaire's attention."

Chelsey shook her head as if India could see her. "Even if I wasn't going to be on the clock tomorrow night, I wouldn't be looking for a man. I'm done with the male species, at least for a while. I'm going to focus on my new career, show the peeps at Supreme that I'm an asset, and enjoy some of the perks that come along with working for them."

They talked a few minutes longer, and by the time the call ended, Chelsey felt better than she had all day. Excitement filled her, and she couldn't wait for her gig tomorrow night. Hopefully, if she stayed busy enough, thoughts of Parker would be a thing of the past.

At least she could hope.

Chapter Seven

Parker shook his head in disgust as he entered his house from the garage, dumped his gear in the mudroom, and rearmed the alarm.

Maybe I am crazy.

He bypassed the kitchen, living room, and headed down the hallway to his bedroom, replaying the disastrous evening in his mind. What the hell had he been thinking? Actually, he hadn't been thinking. He'd just reacted. Nothing had gone right tonight, and it was his own damn fault.

The plan had been simple: stop by and talk to Chelsey before she went to bed. He had parked his truck around the corner, thinking it would be a better chance of her letting him in if she didn't see it. Either way, there'd been no guarantee that she'd hear him out. But he'd had to try.

All he'd wanted to do was make things right between them, but he hadn't counted on her being out with Terrance. Parker had been just about to ring the doorbell when the car pulled into the driveway. He slipped into the shadows on the porch and had planned to stay there.

He figured Terrance didn't stand a chance with Chelsey. She was smart, despite the fact that she'd gone out with the guy again. Parker assumed she'd thank him for getting her home safe, and then send him on his way. But no...the jerk went in for a kiss, and Parker couldn't let that happen. Before he realized what he was doing, he'd held the guy at gunpoint.

Chelsey had been right to ask if he was crazy. That had been a bonehead thing to do. He might be crazy in love with her, but he didn't go around brandishing a weapon like some lunatic. At least he didn't make a habit of it. Yet, seeing another man with his woman didn't sit right with him, especially Terrance.

"I should've handled his punk-ass weeks ago," Parker murmured into the quietness of his bedroom. He didn't bother with lights. Just walked in and fell face first onto his king-size mattress.

He sighed, still mentally kicking himself. Yes, he should've dealt with Terrance the moment he'd dug up the information on him. He could've paid the guy a visit and threatened him without Chelsey knowing. Or he could've made sure she knew what type of man she was spending time with.

Parker had done neither because he hadn't expected her to go out with the man again. Normally she was a good judge of character, and her instincts were usually on point.

Apparently, not this time.

He sighed again and closed his eyes as the hum of the air conditioner lulled him into a peaceful moment. He was going to have to make Chelsey listen, because he couldn't keep up this irrational behavior. Even if she didn't take him back, at least he'd know that he did what he could to make things right with her. He might not want to live the rest of his life without her, but he would have to respect her decision.

Exhaustion settled around him like a heavy blanket and his

eyes drifted closed. He couldn't get Chelsey out of his mind. She was his. They belonged together. He loved her too much to walk away and had been a fool to think he could ever live life without her.

Impossible. He needed her. No one had made him feel as loved as she had, not since before his mother died.

God, he missed her and his mother. He couldn't bring his mother back from the dead, but there was plenty he could do about Chelsey. He had to show her that they belonged together.

That was his last thought before he drifted off into a fitful sleep.

Junior hurried into the kitchen where his parents were arguing, and the incredible smell of fried chicken, his favorite, greeted him at the entrance. Unfortunately, food would have to wait.

"Why are y'all arguing?" he asked, his gaze darting between his mother and father. They used to never argue, until lately. It was because his mother didn't like that his father was making him stay out late to sell drugs.

"Hi, baby. I didn't know you were home." His mother kissed his cheek, then patted it gently the way she always did.

"Junior, this is grown folks' business. So get the fuck out," his father shouted, anger sparking his dark brown eyes.

The menacing look he gave Junior was why everyone on the streets called him Wolf. Well, that, and the fact that he resembled a wolf with the intense slant of his eyes that were a little too close together. Also, the stealth-like way he moved probably added to the moniker.

"I told you about walking around here acting like you own the place."

"Maverick, honey, please. Our son just got home from

school. At least let him get something to eat," Junior's mother said and grabbed a plate from the cabinet.

His dad snatched the plate from her and shoved it back into the cabinet, probably breaking it.

"Mina, he can fix his own damn plate, but I told him to get the fuck out. And here your ass was getting ready to—"

"Don't talk to my mother like that!" The words were out of Junior's mouth before he could pull them back.

He never talked back to his father. Never.

But Junior also never heard his father be this mean to his mother. He never talked to her like this. She was the only person who could usually calm Wolf down, and he always called her his queen.

Before Junior could brace himself, his father backhanded him.

Pain shot through his face and rattled his brain as if an explosion had detonated inside his skull. But on reflex, Junior hit him back. He jabbed his father in the jaw, putting enough power behind the punch to cause his dad's head to snap back. Yet, it was as if Junior hadn't touched him. The man stayed rooted in place.

He met his father's gaze. At first, pride radiated in the man's eyes, but his expression quickly turned to hatred. Junior was tall for his age, but Wolf had several inches on him and at least sixty pounds of pure muscle. He was also the meanest, nastiest person Junior knew. It didn't matter that he was his father. Wolf wouldn't hesitate to stomp him into the ground.

Junior might only be twelve, but he had already seen and done more than most kids his age, including staying out all night to sell drugs for his father. And one thing he had already learned from his dad was to never back down from a fight, and he never would.

"If you're big, bad, and man enough to fight me, boy, then

you need to pack your shit and get the fuck out of my house,"
Wolf growled.

"You said mom is your queen, but you've been yelling at her
and treating her like shit," Junior shot back.

"Get. Out!"

"No! I'm not leaving." Even though inside his bones were
rattling like an overstuffed washing machine, Junior refused to
show fear. His father could smell fear.

Wolf moved so fast, he was a blur when he grabbed Junior by
the front of his shirt and slammed him against a nearby wall.
Mina screamed from across the room.

"Your ass is leaving even if I have to literally throw you
out."

"Stop it, Maverick! If my son leaves, I'm leaving too." Mina
might've only been five-four and maybe a hundred and ten
pounds, but she shoved her way in between them, forcing his
father to release him. "I mean it. He's just a child."

"Mina, get out the way," Wolf barked. "This is between me
and the boy. You can't keep babying him. If he's man enough to
talk back to me, then he's man enough to fend for himself. Now
get out the way!"

He shoved her to the side and got back in Junior's face, but
Mina pushed her way between them again.

"I mean it, Maverick. If you make him leave, I'm leaving
with him!" she yelled, poking him in the chest.

"Shut up, woman! I will never let you leave me," Wolf
roared.

He drew his hand back and slapped her so hard, her feet left
the floor as she went flying.

"No!" Junior screamed a second before the side of Mina's
head connected with the counter, and a loud crack pierced the
air before her body crumbled to the floor.

"Mama!"

"Mina!" His father pushed him out the way and ran to her. "Oh, my God. Mina, baby, I'm sorry. Please don't be..."

"Mama!" Junior dropped to his knees next to them as tears blurred his vision. He kept screaming her name over and over, but she wasn't moving.

When his father released her and started howling and crying, Junior moved him out the way. He gathered his mother into his arms.

"Mama. Wake up," he cried, shaking her. "Please wake up, Mama, please." When he looked at her face, Junior froze.

He blinked several times, trying to clear the tears from his eyes, but then...

Chelsey.

What? How?

Chelsey! His heart slammed against his chest, and his body trembled as blood poured from the side of her head.

"No! No! Chelsey!" he screamed over and over. "Chelsey! Please, baby open your eyes. Please don't leave me. Chelsey!"

Parker bolted upright in bed with a pillow in his arms as he struggled to catch his breath. His gaze darted around the darkened room, but all he could see was blackness.

His chest heaved as his heart pounded hard enough to be heard in the next room while sweat dripped down his face.

It's a dream. It's just a dream.

He kept telling himself that over and over, but it seemed so real. He hadn't dreamed about his mother's death in years, and then to see Chelsey's face...

Shit.

Parker tossed the pillow he was holding to the other side of the bed and dropped back down as he continued gasping for air. It was only a dream. His mother was dead, but Chelsey was alive.

The hum of the air conditioner kicking in was the only sound in the house as he forced himself to take deep, steadying breaths.

His eyes had adjusted to the darkness, and Parker didn't know how long he stared at the ceiling. He just tried focusing on breathing normally.

Chelsey's okay. She's fine.

He knew that. Still, he was on edge. His woman might be fine now, but if Wolf ever found out Parker was alive, no one he cared about would be safe.

"I can't live like this anymore," he mumbled into the darkness.

He also could no longer keep his secrets buried. Those who were close to him might one day be in danger, and they needed to know why.

Parker had never been the type to sit back to wait and see what happens. He was the type to make things happen. If he wanted Wolf to no longer be a threat, it would be up to him to get rid of his father.

Even if it means I start another war.

Chapter Eight

The next day, Parker strolled into Supreme Security still shaken from the dream he'd had of his mother. Her death had traumatized him. It had been one of the darkest times of his life. He'd been a twelve-year-old kid living in an adult world doing adult things. Illegal things forced upon him by his father.

But the hardest part about his mother's death was keeping the "incident," as his father referred to it, a secret. Parker wanted to call the police and have him arrested. He didn't care if it meant ending up in foster care. Unfortunately, he couldn't and he hadn't said anything to anyone. Being a member of the Kingz meant you kept their business in-house, and you sure as hell didn't snitch.

His dad hadn't meant to hurt her, and he sure hadn't meant to kill her. Wolf had been obsessed with Mina and treated her like fine china. Then, as Parker got older, his parents' relationship started changing. It started when Wolf insisted that he wanted his son to one day rule over the Diego Kingz. That meant Parker had to work his way up the ranks, starting with selling drugs at a young age.

He ambled through the quiet halls of Supreme while trying to forget about his past, the memories. But his mind kept being pulled back. After he and his father cried over Mina's body, willing her to wake up, Wolf moved into action as if on autopilot.

One of Wolf's roles in the Diego Kingz, before he became the leader, was a cleaner. He was responsible for disposing of bodies and then cleaning up afterward.

By the end of that day, Mina's body had disappeared, and the kitchen was spotless. As if nothing had ever happened. No funeral. No memorial. Nothing.

Wolf attempted to placate Parker with promises that it would all be okay, but even at that age, Parker knew it wouldn't. Nothing would ever be okay again.

If anyone asked about his mother, he'd been instructed to say that she was in Europe taking care of her sister who was sick. Months later, if anyone asked about her, he'd been instructed to say that she had decided to move there.

It wasn't like she had many close friends outside of other wives who were a part of the Diego Kingz crime syndicate. Parker was sure others knew he and his father were lying about Mina, but no one was bold enough to question them in depth.

Accidental death or not, Parker would never forgive Wolf for killing his mother. Even as a teenager, he had vowed that he'd make Wolf pay one day. It had taken Parker five years to learn everything he could about his father's business—the Diego Kingz's business. Five years to drum up enough courage to take his father down, and five years to put a plan in action.

What had initially been a solid plan, ended up backfiring, though. Somehow, Wolf found out about Parker's betrayal, and how he had started a war between the Diego Kingz and their biggest rival—Euclid Disciples.

Parker's cell phone vibrated and snapped him out of his thoughts. Digging the device from his pocket, he glanced at the screen.

Laz: *meet me in the kitchen*

Parker had been on his way to the small conference room where they usually met before an assignment but turned back the way he had come. Passing several pieces of artwork hanging on the walls, he barely spared them a glance as he mentally got into work mode.

They still had over an hour before they needed to pick up the client, but it wasn't unusual for them to eat before a job. One of many things he loved about working at Supreme—they took good care of their employees. Egypt and her admin team were great at having a fully stocked kitchen at any given time.

When Parker entered the large space, with its cream-colored walls and top-of-the-line appliances, the blend of various spices reached his nose. Inhaling deeply, he could tell the scent included garlic, cloves, and maybe cinnamon, but also something sweet and savory.

Laz was peeking inside of several white Chinese food boxes. There had to be at least ten of them spread out on the center island, along with spring rolls, crab rangoon, pastry puffs, and potstickers, to name a few. Considering all the food, no doubt there were other teams on assignments tonight.

His gaze traveled over Laz, and the way his thick, dark hair was slicked back brought more attention to his olive skin. He no longer sported a ponytail at his nape, but it was still long enough to brush his collar. Both men were similarly dressed. They'd all been fitted with tuxedos years ago specifically for jobs like tonight, but their styles were very different. While Laz's tux was single-breasted with peak lapels, Parker's tux was double-breasted with notch lapels. His was more of a slimmer cut and presented a bolder appearance. Neither of them should have a problem blending in with tonight's wealthy crowd.

Laz glanced up. "Well, well, well, look who finally got off of punishment." He moved to the refrigerator and pulled out a couple of flavored waters and set them on the counter. "For a while there, I thought you'd be on front desk duty until you retired."

"Man, don't start with that crap. Remember, it's because of you Mason punished me in the first place. Now that I think about it, I'm always getting into trouble because of you," Parker said, and greeted his friend with a handshake and a one-armed hug.

Laz chuckled. "I'll admit I've gotten us jammed up a few times, but whatever the hell you did to get on desk duty for *months* was all on you. Come on, dig in so we can talk about what to expect tonight. Egypt said I'm lead on the assignment and there's been a couple of changes."

Parker glanced at all the food and grabbed one of the bottled waters. "Not hungry," he said.

Laz was scooping shrimp fried rice onto his plate, but stopped. "What's wrong with you? You're the greediest person on our team. Normally, if you found out there was a spread like this, you would've been in here before anyone could tell you what was on the menu."

Parker snorted at the truth in that statement. He had an active metabolism and had always loved food. He could eat all day and night and never get full. It was like a going joke around the building that his stomach was a bottomless pit.

But since finding out that the media had snapped a photo of him, and breaking up with Chelsey, he hadn't had much of an appetite.

Parker waved him off. "I'm fine."

"Yeah, if you say so, but these last few months, you haven't been eating, you've been quieter than usual, and clearly you haven't been sleeping."

All true statements, and Parker waited for Laz to say more. He didn't. Instead, he moved over to the long table near the window and dug into his food. The silence between them was almost deafening, and unease crawled through Parker.

Lazarus Dimas going quiet without giving him the third-degree was as unnerving as going to the dentist for a root canal. He and Laz had worked together for years, and Parker knew his friend's tells. Like when he was thinking about doing something crazy, his hazel-green eyes darkened and looked like the color of a malachite crystal. Or when he was mad, he had several tells, but one was a tick in his left jaw. And when he got angry enough to murder someone, he put a gun to their head. Kind of like Parker had done to Terrance the night before, which still bothered him.

But this eerie silence? Nah, something was up. Laz didn't just ask a few questions and drop the subject. It wasn't in his nature. Normally, he'd be giving Parker a hard time about front desk duty, or not eating, or even...

Wait a minute.

Parker carried his bottle of water over to the table and sat across from Laz. "What do you know?" he asked. "And don't insult my intelligence by saying *nothing*."

Laz's lips twitched as if trying to hide a smile, and he hesitated before saying, "So your dad's a gangster, huh?" He stuffed fried rice into his mouth and chewed while shaking his head. "A damn O.G. on the streets. That explains a lot about you."

Parker narrowed his eyes. "What's that supposed to mean?"

He wasn't surprised Laz knew about his past, but he was curious to know just how much he knew. The man was like a bloodhound when he wanted information, and he wouldn't stop until he got what he wanted.

"What do you mean by *that explains a lot?*"

"Learning your dad is the leader of one of the most notorious crime syndicates on the west coast explained a few things I hadn't been able to figure out. Like that edginess about you that doesn't come from just being a cop or a former SWAT officer. I had a feeling you came from the streets despite what we knew about you on the surface."

Thanks to Mason and a few of his connections, Parker had been given a whole new life. It was a bit unnerving that Laz knew anything about his past.

Parker's identity had been scrubbed and changed. Mason and his buddies had hooked him up with a plastic surgeon, a psychiatrist, an etiquette specialist, and a few other people who helped him go from street thug to almost cultured. That included him getting his GED, as well as a bachelor's degree in criminology that he earned online.

Parker had decided to go into law enforcement, determined to be the opposite of everything he'd been raised to be. He was committed to being a better person and upholding the law, not breaking it. Getting thugs off the street and drug dealers behind bars had been paramount, and for years, he helped in that cause. Until Mason recruited him to join his Atlanta's Finest team.

"It's the way you carry yourself," Laz continued while eating. "Your head is always on a swivel, which isn't unusual in our line of work, but you're different, man. You have the type of street smarts that can only be learned one way—on the streets."

Laz would know. He'd been a cop in some of Atlanta's roughest neighborhoods, a white cop at that, and he'd seen it all. He was one of the coolest dudes Parker knew. He might still be somewhat of a hot head, but being married to a former prosecutor, he had cleaned up his act.

Well...somewhat. He still toed the line between right and wrong, especially when it came to family or protecting people he cared about. Nothing was off limits, even murder. He was a good-bad guy in every sense of the imagination.

"Is that where your street smarts and fearlessness came from, the streets?" Parker asked, even though he was sure he knew the answer. No way Laz could be the way he was without having similar experiences as Parker. Maybe he'd been in a gang, too, or at least hung around gang members growing up.

Laz gave a nonchalant shrug. "We're not talking about me. We're talking about you."

"How much do you know?" Parker asked. "And how did you find out?"

Laz's left eyebrow quirked, and his mouth twitched like earlier when he'd been trying to hide a smile. "What makes you think I know anything more than what I told you?"

"Because you're you, and please tell me you were discreet when digging into my life."

Laz sat back in his seat and wiped his mouth with a napkin. "First of all, I never reveal my sources. Second of all, I'm always discreet, but let me just say, I never would've guessed that Maverick Fucking-Wolf Farron was your father. That shit is *crazy*, but before I tell you what little I know, what do you know about your father?"

Parker cringed each time Laz referred to Wolf as his father. He hated his sperm donor and everything the bastard stood for. "All I know is that he's alive, and he's not in Atlanta."

That's all Parker cared about. He wanted to know the moment the asshole took his last breath and until recently, he'd wanted to make sure they were never on the same side of the continent.

Laz nodded. "I know he's deep in the drug business which has quadrupled over the last fifteen years. That's partly because he's not just dealing cocaine. He's connected to a producer of some of the purest fentanyl on the market."

Parker cursed under his breath. Knowing his father was continuing to get rich while slowly killing people with his products angered him. He had to stop him, which was something he should've done years ago.

Soon, though. Soon Wolf would get everything that was coming to him.

"Authorities have tried to connect him with a new cocktail drug that hit the streets of San Diego two months ago. It's linked to ten deaths already, and authorities fear there will be more. Your father's name has been tossed around as the supplier. So far, he hasn't been charged with anything because they can't make a solid connection. Probably because your father has dirty cops on his payroll. No doubt they're helping his ass stay out of prison."

Parker wanted so bad to ask Laz about how he knew any of this, but he'd be wasting his time. "What else do you know?"

"Rumor has it, he partnered up with a gun trafficker a couple of years ago. A guy named T.B. Barron out of Arizona, and he's been in the game a long time but is currently under federal investigation."

Hope bloomed inside of Parker, and he sat up straighter. "Does that mean Wolf is also—"

"Nope. He's not listed in the investigation report. At least not yet. That's pretty much all I know. What I don't know is what you did to piss off the Kingz and why they think you're dead."

Parker broke eye contact and gave his head a little shake. *Damn.* The fact Laz knew anything was unnerving.

At least he didn't seem to know how Parker had gotten free

69

of the Kingz. Meaning, his own contact in the Kingz was still keeping his mouth shut. He and Luis were the only ones who knew exactly how that went down. Mason didn't even know that part. At least, not all of it.

"Oh, and does Kenton know you've been fucking his sister?"

Anger lit inside of Parker, and he jerked his gaze to meet Laz's. "Careful, man. Don't talk about her like that," he said, hating the way those words sounded coming out of Laz's mouth. The guy made it sound as if Parker had been using Chelsey for sex, when that was the furthest from the truth.

Laz grinned. "I figured it was more than just sex. Considering how you've been moping around here like you lost your best friend. I assume you're in love with her."

Parker didn't respond.

"So, let's recap. The Kingz think you're dead. You're in hiding, sort of. Chelsey has threatened to kick your ass, and she isn't speaking to you. Then there's Kenton. Since your ass is still alive, it's safe to say he doesn't know about you and Chelsey. Did I miss anything?"

Parker glared at him. "Sometimes I hate you. Who else knows about my past?"

"I have no idea. I haven't said anything but like me, the guys know something's up with you, but no one has said anything."

Parker nodded. "Good. I need to talk to Chelsey first, but once I fill her in, then I need to run something by you and the guys. I want to take Wolf and the Kingz down once and for all, but I might need some help."

Laz released a long whistle. "*Dude,* I'm good, but going after the Kingz? That won't be easy, but you know I got your back and so do the others."

Parker knew that. He just had to decide if he wanted them to risk their lives and their families' lives for him.

"Oh, and as for Chelsey, she's working with us tonight," Laz said nonchalantly.

Parker stiffened. "She's not a security specialist."

Even if she'd already gone through the extensive training, she wasn't ready. Well, maybe she was ready, but Parker wasn't ready for her to be on anyone's detail. Their job might not be as dangerous as a police officer protecting the streets, but they had their moments. When she first mentioned applying for a security specialist position, Parker had hoped she'd change her mind. She hadn't. Not only had she applied for the position, but she had voluntarily gone through the training.

"What happened to Ashton?" Parker asked. "He was scheduled for this assignment."

Laz shrugged. "Don't know. Didn't ask. But what I do know is whatever shit is going on between you and Chelsey will have to be tabled. The only fights I'm breaking up tonight are those involving our client."

A noise at the door caused Parker to glance over his shoulder, and he almost swallowed his tongue at the sight before him. Chelsey stood there looking like a wet dream in a red halter evening gown that caressed her curves like a second skin. The fitted garment showed off one long, smooth, shapely leg, and Parker bolted out of his chair, causing it to tip over in the process.

"You can't wear that!" he snapped before he could stop himself.

Chelsey glowered at him, then turned her attention to Laz. "Why the hell is he here?"

71

Chapter Nine

God must hate me.

Why else would He open up doors for her to get her dream job, then drop Parker dead smack in the middle of her first real assignment? It wasn't fair. Even more than that, she had to be near the man while he was looking like he had just stepped out of a GQ magazine photo shoot.

Sometime between last night, when he threatened her date, until now, he must have visited the barber shop. His low fade haircut looked fresh and showed off his natural waves, and his mustache and goatee were perfectly groomed.

Chelsey had always been drawn to dark chocolate men, and they didn't come any finer than Parker Wilcox. The man was beautiful, and he had the body to go with it. He always wore his suits fitted, and they showed off his wide shoulders that tapered to his narrowed waist.

Tonight, though, everything about him was popping, including his muscular biceps pushing against the dark fabric. As her gaze took him in, a deep longing for him burrowed into her and landed dead smack into her chest.

Damn him!

"You can *not* wear that," Parker ground out, his words and tone jolting her out of her perusal of him. "This is a security assignment, not some...some party! You shouldn't be going anyway until you've had more training."

Chelsey stepped further into the kitchen, barely hanging on to her anger. "Clearly you have forgotten that I was once a cop. But why am I even talking to you? You're not my boss, and in case no one told you, I belong on this detail!"

His long legs carried him across the room in three steps, and he stopped in front of her. She had opted for dressy wedge-heels since she could run better in them, and they added a few inches to her 5'8" height. Still Parker had a few inches on her. Between his gorgeous eyes that were boring into her, and his enticing woodsy scent, she lost herself in his presence. But then he opened his mouth.

"No one is going to take you seriously if you're wearing that and claiming to be a security specialist. Every asshole in that place tonight will be pawing at you like you're their next meal, and what are you going to do? Like you, Laz and I have a job to do, and we won't be able to keep an eye on you while protecting our client."

Chelsey gritted her teeth, refusing to let his words turn her into a screaming lunatic. But she was seriously tempted to knock him upside his big head with her handbag. The handbag that held one of her weapons. She had another strapped to her inner thigh with a garter holster that was well hidden but easy to reach.

"Parker, you don't have to worry about me. *Ever.* I can take care of myself while also doing my job. So keep your focus on our client and worry about your own damn self."

She wanted to ask him who was going to keep the lonely women attending the event from grabbing his gorgeous ass.

Because no doubt he'd be luring all the honeys his way tonight. The man was too fine for his own good.

"And another thing, why do you even care?" she snapped. She wanted to add that he'd given up any right to anything about her, but she kept that thought to herself.

"Because..." His eyes blazed with anger as his chest heaved. "Because I love you, dammit." He moved closer. Close enough to kiss, and Chelsey stilled. "And I care because if anything ever happened to you, it would kill me!" he roared and shoved past her before storming out of the room.

Startled by the conviction in his tone, Chelsey stood stunned. Parker had professed his love for her numerous times, but this time was different. The emotion behind the words was different.

She turned to Laz who was standing near the center island, shaking his head. "Exactly what did I just walk in on?" she asked, because Parker's overreaction seemed a bit over the top.

Laz tossed his paper plate in the trash. "It doesn't matter. All that matters is that I should be getting hazard pay for dealing with you two nutcases tonight. Let's go." He started for the door but stopped and pinned her with a serious look. "Try to go easy on him tonight, okay? He's not himself."

"Ya think?" Chelsey said sarcastically as they left the room only to run into her brother, Kenton. She sighed before he could even open his mouth.

"What's up with our boy?" Kenton asked Laz, but Laz shook his head and kept walking. Then Kenton turned his attention on her.

At 6'4" with broad shoulders and a linebacker build, Kenton Bailey had always been an imposing sight. Today was no different, especially seeing him in a black suit, shirt and tie. His low-cut hair, perfectly trimmed mustache and goatee high-lighted his smooth dark skin and had him looking more like a business executive instead of someone who provided personal security. Apparently, he was either returning or going on an assignment this evening, too.

His gaze took her in, and then he frowned. "Egypt said you'd been assigned to a job tonight, but what the hell are you wearing?"

"Hello to you, too," Chelsey said, holding back what she really wanted to say to her overprotective brother. Instead, she hugged him and kissed his cheek. "I don't have time to argue with you. Have a good night. I know I will."

"Chelsey, you should probably change into..."

She ignored whatever else he had to say and headed to the parking lot where the company SUVs were located. As she approached their vehicle, where Parker was holding open the back door, she exhaled. He hadn't been himself in months. At first, she was ticked off at him for more reasons than one, but now she was a little worried. Not worried enough to ask what was going on with him, but worried nonetheless.

"Thank you," she said and climbed into the front seat. When he nodded and closed the door, she decided it was time to put on her professional demeanor. She wasn't going to let him, or Kenton's concerns get in the way of her doing her job.

As they drove to the client's home, the three of them discussed the details of the assignment. When the part about her being Jeff Hawkin's fake date came up, Parker mumbled something under his breath that she couldn't make out. She could just imagine what he'd said. Probably something about the guy not putting his hands on her, but she ignored him as Laz continued laying out the plan. He and Parker would be there to provide the security for her and her *date*. She'd only get involved in that aspect if necessary.

Before they arrived at the client's home located in Buckhead, an affluent suburb of Atlanta, they inserted their earpieces. The devices were designed to be almost unde-tectable, allowing them to communicate with each other easily.

When they reached the client's address, Laz drove through the opened gate and a short while later pulled up to the stately brick home. They all climbed out of the vehicle. So that Chelsey could introduce herself to Hawkins as his date, she'd gone to the front door while Parker and Laz stayed at the SUV.

She rang the doorbell and within seconds, the door swung open.

"Good evening, Mr. Hawkins. I'm Chelsey, your date for the evening. Are you ready?"

He wasn't as old as she had expected. Looking to be in his mid- to late thirties, he had a fair complexion, maybe mixed-race, and had short, dark wavy hair, attractive hazel eyes, and he was clean shaven.

Totally not her type.

"My date, huh? You're gorgeous," Hawkins said approvingly. "Mr. Crosby mentioned that the team would be armed. Where's your weapon?" he asked as his appreciative gaze traveled from the top of her head and did a slow trek down her body.

"I have several weapons, including my hands," she said, trying not to let her irritation show. "Are you ready to leave?"

He chuckled. "I am." He offered her his arm as they climbed down the few concrete stairs. She only accepted his assistance because it was time she got into character. Hopefully, he'd be a gentleman the whole evening. Then they won't have a problem.

They were in the back seat with her sitting behind Laz, giving her a good view of Parker's profile. He glanced back at her periodically making it hard to breathe the same air as him. No way would she make eye contact and end up flustered for the rest of the evening. It would throw her off her game, and she was trying to prove herself.

Laz's opinions went a long way when it came to Mason, Hamilton, and even Egypt. If Chelsey could show him that she was willing and ready to be on the Atlanta's Finest team, she wouldn't have to take the office position Egypt had hired her for.

But Parker's words from earlier ping-ponged through her mind. He was worried for her safety like she was often worried for his.

How did they get here?

Months ago, everything had seemed so perfect. They were going to go public with their relationship, she was going to move in with him, and they were going to live happily ever after. Then all of a sudden it was over, and he had crushed her heart.

Even if she allowed him to explain his actions, she couldn't go back. She couldn't risk him stomping on her heart and her feelings the way he'd done months ago.

"How's this supposed to work tonight?" Hawkins asked.

Laz repeated what they'd discussed earlier, explaining that Chelsey would remain at his side throughout the night. If for some reason he needed to have a private conversation with someone, he'd be expected to insist that either he or Parker be nearby since they were his security.

A short while later, they arrived at the historic mansion where the art exhibit and fundraiser was taking place. As they entered through the wrought iron gates, Chelsey took in the magnolia trees that lined the circular driveway. The mansion wasn't as impressive as the landscaping that included beautiful trees, an abundance of flowers, and a large fountain in the center of the yard.

Even if the outside of the home was understated, she'd seen beautiful pictures of the interior. If nothing else, she was looking forward to touring the mansion. With her arm looped through his, Chelsey walked along side Hawkins as they entered the venue.

Numerous people dressed in formal attire had already arrived and were roaming around the semi-open space. A wide staircase leading to a second floor was one of the first things Chelsey noted. The artwork, abstract expressionism, on the walls stood out thanks to spotlights shining on each piece as they were led to the ballroom. There, she took in stunning chandeliers, a coffered ceiling, crystal sconces, and shiny hardwood floors.

Belly bars covered with tablecloths took up the middle of the floor, and at the far end of the large space were food tables. Servers floated around with trays of drinks and hors d'oeuvres. The artwork in this space was more in line with realism. From what one of the hosts was saying, each room they visited would showcase different types of art.

Hawkins leaned over and whispered in her ear, not knowing that whatever he said to her, the guys would be able to hear also.

"If at any time you want to make this date real, let me know. Or maybe when we leave here, you'll join me for a nightcap."

"Thanks, but I'm not interested," Chelsey said while giving him a smile to soften her words.

He returned the smile. "You might not be interested now, but—"

"If he tries anything with you, he's a dead man," Parker growled low in her ear, probably speaking without thinking since Laz was on the coms, too.

Then again, Laz clearly knew that she and Parker had a history. He hadn't seemed surprised by Parker's declaration before leaving Supreme.

She just hoped Parker didn't confront the client the way he'd done with Terrance. That's all she needed was for word to get back to Mason or Hamilton that they let their personal issues get in the way of them doing their jobs.

Nope. She wouldn't let that happen. Parker wasn't going to ruin this for her. Not if he wanted to live to see another day.

Chapter Ten

Frustration pulsed through Parker as he kept close tabs on Hawkins and Chelsey. He was annoyed with himself for being pissed that she was pretending to be the guy's date. She was doing her job, but she was doing it a little too well. Laughing at his jokes. Touching his arm periodically and smiling up at him like he hung the moon. Anyone looking in from the outside would think they were actually a couple.

The other thing that bugged Parker was Chelsey's evening gown. He couldn't stop looking at her in that sexy-ass dress. The front appeared conservative with the high collar that covered her neck and fastened in back. Her toned arms and shoulders were bare while the silky, red material glided over her curvaceous body and showed off her perky breasts and perfectly round butt. The back of the dress was nonexistent, and it was pure torture each time Parker glanced her way and saw all that smooth, dark skin.

All he wanted to do was gather her into his arms, kiss her senseless, and then bury himself deep inside of her.

He shook that last thought free. It wasn't doing him any good to think about how much he missed her long legs wrapped around his waist while he thrust in and out of her until she screamed his name.

Images of their last time together immediately flooded his mind. He'd made love to her like a man possessed, while burying his nose in the crook of her scented neck. It was like he could still smell the combination of coconut and vanilla mixed with her sweet natural scent and...

Dammit. He had to stop this and focus.

Not just on her, but he also needed to keep eyes on Hawkins. Why the guy actually hired them for this event was a mystery. It wasn't like this was some type of hip-hop party where things could jump off at any given moment. No, this was a three-hundred-dollars-a-ticket event with top-shelf liquor, amazing finger-food, live music, and an art exhibit. All to raise money for children with special needs.

It didn't make sense that he needed personal security. It wasn't like any of the people his company had laid off would be attending an event like this...

Wait. Maybe Jeff was expecting someone to be in attendance who wanted to do him harm. Someone he knew would be there and that same someone who might've threatened his life.

Parker straightened as he gazed around at everyone who was near Hawkins, looking for anyone who seemed out of place. That had to be it. He had beef with someone he was expecting to be there. Nothing else made sense. This event was too low-key to be expecting trouble.

As Parker studied the people in their vicinity, no one stood out. Then his attention went back to Chelsey. Every time he stole a glance at her, his heart flipped and knocked against his rib cage. She was his. All he had to do was win her back, especially before some other guy like Terrance tried to get with her.

Watching her now, he hated that she was putting her life in danger, and he didn't care that she'd once been a cop. It didn't matter that she could handle herself. He still worried about her.

It had been so long since he cared about someone, he wasn't sure how to act. The helplessness that he was currently feeling was foreign to him, and now he knew how the other guys on his team felt. They all were protectors by nature, but he always thought they were overprotective when it came to their wives.

Now he understood since Chelsey was a part of him. She meant everything to him, and he hadn't been kidding when he told her that if anything happened to her, it would kill him.

He just had to make sure nothing ever happened to her.

As he stood near the bar set up in the corner, not too far from Chelsey and Hawkins, an eerie sensation he had experienced earlier in the evening was back. The first time he'd felt it was shortly after they'd arrived.

Now that sensation was stronger, as if someone was watching him. He looked around. There were too many people in the ballroom to determine if anyone was focused on him.

Until now.

To his left was a guy wearing a white dinner jacket and black tuxedo pants. When Parker made eye contact, the man quickly glanced away.

Interesting.

The guy stood out because he was taller than those near him, over six feet tall.

Parker kept his attention on him, predicting that he would look at him again. Sure enough, he did. Parker cataloged everything he could about the man. Mid-forties. Low haircut. Sepia skin tone. His height and build were close to Parker's.

He didn't look familiar, but he'd definitely been staring, and now he had Parker's full attention.

Who the hell is he?

Seeing Laz strolling along the perimeter not far from the man, Parker discreetly pulled out his cell phone and shot off a quick text.

My ten o'clock. Black guy. White jacket. My height.

Laz glanced at Parker, then immediately spotted the guy. He would also know what the text meant—keep an eye on him.

Parker wasn't sure what interest this man had in him, but it could also have something to do with Hawkins. Anyone watching long enough could probably figure out that Parker was with him, and maybe even his security.

The guy was still watching, and Parker didn't look away until two women approached the man, and they all started talking.

Parker's attention went back to Chelsey and her *date*. The jerk was still trying to talk her into going out with him once she was off duty. This time, Parker didn't say anything. He needed to keep things as professional as possible, and threatening to kill the guy had been the wrong thing to say. Even if he did mean it.

A man and woman strolled over to them.

"Jeff, I was wondering if you'd be here tonight," the guy said, greeting Hawkins with a handshake.

"Of course I'm here." Hawkins greeted the man's companion, then kissed her cheek. "You two know I couldn't miss this fundraiser. The organization was a godsend to my family when I was growing up, and I don't know what my parents would've done without their financial assistance. Thanks to them, my brother got the treatment he needed.

"Oh, forgive my manners. Let me introduce you to my

83

date," he said, wrapping his arm around Chelsey's waist as if he had every right to do so.

Parker kept his cool. *This was a job*. He'd just keep telling himself that.

As for what Hawkins had said about his brother, that information hadn't been in the client's dossier. Parker only knew the basics about his extended family; Hawkins was single, his parents were retired, he had an older sister and a younger brother, who all lived in town. There hadn't been any information about his brother being special-needs.

"Excuse me," Parker heard Chelsey say, "I'll let you all catch up. Jeff, I'll be right over here." She pointed a few feet away to a table that held desserts.

"Okay, baby," Jeff said and pulled her close, placing a kiss on her cheek.

Parker growled before he could stop himself. "You should've decked him for putting his hands and mouth on you," he mumbled, and Chelsey smirked while shaking her head.

"Parker, your guy is heading your way," Laz said quietly through the earpiece. "I'll keep eyes on our client."

"Me too," Chelsey said, but glanced Parker's way.

He turned to see the man from earlier walking toward him with purpose, and Parker dropped his hands to his sides prepared to reach for his gun if necessary.

As if reading his mind or recognizing his stance, the man slowed and lifted his hands out in front of him as if to say, *relax*.

"Hey, man. I'm not looking for trouble," he said when he got closer.

His voice carried over the live music that sifted through the speakers, but not loud enough to catch anyone else's attention. Parker still had to strain to hear him.

"It's just that you look so familiar. Have we met?"

Unease coursed through Parker, aware that the man had

moved even closer. Now he was in striking distance. Parker rarely forgot a face, and he was sure he didn't know the guy.

"My name is Sean. And you are?"

"Lance," Parker said, using an old alias from back in the day.

"Did you ever live in San Francisco?" Sean asked.

"No," Parker said simply, planning to make that his answer no matter what question was thrown at him.

"What about LA or Champagne, Illinois?"

"No."

"Are you in law enforcement?"

"No," Parker said again, that unease from earlier returning. The last two questions hit a little too close to home.

"Oh, well." The man shrugged. "Sorry to bother you. Have a good evening."

"I took a photo of him," Laz said, and Parker's lips quirked, trying to keep from grinning. His friend was thorough if nothing else, and he knew Parker would want to gather some information on the man even if it didn't lead anywhere. They could get Wiz, Supreme's computer guru who lived in Chicago, to plug the photo into his facial recognition system.

"I saw you come in with Jeff. Apparently, you don't know the type of man you're dating." The low, menacing voice sounded through Parker's earpiece, and his gaze shot to Chelsey.

A stocky, fair-complexioned man, maybe in his late forties with reddish-blond hair, was standing a little too close to Chelsey. "He's a homewrecker," the guy continued, his words slurring a bit. "He thinks he's going to get away with it. He won't. Not when I'm done with him."

"Who are you?" Chelsey asked, slowly setting down the plate in her hand.

"I guess you don't recognize me," the man said with a shrug. "That's all right. I'm just warning you. Jeff is a user."

85

"His name is Troy Warrenberg. He owns several businesses in Georgia and is known around town for his philanthropy," Laz said in their ear. "Not sure what's up with him and Jeff, though."

Parker didn't care who the hell he was. He didn't like the way the man was looking at Chelsey. It wasn't necessarily a look of desire. No, it was more like he was sizing her up, and when the corners of his mouth kicked up into a smarmy smile, Parker knew he was up to something.

Troy ran the back of his hand up Chelsey's bare arm, and Parker didn't feel himself move until Chelsey whispered, "Stand down."

Parker pulled up short but didn't take his attention from them.

"I don't know what you're talking about," she said coolly to Troy as she moved her arm from his touch.

"I'm talking about your boyfriend over there—Jeff Hawkins. The bastard slept with my wife. I've warned him to stay away from her but apparently, he thinks he's untouchable. Like he can do whatever the hell he wants without consequences."

"That's between you and Jeff. So take it up with him."

"Or maybe I'll just take his woman."

The guy moved fast. He grabbed Chelsey's upper arm in a death grip, and Parker heard her as she hissed in pain. He skirted around a few people and was moving toward Chelsey before his brain was completely engaged. But before he could reach her, she grabbed Troy's wrist and twisted it while simultaneously kicking him behind the knee and forcing him to the floor. He cried out in agony as she twisted his wrist harder.

"I don't care what Jeff has done to you or your wife," Chelsey ground out close to the man's ear, ignoring his pleas to release him, "but if you *ever* put your hand on me again, I will break it in multiple places."

Knowing Laz still had eyes on Hawkins, Parker grabbed the back of Troy's tuxedo jacket and yanked him to his feet.

"You're lucky she handled you before I got over here. Otherwise, they'd be carrying you out on a stretcher," Parker said between gritted teeth, trying to keep his anger in check.

He glanced at Chelsey, and she met his eyes.

You okay? he mouthed.

With her hands on her hips, she gave him a head nod and a cocky smile.

Damn. She was amazing.

His woman literally brought a man to his knees and looked sexy as hell in her evening gown while doing it. Parker was an idiot. The stupidest thing he'd ever done in his life was walk away from this incredible woman.

He had to fix this...fix them, because there was no way he was living the rest of his life without her in it.

Three security guards rushing toward them snagged his attention.

"What's going on?" one of them asked.

"These people assaulted me!" Troy yelled, trying to jerk free of Parker's hold. The man swayed, making it clear that he'd had too much to drink.

The commotion caught Jeff's attention, along with others in the room. Especially when security led Troy, Chelsey, and Parker out of the ballroom. Jeff followed behind them, and they all were taken to a room at the back of the mansion. It was interesting watching as Jeff played Chelsey's doting date, insisting that he wanted Troy arrested for assault. Pointing out the bruise on her arm that made Parker want to snatch Troy up and choke him.

For the next few minutes, security listened as they

explained how everything played out. Parker backed up Chelsey's account of what took place, telling them he witnessed everything and only got involved because the guy tried to manhandle her.

Chelsey insisted that she was fine and had no intention of pressing charges. It was clear the guy had too much to drink, especially when he started crying and saying that Jeff broke up his marriage and ruined his life.

Jeff never admitted to anything; he also never mentioned that he had hired personal security for the event. Instead, he had referred to Chelsey and Parker as his guests for the evening. He didn't mention Laz who had hung back but was nearby.

When Parker, Chelsey, and Jeff were free to return to the fundraiser, they stepped out of the room and found Laz leaning against the wall at the end of the hallway. He didn't say anything as they approached, but he had heard everything through his earpiece.

"Let me leave a check with one of the organizers, and then we can leave," Jeff said, and Chelsey walked away with him while Parker and Laz trailed a short distance behind.

"Well, this has been interesting," Laz mumbled, and Parker agreed.

Part of him wanted to take his frustration out on Jeff, but he had to remind himself that this was a job. If anyone had anything to say to their client, it would be Chelsey, and he'd follow her lead. She had handled herself well tonight, but he decided that if she got a permanent position doing security, he couldn't work with her. She was too much of a distraction. A good distraction, but a distraction, nonetheless.

Twenty minutes later, Laz brought the SUV around and they all climbed in.

Silence filled the vehicle until Jeff spoke. "I'm sorry

about what happened back there," he said, then turned to Chelsey. "I'm glad you weren't seriously hurt. As you've probably figured out, there's bad blood between me and Troy. I didn't knowingly sleep with his wife. She never told me that—"

"Wait," Chelsey said, and Parker stole a glance at her without turning all the way around. She lifted her hands to stop Jeff from continuing. "You don't have to explain. Our job was to keep you safe this evening, and that's what we did. Yes, it would've been nice to know up-front that Troy had been threatening you, and that he was there and might cause trouble. But it's over now, and whatever happens between the two of you is between you guys. I hope you'll be willing to give Supreme a good review."

Parker exchanged a look with Laz, who snorted. None of them, their security team, had ever asked a client for a review. They did their jobs, did it well, and were rewarded when the clients hired them again.

But a review? If reviews were requested, they were requested by Egypt or someone else in the office. Never the security specialists.

"Of course. That's the least I can do. You were great tonight, and I know you don't want to go out with me outside of your job, but I'll be requesting you if I ever need a date who can also provide security."

Parker growled under his breath and ignored the rest of their conversation. Nope. He definitely couldn't work with Chelsey going forward. He'd end up getting himself fired for doing something stupid like beating up a client.

He released a quiet, long, drawn-out breath and stared out the SUV's side window as the city flew by in a blur. He replayed the evening back through his mind.

What if Chelsey hadn't been able to defend herself? What

if that jerk had seriously hurt her? Parker would've lost his shit, and who knows how the evening would've gone from there.

Now that he was thinking straight, something else came to mind. Though the altercation had ended quickly, what if someone had videotaped it? They were living in a day and time when people were capturing everything on their cell phones. He'd been so caught up in the moment that he didn't do his usual due diligence in making sure to keep his head down.

The last thing he wanted was for Wolf to find out he was still alive. At least not before Parker was ready to reveal himself. He didn't want his father to have a heads-up.

Not yet. Not until Parker had a plan in place that would destroy Wolf once and for all.

He was ready for a normal life. No more looking over his shoulder or fearing that his father would find him.

He was done hiding.

Chapter Eleven

The next day, Parker jogged up Chelsey's front steps and rang the doorbell. He was determined to talk to her even if it meant doing so through the door. It had to be today. It had to be before he told his Atlanta's Finest team about his past and then asked for their help.

In hindsight, the secrets he planned to reveal to everyone was something he should've done already. He trusted all of them more than he ever trusted anyone, but he honestly thought his past was behind him, and maybe it still was. Either way, it was time they knew who was in their midst.

"I don't want to talk to you," Chelsey said by way of greeting when she swung the door open.

"But I need to talk to you, and it needs to be today," Parker countered.

Her hair was in two messy ponytails on each side of her head, and based on the yellow, rubber gloves in her hand, she'd been doing some cleaning. He took note of the old ratty Atlanta Hawks T-shirt and cutoff jeans that showed off her sexy legs.

He had always been a leg man, and hers were the first thing he'd noticed on her.

She definitely didn't look like the sex goddess from the night before. Still, Chelsey was the most beautiful, sexy woman in the world. Even when she was glaring at him, like now.

Any sane man would probably walk away until she was in a better mood. Parker couldn't. She was his heart, and he couldn't go another day without her in his life. He wanted a second chance with her but first, there were things she needed to know about him.

Chelsey knew the good. Unfortunately, he now had to tell her some of the bad. He just hoped she gave him another chance once she learned about his past.

"Please, Chelsey. I need you to know why I broke things off between us. I need you to know the truth about me."

He wasn't sure what she saw on his face or heard in his voice, but her expression softened. Without a word, she let him into the house.

The place smelled like pine cleaner and furniture polish, and as he glanced around the open floor plan, it was clear that she'd been doing some deep cleaning. She wasn't the neatest person in the world, and it wasn't unusual to see a jacket on the arm of the chair or shoes in the middle of the floor.

Not today, though. Today everything was in its place. Pillows on the sofa and love seat had been fluffed. The hardwood floors gleamed, and the family pictures on the mantel had been reorganized and shined up. She'd been busy.

Chelsey dropped the gloves onto a nearby table and folded her arms across her chest. Parker's eyes immediately zoned in on her luscious breasts. This was not the time for him to be lusting after his woman, but damn. He couldn't ignore the way her pebbled nipples pushed against the thin material of her T-shirt. Nipples that he had teased, licked, and sucked into submission more times than he could count.

His body stirred at the memory of how good her full breasts used to feel in his hands. How amazing she'd felt hugged up to him, and how much he missed what they'd had. More than anything in the world, Parker wanted her back, but it wasn't just because the sex had been incredible. No, it had more to do with the fact that she completed him. His life had been empty before she came along, and she filled it with love, compassion, and fun times. The last few months without her had been hell.

"Eyes up here, Buster," Chelsey bit out.

Parker's gaze shot up, and he had to bite the inside of his cheek to keep from laughing. Damn, he missed her sass. He missed everything about her from her bow-shaped, kissable lips, to the way she screamed his name whenever he was buried deep inside her sexy body.

He sighed. This was not why he came over here, but being this close to her, made him want to carry her to the nearest bed or any flat surface. It didn't help that he hadn't been with another woman since the first time he'd made love to Chelsey. No one else would do. She was it for him. The complete package.

"Parker, I don't have all day to stand here, and if I'm honest, I don't give a—"

"My father killed my mother," he interrupted, knowing he had to talk fast. "And I couldn't tell a soul. To this day, no one knows she's dead and died at the hands of my father."

Chelsey's mouth dropped open, but then she closed it quickly. She stared at him, horror in her eyes and her hand over her heart. Each time she opened her mouth to speak, she closed it again.

Okay, maybe he could've figured out a better way to start, but this was going to be one of the hardest conversations he'd ever had. He wasn't exactly sure how to share everything he wanted and needed to tell her.

"Oh, my God, Parker, I..." she started but stopped and shook her head. Then she reached for him, linking her fingers with his and pulling him further into the living room. "I am so sorry. I knew your mother passed away, but I had no idea she was killed."

That was something they had in common. Her mother had been killed during a bank robbery when Chelsey was an infant. While he'd had twelve years with his mother, Chelsey never knew hers.

Another difference in the way they'd grown up was that she'd been raised by a father and three older siblings who adored her. She had once told him that they had showered her with so much love that she never got a chance to miss the mother she never knew.

"How? Why? We've talked about our mothers. Why didn't you tell me this before?" she asked.

Parker rubbed the back of his neck. He'd had more than enough opportunities to tell her the details about his mother's death, as well as the other stuff about his past. Yet, he had kept quiet.

"I wasn't ready, and if I had told you, it would've led to more questions that I couldn't discuss."

"Couldn't or wouldn't?" she asked quietly, and he didn't miss the hurt in her eyes. "You claimed to love me. Yet, you didn't love me enough to trust me with that information."

"Wait!" he said, the word snapping out like a whip crackling through the air. He got in her face so fast that Chelsey tensed and took a step back. Which put her against a wall.

Parker placed his palms against the wall above her head, locking her in before bending slightly to make sure they were at eye level. He needed her to see the truth in his eyes and hear what he was about to say.

"I love you more than I have *ever* loved another human being! So get that thought about me not loving or trusting you out of your head," he growled, but seeing her wide eyes, he reined in his emotions enough to not totally freak her out.

"Chelsey, I know my behavior lately has been all over the place, and I'm so sorry about that. I'm hoping to clear some of that up today, but baby, don't ever think that I don't love you. I love you so damn much it hurts," he choked out, then swallowed hard. "I will *always* love you; whether you give me another chance or not, you will *always* own my heart."

She nibbled on her lower lip and blinked rapidly as if trying to hold back tears. None fell during the seconds that ticked by as silence fell between them. But then she caught him off guard and pounded her fist against his chest with enough force to have him stumbling back.

"Ow," he said, rubbing his chest.

"Dammit, Parker! I'm trying to stay mad at you, but when you say mushy stuff like that..." Her words trailed off and she dropped her gaze.

Relief flooded through him, and Parker couldn't stop the smile that spread across his lips. He stepped forward and got back in her face, glad to see she was softening toward him.

He lifted her chin with the pad of his finger, and when their eyes met again, his heart squeezed. The love brimming in her dark orbs matched what he felt for her to the depths of his soul.

"Baby, I am so sorry I hurt you," he said. "I'm an idiot, and hopefully after we talk, you'll understand why I thought I had done the right thing by breaking up with you."

Her dark eyes met his before her gaze dropped to his lips, lingered, and then returned to his eyes.

Parker wasn't exactly sure what she was thinking, but he was sure they wanted the same thing. Without hesitation, he cupped her face between his hands and lowered his head until his mouth covered hers. He marveled in the softness of her pillowy lips that were warm and sweet. This was what he needed. His emotions had been out of balance before he arrived, but in this moment, he felt a calmness settle over him. A calmness he hadn't felt since before they parted ways.

He tried to tame his eagerness, but it had been weeks since he had tasted her. Weeks since he held her in his arms, and weeks since he'd known that she wanted him as much as he wanted her.

As their tongues explored the inner recesses of each other's mouth, Parker slid one hand behind her neck and lowered the other to her waist. He pulled her flush against his body and deepened their connection.

Chelsey might've drove him crazy with her sass, but no one soothed his tattered soul the way she could.

His heart thumped uncontrollably as the kiss turned more intense, and a rush of pleasure pulsed through him. She filled him with hope, while also making him long for more. There was no doubt she felt his erection pressing against her stomach. It was impossible for him to be this close to her and his body not react to her nearness. She felt too damn good, and all he wanted to do was carry her upstairs and make mad, passionate love to her.

But he needed to get back on track. Not only did he want to tell her the rest, but he wanted to make something else clear.

Though he didn't want to break their connection, Parker slowly lifted his mouth from hers and gazed into her eyes. "I've missed you so much, and I know I mishandled things between us. I just..."

Compared to the type of family Chelsey had and the way

she'd grown up, Parker knew he wasn't good enough for her. Whenever he thought about his upbringing and the man who had raised him, he didn't feel worthy of someone like Chelsey. But that didn't stop him from wanting a chance to prove to her that he could be everything she wanted in a man.

"Hear me out for the next few minutes, and I'll explain where my head was at when I thought it was best to put some distance between us."

"You've had plenty of time to tell me what's going on. Why now?"

He released a long breath, unsure of what to say.

Yes, he could've told her months ago, but when he'd broken up with her, he thought he'd be leaving town. He thought he'd be protecting her and everyone else around him. Back then, he thought the less they all knew, the better. Now he wasn't sure. There might not currently be a threat to his life. Yet, that could easily change.

"It was too dangerous."

"And it's not dangerous now?" she shot back.

Even when he told her months ago that they had to break things off, he suspected she knew he hadn't told her everything. His reasons had been lame, even to his own ears.

"It might still be too dangerous, but I'm ready now. I'm ready to tell you everything about my past that I wasn't ready to tell before."

Silence pulsed between them before Chelsey nodded. "Okay, we can talk but have a seat and give me a minute. I need to freshen up a bit."

Parker took a step back. "All right, but I could come with you and help," he said, trying to lighten the moment some.

"No, absolutely not. I don't trust you or myself to be anywhere near a bed right now."

Parker laughed. He didn't bother telling her that anything

97

he'd do with her on a bed, he could easily do on the sofa. Hell, they could even do it on the floor, on the stairs, and even in the bathtub. It didn't matter as long as he was with her, and they were naked.

Instead of saying any of that, he kept his mouth shut and watched her fine ass swish back and forth in those short shorts as she started up the stairs.

She glanced over her shoulder at him. "Give me five minutes."

Ten minutes later, Chelsey returned with her curly hair hanging loose around her shoulders and mascara making her pretty eyes pop. She was still wearing the same T-shirt, but to Parker's disappointment she had put on a bra. A lace one, based on what he could see through the thin material of the shirt, and her bare feet were now covered in thick red socks.

"Now, I'm ready for us to talk."

"God, you're beautiful," Parker said, his heart squeezing as he stared into her gorgeous brown eyes. It didn't matter what she wore, she was the most alluring woman he'd ever met.

Her features softened and she gave him a small smile. "Thank you."

He gave a slight nod. They were off to a good start. That should excite him, but he was anxious about their talk. What would he do if she decided she didn't want to be with him? What if she blew a gasket at the fact that her life could've been in danger while they'd been dating?

He didn't have the answers to those questions, but if he wanted a future with her, it was past time to come clean.

"Do you want something to drink or eat?" she asked.

"No, thanks. I'm not hungry."

She stared at him. "In all the time we were together, you have *never* turned down food. Even when no one offered you food, you wanted something to eat."

He chuckled and sat on the sofa, patting the seat next to him for her to sit.

"Yeah, I've been hearing that a lot lately. Let's just say, I've been having some stressful months, and I guess I just haven't had an appetite."

Instead of sitting next to him, she sat in a wingback chair across from the sofa. That was probably best, because if she sat near him, he'd want to touch her. Actually, he'd want to do more than touch her. So, yes, keeping some distance between them was good.

For the next few minutes, he told her about the day his mother was killed. Parker didn't leave anything out, including how he couldn't tell anyone about what had happened and how Wolf made the body disappear. It had been such a dark time in Parker's life, and talking about it brought back all the hurt, anguish, and hatred he had for Wolf. There was no doubt Chelsey could feel what he felt for his father.

Parker told her about Wolf being the leader of the Diego Kingz, and how he'd been grooming him to take over the organization one day. The sick bastard hadn't given a damn about him except for when Parker did something to make him proud. Like sell drugs or beat the crap out of someone who was encroaching on the Kingz's territory.

"Even before my mother was killed, I hated Wolf. I hated everything about him and the Kingz. I vowed then that I would one day destroy him and the organization."

"Dear God," Chelsey said, looking at him with horror in her eyes. "You were a child. How could he treat you so...so..."

"Like I was a worthless piece of shit?" Parker said, knowing that wasn't what she was trying to say, but that was how Parker felt at the time. There was never any love between him and his father, and there never would be.

"I had no idea," she said quietly as if talking to herself. "I can't believe your father is the leader of an organized crime syndicate. And his name is Wolf?"

Parker knew this was only the beginning of her questions; questions he really didn't want to answer.

"That's his street name," he said. "Chelsey, I don't think it's a good idea for you to know his real name. Baby, you can't discuss him with anyone. You can't Google him. You need to act as if you've never heard of him. If you start poking around —"

"I won't, and I won't say anything about him to anyone. Tell me. What's his name?"

After a long hesitation, Parker conceded. "His name is Maverick Farron, Sr., and he's an evil, self-serving, narcissistic, SOB. I hope you never meet him."

"Senior?" she said with her perfectly arched eyebrows scrunched together. "Does that mean you're a—"

"I *was* a junior before I changed my name."

"*Maverick,*" she said, as if testing out the name.

"Don't even think about calling me that," Parker said, his tone hard. "I'll *never* answer to it."

"Okay, I won't, but what was your street name?"

Again, he hesitated. Why'd she want to know? That was part of his past life. A life he had completely removed himself from, and it was painful and unnerving to think about any of it.

But when Chelsey continued watching him, patiently waiting, Parker said, "My street name was Knuckles."

"*Knuckles?*"

"Yeah," Parker shrugged. "I fought a lot."

Which was putting it mildly. After his mother's death, he acted out and fighting was his therapy. How many times had his principal threatened to kick him out of school?

And on the streets? Everyone knew not to fuck with him. He'd been out of control and hadn't settled down until he got to high school. He couldn't afford to get expelled from school. Otherwise, it would've messed up his future plans of getting away from California and making something of himself.

As if knowing he didn't want to discuss name changes, his street name, or even fighting, Chelsey didn't ask him anything else about that subject.

Instead, she asked, "What does any of this have to do with you breaking up with me? I don't understand."

Parker released an unsteady breath. Now came the tough part of the conversation.

"When I was seventeen, almost eighteen, my father tried to kill me, and he thinks he succeeded. He thinks I'm dead."

Chapter Twelve

Chelsey could only stare at him.

How the hell had they dated for months, and she did not know any of this?

Her mind was spinning with so many questions, she didn't know what to ask first. All this time, she thought he had grown up in Chicago. All she'd known about his parents was that his mother had died when he was younger, and he was raised by his father who he no longer had a relationship with.

But *this*? He'd been brought up in an organized crime family...which was insane. A drug dealer by the age of eight, he was involved in stuff that could've gotten him thrown in jail for the rest of his life. Or worse, could've gotten him killed.

Parker leaned forward as he ran his hands up and down the thighs of his jeans. Normally, he was calm and laidback, but in the last few minutes, his anxiousness was palpable.

He thinks I'm dead.

His words rattled her, but she couldn't let it show. She needed to hear everything he had to tell her. No matter how shocking or painful it might be.

He lifted his gaze to hers. "Do you remember a few months ago when Laz was shot, and I was assigned to protect Journey?"

"I remember."

Journey was Laz's wife, who'd been a US prosecutor at the time. Now she was with a private practice firm who worked with nonprofit agencies. It had been a tough time for their family and friends because someone had been gunning for Laz. He had feared they'd go after Journey and their daughter. So the guys of Supreme provided around-the-clock protection.

Parker explained that when he was escorting Journey from the courthouse once, they were bombarded by the media. Though they were able to get her in the vehicle without incident, a news station had posted a photo, that included her with him and another security specialist.

"Why did it matter that there was a photo of you? You don't usually do undercover work."

Supreme offered personal protection, and on occasion, some of the specialists had been tasked with undercover work, but not Parker.

As for pictures, Chelsey had plenty of photos of her and Parker, but she never had a reason to share them with anyone. Neither of them posted to social media, and she probably never would, but she didn't understand where this conversation was going.

"Because my father doesn't know I'm alive," he said again. "If he did, he'd come after me. If that happens, he'll stop at nothing to make sure he kills me next time. Which was why I broke up with you.

"Chelsey, Wolf doesn't give a damn about anything, and revenge is his love language. I'm a dead man if he ever finds out I'm still breathing."

Unease clawed through Chelsey as she started to understand what he was saying. If this man killed Parker's mother, whether intentional or not, it was safe to say that he had the ability to take Parker out, too.

"Wiz and his people have scoured the internet for photos of me," Parker continued. "That one with me and Journey were the only ones they found, and he did the best he could to make sure it was no longer on any sites," he said, referring to Cameron "Wiz" Miller, one of the owners of Supreme Security-Chicago. He was also a former Navy SEAL and a computer guru. "If Wolf saw that photo, he'd come for me and anyone I care about. I couldn't risk anything happening to you. That's why I had to put distance between you and me."

Chelsey stood and moved over to where he sat on the sofa. She started to sit next to him, but he pulled her onto his lap. She wasn't sure what to say about what he had just shared. What could she say? The idea of someone interested in killing him didn't make sense. The man she knew was the sweetest, gentlest person she'd ever been with. It was hard to believe someone wanted him dead.

She wrapped an arm around Parker's neck and placed her other hand on his chest as she stared into his eyes. There was so much love staring back at her that it almost made her want to cry.

"You should've told me," she whispered. "Instead, you broke up with me and made both our lives miserable."

He pulled her close and placed a sweet kiss on her lips. "I thought it best to walk away, because I couldn't keep taking a chance with your life, baby. I was serious about what I said last night. If anything ever happened to you, it would kill me, and if I was the cause..." He dropped his gaze and shook his head. "I didn't want to break things off with you. I felt I didn't have a choice."

She understood why he thought that was the only choice, but it was the wrong one. Instead of telling him that, she laid her head against his shoulder and snuggled against him. His strong arms held her close, while the clean, fresh scent of his cologne swirled around her like a calming elixir. This was where she was meant to be, in his arms like this.

They stayed that way for a few minutes until Chelsey noticed how Parker rubbed his right thumb over the inside of his left wrist. There was a tribal tattoo there and on occasion, she'd notice him rubbing that spot.

Never go back. That's what he'd told her the tattoo meant.

Both of his arms and his back were littered with elaborate tattoos, but the tribal one was the only one that seemed to hold something more to him than its actual meaning.

Then she remembered something.

She sat up. "You once told me that you had gotten that tattoo to cover up another tattoo that you'd gotten when you were younger. Did it have something to do with the Kingz?" she asked carefully, not wanting to trigger him. For all she knew, the question might cause him to remember something he might not want to.

"Yes. Every member of the Diego Kingz has a six-point crown tattoo with flames shooting out of the center point. Right here," he said, pointing at the spot that was now covered with the tribal tattoo. "I got that tattoo when I was ten, and it was to let people in our world know what crew I belonged to. At the time, I thought it was cool since Wolf had one. The older I got, though, and the more I had to do within the Kingz's crew, the symbol felt more like an anchor weighing me down."

Silence fell between them again until Parker yawned and leaned his head back. Chelsey had noticed his exhaustion last night while they were working, and again when he arrived today. It was clear he hadn't been sleeping well, but even though he probably needed some sleep, she needed him to finish telling her about his father.

Chelsey placed a kiss on the light scruff covering his cheek, then moved from his lap to sit next to him on the sofa, which had him lifting his head.

She slipped her arm through his and rested her chin on his shoulder, and he glanced at her. "I know you're tired. I can see it in your eyes, but tell me the rest. Why did Wolf try to kill you? Why does he want you dead?"

He studied her for a few seconds, and then he kissed the tip of her nose. It was so out of character for him, yet so sweet and gentle, that she almost purred.

"I love you so damn much," he said, gruffer than it had been moments ago. "But I never planned to tell you or anyone any of this. Mason is the only one who knows everything. Well, mostly everything that I remembered."

That last comment only sparked more questions for Chelsey, but she held back from asking them. There would be time for asking questions. If not today, then soon.

"I was seventeen, almost eighteen, and a punk kid out for my own revenge. Basically, I had turned into my father. My anger was so deep toward Wolf, I had tunnel vision when it came to destroying him. For years after my mother died, I had bided my time until I could take Wolf down.

"So I found out that the Euclid Disciples thought that the Kingz had gotten to their suppliers. Which was probably true, but I wasn't sure. Still, I figured I could use that information to my advantage. Since the Disciples weren't receiving their usual amount of product, they were struggling to keep up with demand in their territory. They were desperate."

Chelsey wondered where he'd gotten that information about their suppliers, but again she remained quiet.

"This was around the same time the Kingz were preparing to get a major shipment. I'm talking huge, to the point that Wolf wanted all-hands-on-deck to receive it. I leaked that information to someone who I knew was connected to the Disciples. I knew once they found out, they'd ambush the Kingz. It had been the perfect scenario, and like I suspected, the Disciples went in hot. That incident was the start of one of the biggest wars the Kingz had ever been a part of."

Parker shook his head. The tension rolling off him let Chelsey know that it was probably worse than he was letting on. She also had a feeling he wasn't telling her everything.

"I wanted," he started, his voice full of emotion as he rubbed the back of his neck. "I wanted Wolf to suffer as much as I had suffered when he killed my mother. I wanted him dead, but I had no intention of sticking around town to see how everything shook out. I conveniently didn't make it to the delivery sight, and I was heading out of town. Everything was planned out perfectly. Or so I thought." He cleared his throat. "Wolf somehow found out that I had betrayed him and the Kingz, and he tracked me down not too far from one of his warehouses."

Parker glanced at Chelsey before looking away, but not fast enough. The torment she saw in his eyes broke her heart, and she felt helpless. Whatever happened that day clearly still haunted him.

He leaned forward, his elbows on his thighs. When he trembled, Chelsey wrapped her arm around him, trying to provide some comfort while a few tears slipped from her eyes. He hadn't even told her everything, but she knew whatever happened had been bad.

"I thought watching my mother die was the worse day of my life," he said, emotion clouding his words, "but it hadn't been. The day Wolf kicked my ass, I prayed for death. Chelsey, I wanted to die, and I thought I would."

Chelsey didn't know how to comfort him. Parker was hers.

It didn't matter that they'd been estranged for months. In

her heart, he would always be hers. The thought of anyone trying to hurt this man, her man, scared her to death while also making her angry enough to kill someone on his behalf.

He might be able to take care of himself, but that didn't stop her from worrying about him. Wolf was still out there. Maybe he didn't know Parker was still alive, but what if he one day found out? Then what? Was Parker right, would his father hunt him down and try to kill him again?

"Wolf literally left me for dead," Parker said, interrupting her thoughts. "My face was a bloodied mess. I couldn't see out of one eye, and I could barely see out of the other. My nose was broken, and I had missing teeth. Broken ribs, a punctured lung, a broken kneecap, and some internal injuries had me in bad shape."

"Dear God. I just don't understand," Chelsey said, her heart breaking for him even more. "What type of person would do something like that to their only child?"

"A low-down, heartless bastard who put the Diego Kingz before anything else, including his son. Remember, I had betrayed him and the crew. In Wolf's world, that was punishable by death."

"How'd you get away?" She couldn't help herself, she had to ask. "If you were almost dead..."

"Chels, with everything that happened after that, I truly believe my mother was watching over me," he said shaking his head. "There is no other way to explain the events that followed. In the warehouse—where there's a torture room—there's also an incinerator."

"Oh. My. God." The words slipped out, and Chelsey covered her mouth with her hand as her active imagination took her down a dark road.

"Let's just say, I believe in angels."

Chapter Thirteen

Drained, Parker wanted nothing more than to close his eyes and not think for at least an hour. Or better yet, getting some fresh air might recapture some of the energy he had expended during this conversation.

But knowing Chelsey would pitch a fit if he even thought about walking outside, at least before they finished talking, he ambled over to the window instead. Leaning a palm against the window casing, he released a slow, cleansing breath.

He had shared most of the story with Chelsey, but there was one part he had locked away in the back of his mind. The part that came with the type of guilt that could cripple a man.

He hadn't lied about leaking the shipment information to the Disciples, but it had been more than that. The truth was, he had worked with someone closely connected to the Disciples. Someone who wanted to inflict the same type of revenge as he'd wanted to do against the Kingz.

Elena. He hadn't thought about her in years, but she'd had just as much at stake as Parker did. She'd been all in on the deceit for her own reasons that were similar yet different from his. The plan had been perfect. They'd share enough information to start a war, then they'd let the syndicates destroy each other. While that happened, they'd get as far away from California as possible.

Parker wished he knew what happened to her. He had no clue if she was alive or dead, because instead of him meeting up with her, Wolf had intercepted him. Had she been able to disappear? Or had the Disciples done to her what Wolf had tried to do to him? Was she dead because of his idea to start a war? Parker didn't know, and he'd been carrying that guilt around with him ever since.

Talking about his past felt as if he was reliving those dark days all over again. Especially when he recalled the beating he had received. The pain. The majority of his body had been covered in blood and throbbed while he had struggled to breathe.

Even now, as he rubbed his chest, it was as if he was back there. Back in that warehouse with Wolf, Elder, and three other people, one being his best friend, Luis. Or as close to a best friend he could have. That day was what nightmares were made of.

Parker startled when Chelsey wrapped her arms around him from behind and laid her head on his back. He covered her hands, which lay against his stomach, with his and released a pent-up breath as he relaxed.

It was hard to admit how jacked up his youth had been, and how horribly it almost ended.

"I'm so sorry for everything you went through," Chelsey murmured. "But I want to know as much as you're able to share. Right now, give me the short version."

Her voice was muffled against his back, and he couldn't help but smile a little at her words. Her saying he could give her the short version now meant she'd be asking more questions later or in the very near future.

She had a right to, though. If they were going to be a couple, it was only fair she knew everything about him. Even the parts he wanted to forget. He just didn't realize how much remembering would bother him.

Before he continued with the story of his almost-death, he decided to tell her about Elena. He shared how guilty he felt pulling her into the plans, even though it should've benefited them both. But not knowing if she made it out of San Diego would forever haunt him. Especially when he tried to find her years later with no luck.

"Getting back to the warehouse situation..." he said, "Luis, one of the guys in the crew I was closest to, was a few years older than me. We clicked and often hung out. I didn't tell him my plan about the ambush, because I didn't want any blowback to touch him if Wolf ever found out. Anyway, Luis happened to be one of the guys in the warehouse watching me get my ass kicked. He was also one of the cleaners Wolf often used to make dead bodies disappear.

"I don't remember much after Wolf beat me, but years after everything took place, I reached out to Luis, who filled me in. He was shocked I was alive."

"What do you mean?" Chelsey interrupted. "If he was there, wouldn't he know you were still alive?"

"When Wolf and the others left my body with Luis, they all thought I was dead, including Luis. But after Wolf walked out, Luis said he saw my fingers move."

"Oh, my goodness," Chelsey breathed, and her arms tightened around his waist. "Oh, Parker."

"He said I was in and out of consciousness and my pulse was thready. He didn't think I'd last long, but he said he couldn't toss me in the incinerator like Wolf had instructed

111

since I was still alive. Instead, he wrapped me in a tarp and drove me to the beach." Parker shook his head at the memory, still finding it hard to believe that he had lived.

Needing to hold Chelsey, he turned in her embrace, and then gathered her in his arms. When he glanced down, he was surprised to see tears running down her cheeks.

"Ahh, baby, don't cry," he said, wiping away her tears with the pad of his thumb.

"I can't help it. You almost died," she said, her voice trembling as she swiped frantically at a few more tears. "If that would've happened, I never would've met you, and that's something I can't...I can't imagine my life without you in it."

The anguish in her voice was like a knife twisting in his gut, but Parker didn't want her sympathy. He'd done so much shit over the years, he probably had that beating coming.

The only reason he was telling her about any of this was because he wanted her back, and he needed her prepared for what was coming soon.

Parker placed a lingering kiss on the side of her head as he cradled her against him. She was everything to him, and he almost blew it when he broke up with her.

What an idiot.

Never again.

He was never letting her go again.

Chelsey lifted her head from his chest and exhaled. "I'm sorry. You can continue."

Parker smiled down at her and kissed her sweet lips. His woman was tough. If that weren't the case, he wouldn't have shared as much as he had so far. She might not have much experience with gang life, but as a former cop, she understood their ways more than most.

Gangs operated through a different moral compass than the

average person. Their beliefs, thought processes, and ways of life weren't necessarily in line with society's values.

"Long story short, Wolf's warehouse is not too far from Oceanside, California. Luis and I used to hang out near a beach in that area. Usually in the middle of the night doing stupid shit. Anyway, a few times we'd see military guys jogging before daybreak along that stretch of beach. Probably because it wasn't too far from Camp Pendleton," he said, referring to a military base in that area. "Counting on someone finding me sooner rather than later, Luis left me at a spot where a jogger would see me.

"It was a major risk and a gamble on so many levels, but he felt that was my only chance for survival. According to him, he stayed nearby until he saw a guy stop. Then he took off before the man spotted him."

Chelsey jerked out of Parker's hold and backed away from him. Her eyes were wild and furious as she glared at him.

"Are you kidding me?" she spat, her beautiful face a mask of fury. "How could you call that guy a friend? A friend wouldn't do shit like that and just leave you, Parker! That's the craziest thing I've ever heard! I understand your crew stayed away from hospitals or any place else that would alert cops, but... Dammit. There had to be something else that guy could've done for you. I can't believe he just left you!"

Parker rubbed his forehead as a yawn slipped through. A person would have to have grown up in gang life to understand what Luis had done for him. Yes, there was a chance Parker would've died before anyone found him, or someone would've saw him and called 911.

But Luis had ultimately saved his life while risking his own. If Wolf had ever found out that Luis disobeyed an order, he would've put a bullet in his head, no questions asked. Taking

Parker to a hospital had been out of the question. There was nothing else his friend could've done to help.

Parker tried explaining that to Chelsey, but she wasn't hearing it. She put even more distance between them. She now stood on the edge of the living room facing him with her arms crossed in defiance.

"So, what happened?" she finally asked.

"Mason was the one who found me." Chelsey's eyes grew wide, and she started to say something, but Parker lifted his hands to stop her. "I don't remember much, Chels, but he told me that before I passed out, I said—*no cops, no hospital, gang war.*"

Luis and Mason were additional reasons why Parker believed in angels. Mason could've easily called the cops to deal with him. Or he could've taken Parker to a local hospital. If he had done either of those things, word would've gotten back to Wolf, and he would've found a way to finish the job. Then he would've gone after Luis.

But Mason hadn't done either of those things.

Instead, he'd managed to get the emergency care that Parker had needed.

There were times Parker still couldn't believe his luck. He'd been clueless to everything until he was recovering in Germany. That's when Mason had filled him in on all that happened after finding him on the beach. He explained how a voice inside of him had told him not to involve authorities. He'd said the feeling was so strong that he was determined to do whatever he could to save Parker. Even if it meant not doing everything above board.

One of Mason's friends who'd been a medical officer in the Marines got involved. Mason wasn't forthcoming on how they'd managed to get him treated at the hospital at Camp Pendleton. Nor did he share how they'd arranged for a transport to

Germany where he could recover and where Mason had just been reassigned.

As he continued telling Chelsey about his ordeal, Parker once again believed his mother, his angel, had been watching over him. He believed every aspect of that situation had been divinely orchestrated.

That was the only way to explain how his life had been spared. It was a miracle that he was still alive, and that thought was never far from his mind.

He ended up spending years oversees in an apartment near base that Mason had rented. It had taken Parker almost a year to recover mentally and physically before he eventually returned to the States. He came back a different person, a better person inside and out, and it was all thanks to Mason.

"I owe him everything," he said. "Had he made different decisions, I might not be here today. He saved my life, and the only thing he asked of me was to never return to gang life and to stay out of trouble."

Chelsey stumbled back a few inches and leaned against a nearby wall as if needing that extra support to stand. That sadness in her eyes and the fresh tears gliding down her cheeks had Parker's stomach twisting in knots.

Before today, he had never seen her cry. Not even that time when one of her favorite parolees was gunned down while walking home from work.

Parker moved across the room and pulled her into his arms again. "Don't cry, baby. I didn't tell you any of this to make you sad," he said, placing a kiss on the side of her head as he rocked her back and forth.

"I'm so glad Mason stopped to help you," she whispered. "If he hadn't..."

He leaned back, then cupped her face between his hands, forcing her to meet his eyes. "I love you so damn much. Part of me never told you about my past because I had put it behind me. I had completely separated myself from that life and tried to block it out of my mind."

"But then you saw the photo," she said, and he nodded.

"I panicked. All I could think about was that Wolf would see that picture and come for me and everyone I love. I didn't want to leave you or the Atlanta's Finest team, but I seriously considered it for fear I'd put you guys in danger. Once again, Mason was there, talking me out of it and saying if Wolf comes for me, he comes for all of us."

Chelsey ran her hands up Parker's torso and to his chest, and his body tingled from the contact. He would never be able to express how much he missed being with her and feeling her hands on his body again.

"I agree with Mason," she said. "You're not alone anymore, Parker, and I'm disappointed that you didn't trust me enough to tell me everything. Instead, you opted to break up with me."

"I know, baby. I regret how I handled the situation. It won't happen again." He rested his forehead against hers, then lifted it again. "Going forward, I'll always be straight with you. Give me another chance to prove how much I love you. Let me show you that I can get this right."

She searched his eyes as if looking for something before saying, "I'll give *us* another chance. I've missed you too much not to, and I love you, too. That hasn't changed."

"Good to hear," he said and backed her to the wall.

She meant the world to him. More than she'd ever know. Her beauty inside and out, her dry sense of humor that he adored, and even her sassiness. He missed it all.

He reached out and pushed a strand of hair behind her ear. "It's been hell without you."

She ran the back of her fingers over the light scruff on his cheek. "I can tell. You look like shit," she said, and he couldn't help but laugh. "It's easy to see that you haven't been sleeping or eating. Is there something else I should know? Are you sick?"

He shook his head. "Nah. It's just been a stressful few months, but talking to you is the beginning of me getting my life back on track."

She slid her arms around his neck. "Good, because we belong together, and I need you just like you need me. But if you ever break up with me again—"

"I won't. I'm never walking away from you. It's me and you until eternity."

"Yeah, and you better remember that," Chelsey said, and he wasn't sure who moved first, but before he realized it, their mouths were touching.

The kiss started slow and sweet, but within seconds reached a whole different heat level. Desire pulsed through Parker, and he ran his hands along the soft curves of her sexy body as their connection deepened.

He missed this. From the moment they'd met, Parker had known there was something special about this woman. Every day since then, getting to know her and spending time with her solidified that initial assessment. She was like no other, and he had almost ruined the best thing that ever happened to him— falling in love with her.

As Chelsey ground against him, Parker's heart pounded an erratic beat, and their tongues tangled as if trying to find each other's tonsils. The heavy conversation they'd just had was all but forgotten. All Parker could think about right now was how badly he wanted to get reacquainted with her body.

But that wasn't why he had stopped by her house. He wanted to make things right and win her back. He wasn't expecting anything more than that.

Yet, he was only human.

His dick was suddenly hard as granite. And the way

Chelsey literally had him by the balls as she cupped and squeezed him, made him even harder.

There was no resisting this woman.

His woman. Especially when it was clear how much they wanted each other.

Parker winced with the pleasure she was giving him, but if she didn't stop...

"Mmm," he moaned and eased his mouth from hers, but their lips were still only a breath apart as he covered her hand with his. "If you don't stop touching me like that, I won't be responsible for my actions."

Chelsey grinned, *and God help him...*

She slowly released him and then lifted the tail of her T-shirt and tugged the garment over her head before tossing it to the floor. Next, she added the royal blue lace bra to the beginning of a pile.

Goodness. It didn't matter how many times he was blessed with seeing her body, he was still left in awe. The woman's figure was what wet dreams were made of, and she was totally uninhibited as she smiled wickedly at him.

"Damn, baby," he whispered and cupped her mouthwatering breasts with both hands before pushing them together. He loved how heavy they were in the palms of his hands. And the way her dark nipples stood at attention, they were begging for his mouth on them, and Parker didn't hesitate.

He swirled his tongue around the taut bud before he tugged it into his mouth. Then he sucked and teased while being keenly aware of the way she was feverishly trying to get his belt undone as she squirmed against him.

"Parker..." she breathed.

Though she might be uninhibited, his baby was also impatient. She loved quickies but Parker didn't, and she knew that.

He preferred to take his time with her, but occasionally, like now, she made that difficult.

He knew what drove her wild, and her sensitive nipples were one of her erogenous zones. So he moved to the second one, giving it the same attention as the first one. But between her arousing scent surrounding him and the way she was touching him, need and lust charged through his body. He'd prefer to take his time with her, but...

When Chelsey unzipped his pants and pulled his dick out, Parker knew he had to hurry this along. Especially when she started squeezing and stroking his length, and he nearly leaped out of his skin when she ran the pad of her thumb over the tip.

"Okay, okay, baby, you're going to make me come," he said, sucking in a breath as he half laughed and half groaned while easing out of her grip.

He hurried and dug his wallet from his pocket and grabbed a condom while Chelsey rushed to unfasten her shorts. When she released a low growl, he couldn't help but chuckle at her frustration.

"Chels, we have all night to..." his words trailed off as he watched her push her shorts over her hips, then let them pool around her feet.

Parker's mouth went dry. She wasn't wearing panties and stood before him gloriously naked, except for her red socks. He considered himself a man of control in most situations, but this woman... This incredibly sexy human being who was truly a gift from God, tested him in every way possible.

"What were you saying?" she asked with a nefarious grin, and the shapeliness of her naked body taunted him.

Parker didn't bother responding. He yanked off his T-shirt, toed off his shoes, got out of his jeans and boxer briefs in record time. He then made quick work of sliding on the condom.

All the while his gaze never left Chelsey.

He backed her to the wall. "You are still the sexiest woman I've ever laid eyes on."

"I'm glad you think so."

She ran her hands up his bare chest and he shivered under her soft touch, then she smirked and gazed down between their bodies. His erection was standing at attention, more than ready for action, and she chuckled.

"Well, hello. It looks like you've missed me."

"More than you know."

Before she could say another word, Parker claimed her mouth with a savage intensity. He wanted her like a drug addict wanting his next fix, and the way Chelsey was palming his ass and grinding her sex against him, meant she was in a similar state.

But when she wrapped one of her legs around his waist, he knew this was going to be quicker than quick.

He ripped his mouth from hers, hauled her up into his arms, and she wrapped both legs around him. When he slid into her sweet heat, it was like coming home. He glided between her slick folds, loving the way her muscles contracted around him as he moved inside her.

Yeah, this was what he needed, what he wanted.

Her arms around his neck and the cool brush of her fingers at the back of his head, along with the heady kiss she was giving him, had his senses on overdrive. He didn't want to hurt her, knowing her back was against the wall, but he couldn't stop the way he was driving into her.

It had been too long without having her sex wrapped around his dick. It had been too long since he'd been able to hold her close like this. And it sure as hell had been too damn long since he'd heard her moans and whimpers of pleasure. It was like music to his ears, and the way her luscious breasts bounced in front of his face...

He wasn't going to last.

This was going to be over way too quickly.

He might...

"Pa—Parker!" Chelsey screamed and bucked hard against him while her nails dug into his skin. Her body stiffened, and she cried out as she rode the wave of a long orgasm.

Watching her come was always one of the most beautiful sights he'd ever witnessed. It also never failed to push him over the edge of his own control and into an earth-shattering, shuddering release.

His knees went weak as he growled her name, but he managed to stay upright and hold her tightly against the wall. His heart was practically beating out of his chest as his body trembled with aftershocks from his release.

"Goodness," he panted, struggling to get air into his lungs.

"Wow," Chelsey breathed, her chest heaving as she lay limp against him. "Did I mention that I've missed you?"

Parker chuckled and kissed the side of her head. "Yeah. You might've mentioned it a couple of times, but I'll never get tired of hearing it. Now, how about we take this upstairs so that I can show you more thoroughly how much I've missed you."

Chelsey slowly leaned back to look at him, and the sweet smile she gave him sent heat pulsing through his veins.

"I'd like that very much."

When their lips met again, and she kissed him sweetly, Parker knew without a doubt that she would forever be his, and he'd protect her with his life.

No matter what.

Chapter Fourteen

Happy anniversary, my love, Wolf thought as he tossed back a shot of tequila.

Growling, he shook his head at the way the liquid burned the back of his throat. The top-shelf liquor he had requested was even stronger than he'd hoped, and he poured another shot. Three more and he finally felt a buzz.

Just what he needed to get through the evening.

He and Elder were hanging out at a strip club they owned, and based on the music, laughter, and catcalls, everyone was having a good time. This was just one of many prosperous clubs they had but the one they frequented the most.

The dimly-lit building had two floors. Downstairs, the main stage and several smaller stages were strategically placed around the large space. That gave their customers plenty of options to watch naked women shake their asses. The club also had rooms in the back for those who wanted to spend more money on a private dance.

Wolf and members of his crew were on the second floor in the VIP section, but he would've rather had been at home getting sloppy drunk. Liquor could help numb the hole in his heart that he'd had since losing Nina. But Elder had insisted he be at the club with the guys.

He was probably right.

This was a celebration for all of them. Profits were at an all-time high. Not only that, the Kingz were gaining more political and economic power; something Wolf had been working toward for over thirty years. This was as good a reason as any for their crew to celebrate by drinking too much, eating a lot, and watching beautiful women defy gravity on the strip poles.

Finally, the Kingz organization was gaining some traction after taking major hits in the past. They'd grown stronger in the last fifteen years and with the alliances Wolf had made recently, along with those that were in the works, nothing could stop him. All his plans were coming into fruition.

He poured another shot and slammed it back, cringing as the liquor flowed down his throat. The searing burn wasn't enough to stop him from remembering what day it was.

Just that quick, his shitty attitude was back in full force. His successes were great, but his life was just a shell without his queen. Today would've been his and Mina's thirty-second wedding anniversary.

He always got depressed around this time. He missed his wife—so much so that there'd been times when he thought about ending his worthless life and joining her.

That thought made him release a humorless laugh. She was probably laughing too since they both knew there was no way they'd spend eternity in the same place. With all the bullshit he'd done over the years, there was no doubt that when he died, he was going to hell.

Without a word, a pretty, leggy brunette and an equally beautiful, tall chocolate sister approached him. The only thing they were wearing were smiles before they started dancing for him. The high-tempo music they were moving to had them wiggling and jiggling before they started taking turns giving him a lap dance.

They both had tits and ass for days, and any other time, Wolf would've considered taking one or both of them to a private room. Not tonight. Tonight, he wasn't interested. Instead, he poured another drink, planning to get drunk enough to forget reality, at least for a while.

He hefted the almost-empty bottle into the air and caught the attention of the topless server. She nodded in acknowledgement as she set drinks in front of a couple of his men.

"Let us take care of you, daddy," the black woman said while the brunette went for his belt buckle, but Wolf slapped her hand away.

The only person he wanted sucking his dick tonight was dead.

He waved both women away just as the server approached, wearing a barely-there red thong. She had a pretty face and nice boobs, but she was a little too skinny for his taste. That didn't stop him from running his hand up her long leg as she set a bottle of tequila and a platter of appetizers on the table near him and Elder. Then she smiled prettily before moving to another table.

As Wolf bit into a potato wedge, he glanced around the VIP section. There was an oval stage in the center where two naked women were performing on two strip poles. Three long, huge loungers covered in red velvet with high backs were positioned on each side of the stage. Even if he wasn't enjoying the gorgeous women, his men who were whistling and tossing money, were enjoying the show.

Elder started laughing, and Wolf looked over to see him staring at something on his phone.

"What's so funny?" he asked, eating some of the popcorn

shrimp that were also on the platter. His head was spinning, and he had a nice little buzz going.

Still grinning, Elder turned the phone so Wolf could see the message. Apparently, the liquor was finally taking effect, because Wolf couldn't make out a single word.

"My nephew, Sean, asked if you had a lovechild who lives in Atlanta. He saw some guy last night at a fundraiser who looked familiar, and he just figured out why. He said the dude looks a little like you. Says he could be your kid."

"I don't have no damn kids," Wolf growled as anger stirred inside him when he thought about the son he once had. The son who betrayed him in the worse way possible.

Wolf shouldn't have been surprised, though. After Mina died, Junior was never the same. He did what he was told to do out on the streets, but there was always a silent tension between them just below the surface.

Wolf should've known sooner that the bastard had been up to something, but he'd missed it—and the Kingz paid heavily for that oversight.

Elder was still laughing until a photo popped up on the screen. Then he studied it for a few minutes before turning the phone to Wolf again.

"I have to admit, the guy does look a little like you around the eyes. You sure you haven't been spreading your seed around? We could use some more Gs," he said, referring to the low-level members in their crew. There was never enough of them to do their bidding.

"Well, you won't be getting them from me," Wolf growled, and ate one of the jalapeño poppers followed by another.

He didn't have any kids, and there was no way in hell he planned to create anymore, especially without his queen. The last thing he needed was some baby-mama drama landing on his doorstep. Nope. Never gonna happen.

Elder sat forward, still staring at the screen of his phone. "I don't know, Wolf," he said slowly. "There's something about this guy..."

Wolf held out his hand. "Let me see that picture again.

When Elder handed him the phone, Wolf enlarged the photo and squinted. He studied the man's face and kept going back to his eyes. Eyes that were familiar, but there was no way.

No way he could be....

He shook the thought free. Clearly, the alcohol was making him see something that wasn't there, because the kid who came to mind was dead. He'd seen to it himself, but still...

"Who is he?"

"Sean doesn't know."

After studying the photo a few minutes longer, Wolf's curiosity was piqued. He handed Elder his phone back.

"Find out who he is. I want to know everything about him, from who his parents are to everywhere he's lived and worked. Get me some answers."

Better to nip his curiosity in the bud instead of wondering.

Chapter Fifteen

Chelsey slowly opened her eyes, and there were several things she noticed at once. One: there was a delicious ache throughout her body from how thoroughly her man had loved on her. Two: She was in bed alone and the house was quiet.

Turning onto her back, she stared up at the ceiling as memories of lovemaking with Parker flooded her mind. A little tenderness in a certain region definitely wasn't a bad thing. Flashes of the last couple of hours with Parker had her grinning like an idiot. Unable to get enough of each other, they'd gone at it a little harder than usual. There wasn't an inch on her body that his hands and mouth hadn't been on, and Chelsey had loved every minute. Parker had always been a thorough lover, and that hadn't changed.

Even though sex had distracted her for a while, their conversation from earlier in the day was still on her mind. Parker had been through more before he was eighteen than she'd been through in all her life. How he'd managed to become the man she knew, the man she had fallen in love with, was a miracle.

Her heart squeezed at knowing what could've happened if Mason hadn't stopped to help him. Had she been Mason, jogging on the beach in the middle of the morning, she wasn't sure what she would've done had she come across a man who was barely alive. Then again, she probably would've called 911 without a second thought. Thankfully Mason had been in the right place at the right time. Otherwise, Parker might've died.

Nope. Nope. Nope. Don't go there.

She needed to focus on the fact that he was alive. It didn't matter that his heartless father had tried to kill him. Wolf hadn't succeeded, and Chelsey was grateful for that. Now her only concern regarding Wolf was that Parker was planning on revenge. This time, he was confident he wouldn't fail, and she believed him, especially knowing that she and Atlanta's Finest would have his back.

But if she were honest, she wished he would forget Wolf and continue living his life. Because if things went sideways, the way they had when Parker was a teen, she didn't want to think about what could happen. If Wolf was as ruthless as Parker led her to believe, he wouldn't go down without a fight.

What if he succeeded in killing Parker this time?

"Stop it. I'm not going to think like that," she murmured, then decided to just stop thinking period.

Still not hearing any movement in the house, Chelsey sat up, pulling the sheet up over her bare breasts in the process. Glancing around the room, she looked for any signs that Parker hadn't left. The bathroom door was slightly ajar, but the room was dark. Then her gaze moved to the upholstered chair in the corner, and she spotted his shirt, as well as his shoes beneath the chair.

Good. He was still there.

Relief flooded through her despite knowing he wouldn't have left without letting her know.

Yawning, Chelsey started to lay back down, but instead grabbed her cell phone from the side table to check the time. That's when she saw Terrance had texted her, and she had missed two calls.

She opened the text and read.

Terrance: I'm sorry. I shouldn't have lied. Let's talk so I can tell you the truth.

Chelsey snorted and deleted the message. She also deleted the voicemails that he'd left. What made him think she'd ever talk to him again? Especially when she wouldn't believe anything he'd say.

Not only did she delete his messages, she also blocked his telephone number—something she should've done the other night. Terrance had called several times since then, and in the one message she actually listened to, he had sounded like he was sorry. It didn't matter, though. What was done was done, and now she was back with Parker. There was no room in her life for Terrance or any other man.

Chelsey turned onto her side and winced at how tender she was between her thighs. Heck, she had used muscles she hadn't used in months, but she wasn't complaining. That man of hers was incredible, and they had definitely made up for lost time. Chelsey had lost count of the number of orgasms she'd had, and if he was still in bed, there was no doubt they'd get in another round.

Sighing in contentment, she was cautiously optimistic even though she wondered where they'd go from here. Now that she and Parker were back together, they had a few things to discuss. Like if they were ready to go public with their relationship. She hadn't wanted to tell anyone before because her dating track record was horrible. She had introduced a couple of her exes to her family, only to later tell them that it didn't work out. With her and Parker knowing many of the same people, she hadn't wanted that to happen with him.

He had also been hesitant because of Kenton. Apparently, there was a guy code about a friend dating your little sister. Parker insisted her brother wasn't going to take it well. Mainly because he didn't think Parker was the settling-down type since he never brought a girlfriend around them. He'd had hookups, but never dated seriously. Until her.

Knowing that, along with Kenton being ridiculously protective, her brother probably would have something to say about her and Parker being together.

Chelsey jerked her head up and listened. For the first time since waking up, she heard bumping around downstairs. That's when she also noticed the smell of food. As if on cue, her stomach growled. The enticing aroma of barbecued meat, garlic, onions and a host of other smells had her sitting upright.

She hurried out of bed, made quick work of relieving herself in the bathroom, and finger combing her hair before slipping into a pair of lounging pajamas. When she made it downstairs and into the kitchen, Chelsey pulled up short.

Her gaze assessed the space that wasn't very big, and she couldn't believe the amount of food that lay on every flat surface. There were too many carryout containers to count, and she saw that some were from her favorite restaurants.

Parker glanced up from the barbecue ribs he was eating and smiled. "Hey, baby. You're awake."

Chelsey moved further into the room, stopping at the counter that held an apple pie and a cheesecake.

"What in the world have you done?"

"I was hungry," Parker said as if that explained everything.

"Are you expecting an army battalion? Because there's easily enough food here to feed one, if not two."

"Nope, this is for me and you. I figured you might be hungry too," he said and shoved coleslaw into his mouth. "Besides, I had a taste for a few different dishes and figured I'd buy it all."

"Apparently," she said, snagging a chicken wing. "I guess your appetite is back."

Chelsey filled a plate with more chicken wings, a slice of cheese pizza, coconut shrimp, and some broccoli. It was an odd combination, but she was hungry enough to eat a cow.

"Yeah, thanks for your help with that." He winked and her cheeks heated. "I guess I worked up an appetite," Parker said, piling chicken Alfredo onto his plate. He took a long drag of his beer and set the bottle back down on the counter. "I can't ever remember being this hungry."

Chelsey grabbed a bottle of water, and then took her plate over to the two-seater table.

"How long have you been awake? Looks like you've already put a dent in some of this food."

"About an hour. I feel like I haven't eaten in months."

Chelsey chuckled at the seriousness of his expression. "Actually, by the looks of you, you haven't."

Her gaze took in his bare upper body, and the beautiful tattoos covering it. His muscular chest was still drool-worthy and worked like a well-oiled machine, but his face was thinner than usual. Sure, he was still handsome. Yet the sallowness of his skin made him look a little ill. Hopefully, with him back to eating and not dealing with the stress of their breakup and worrying about Wolf, he'd be back to his old self in no time.

As she watched him eat, memories of all that he could do with that body, his mouth and hands, flooded her mind. Yeah, she was a lucky woman because he was all hers, and after spending the last few hours with him, it was as if they'd never been apart. Despite trying, she hadn't been able to scrub him from her heart, and she probably never would.

That's what concerned her. If trouble came his way, she feared that he'd react the same way—cut all ties and run.

"Parker, are you sure this is what you want? Are you sure *I'm* what you want? Because I can't go through months without you again. I can't do this on-and-off again thing with you. If you decide to up and leave Atlanta—"

"I'd be taking you with me," he said and wiped his mouth and hands with a napkin.

He strolled over to the table and pulled her into a standing position, and Chelsey stared up at him. She couldn't miss the seriousness and love radiating in his eyes.

Before they'd started dating exclusively, Chelsey had known he was the man for her. She just hadn't known how powerful their connection would be. Her heart didn't beat right without him, and it was like nothing she had ever experienced.

"I know I shook your faith in me, but I promise you, Chelsey. I'm going to regain your trust."

"I trust you," she said quickly.

Chelsey was hesitant to trust him with her heart again but honestly, she was in too deep to walk away now. What she felt for Parker was a scary, all-consuming, I-would-die-for-you type of love. A first for her. Granted, he had caused her heartache and tears, but it would be worth it in the end if it meant they'd be together forever.

"Good, because I'm not going anywhere, especially not without you. I'm planning to spend the rest of my life with you, assuming you'll still have me."

She wrapped her arms around his waist. "You're all I want."

When their lips met, heat spread through her body like usual. This man's kisses, and the way he held her so gently, always ignited a yearning within her. Nope. She was never letting him go, and he was right about one thing. If he ever left, she was definitely going with him.

With one last peck to her lips, he pulled back.

"Are we good?" he asked.

"Yes, we're perfect." She reclaimed her seat. "So, where do we go from here? We had some plans before..."

She stopped the rest of her words before they could slip out. There was no sense in mentioning the breakup. Again. She was going to have to forgive and forget if she wanted their relationship to work. No way would Parker want her throwing his mistake in his face every other day.

No, she was going to have to do what they'd done earlier when they reacquainted themselves with each other's body. They were going to pick up where they left off in every aspect of their relationship. Except this time, she'd be going into this with eyes wide open, instead of looking at him through rose-colored glasses.

He'd been through hell and survived and was a fighter in more ways than one. She couldn't help but respect all that he'd seen in the last thirty-plus years and still managed to be a kind, loving, and generous human being.

"I've been thinking about that," Parker said, interrupting Chelsey's thought.

He moved back to his plate of food on the counter and returned to the table with it. Then he grabbed a container of some type of pasta and meatball dish and set it on the table.

"I'm thinking that where we go from here is forward. Except, I'm sure you're not ready or interested in moving in with me...yet. However, I want all our friends and your family to know that you're mine. No more hiding our relationship."

Chelsey nodded, watching as he continued shoveling food into his mouth.

"Yes, I'm ready for us to go public. As for us moving in together, I can't right now. I did a year lease on this place with the intent of saving to buy a house next year." That was planned with her thinking that she'd be single for the foreseeable future.

Sure, she could break the lease, but not yet. They needed to be on solid ground before she considered moving in with him. Though, in her heart, Chelsey wanted more than anything to wake up to Parker lying next to her every single morning for the rest of her life. If that made her gullible or even a fool, she didn't care. Deep down, she knew the two of them belonged together.

"Okay," he said, understanding in his eyes. "I'm thinking we can tell everyone next Saturday at Mase's barbecue. Most of my...I mean *our* Atlanta's Finest team will be there."

Chelsey grinned at him. It was great that he was including her when mentioning Atlanta's Finest. But Supreme had grown so much in the last few years, they had more than one team of security specialists. She didn't want to assume that she'd be on the Atlanta's Finest team with Parker and her brother. Right now, she'd just be glad to be assigned to either team. That would mean that she wouldn't be stuck in the office doing the administrative job she was hired to do.

"That's a good idea. London mentioned that the wives will be hanging out separate from you guys," Chelsey said, referring to Mason's wife. "I'll be with them in the guest house."

How weird would it be for her to be around the wives when she was just a girlfriend?

Who knows...if all went well, maybe one day she'd be a wife.

Anything was possible.

Chapter Sixteen

On their way to Mason's house for the cookout, Parker couldn't think of a better way to spend a Saturday evening. Especially when cruising the streets on his Suzuki V-Strom 1000. The motorcycle had been one of his splurges a couple of years ago, and he loved the exhilaration he felt and the power beneath him as he flew down an open road. He didn't get to do that often in the city, but the streets surrounding Mason's huge property gave him that rare opportunity.

What made the ride even more enjoyable was having Chelsey on the back again, just like old times. She enjoyed his bike as much as he did, and often talked about getting her own. Parker selfishly hoped she never did, though. He preferred her soft breasts pressed against his back and her firm thighs hugging his.

Yeah, having her wrapped around him like she was now added to the thrill of the ride.

He slowed as he approached the guardhouse in front of Mason's estate. It didn't matter if the guard on duty knew who

135

you were, they were required to stop you before letting you onto the property. To say security was tight was an understatement. London insisted on it, and there was nothing Mason wouldn't do for his wife.

When London was a child, her parents were killed during a home invasion. The only way she survived was because she had hidden in a closet. Unfortunately, the traumatic experience mentally crippled her from living in a house. She always lived in a condo or an apartment, but after marrying Mason and their family started growing, they had to get a larger place. Mason had to promise to have around-the-clock security for their home before London finally conceded.

After checking in at the guardhouse, Parker cruised up the long and wide driveway. It didn't matter how often he visited, he marveled at the size of the house. Mason called this place home, but the structure was as grand as a castle, surrounded by a lush yard that could easily be featured in *Better Homes and Garden* magazine. Behind the main house was a guest house, and beyond that were oak and pine trees for as far as the eye could see. The property was spectacular.

Parker slowed; glad they were some of the first to arrive. He was hoping that Kenton would also show up early like he usually did. That would give Parker a chance to talk to him before everyone else arrived. The conversation was past due, and to be honest, he should've respected Kenton enough to already have talked to him. Parker would've wanted that same courtesy if one of his friends was dating his sister...if he had a sister.

But hey, better late than never.

He pulled around to the other side of the house near the four-car garage and parked. After shutting off the engine, he extended his hand to help Chelsey off the bike before climbing off himself.

"Are you okay?" he asked as he stored their helmets in the hard-shell saddlebag.

She'd been quieter than usual today. They'd stayed the night at his place, and Chelsey had seemed fine until this afternoon when he mentioned some of his plans regarding Wolf. She admitted to being worried about him despite his assurance that he'd be careful and that he wasn't going after his father alone.

"Come here." He pulled her into his arms and placed a lingering kiss on the side of her head. "What's going on in that beautiful head of yours? Are you having second thoughts about us being here together?"

With her arms around him, she met his gaze, and the corners of her tempting mouth tilted up into a smile. "Of course not. I'm not ashamed of you, Parker. It's past time our friends know that we're together. I guess I'm more concerned about the conversation you're planning to have with the guys. What if they don't agree to help you?"

"Chels, they will," he said confidently.

Even if everyone wasn't on board with him going after Wolf, he already knew a few of his guys would stand by him. Not only that, but they'd also do whatever necessary to help him gain the freedom he needed. Otherwise, he'd have to remain in hiding.

"Keep in mind, with modern technology, I don't have to be anywhere near Wolf to destroy his organization. I'm bringing in the guys because, one, I want them to know about my past. And two, because they're all brilliant in their own way, and I want to make sure I've thought of everything. I have no doubt that they'll have some good ideas to offer."

He had reiterated his reasons for wanting to go after Wolf now. Yes, Parker still blamed the man for his mother's death, but it was more than that. He'd been looking over his shoulder for the past fifteen years, and he was tired of it. There was no reasoning with Wolf. So showing up on his father's doorstep and apologizing about how everything went down years ago was out of the question.

No, this was the only way Parker would ever have a normal life, and since he planned on Chelsey being a part of his future, this had to be done. He wanted her safe.

Chelsey nodded. "I'm sorry. I know you have to do this, and I'm behind you one hundred percent."

Parker brushed his lips across hers. "Thank you, sweetheart. I promise I'll be careful."

They headed to the front of the house, and before they could ring the doorbell, the door swung open. London stood there with her hair smoothed back into a short ponytail and wearing a red short set that made her look like a college student, instead of a mother of five. Her gaze bounced from one to the other before zoning in on their joined hands. Then she grinned.

"I knew it! I knew you two were a thing!" she squealed and started laughing as she hugged first Chelsey, and then Parker. "Why the secrecy? Why were you guys hiding your relationship?"

"Baby, can't you let them in the house before you grill them?" Mason said from behind her. It was clear his friend and mentor hadn't said anything to his wife about them.

After greeting Mason, Parker and Chelsey moved further into the house. The large home with tall ceilings, a double-curved staircase, and high-end fixtures was luxurious. Yet, it was also warm, inviting, and well lived in, probably because of five kids, including a set of twins, under the age of twelve. At that moment, Parker could hear them running and screaming overhead.

"It smells like Aunt Carolyn has been hard at work,"

Chelsey said as she inhaled. "Please tell me that's peach cobbler I smell."

London laughed. "Girl, yes. She's been cooking and baking all day. We offered to have everything catered, and you would've thought we threatened to kick her out of the house."

"Did I hear my name?" Aunt Carolyn strolled down the hallway toward them smiling. She was Mason's aunt, but Parker and all the guys called her Aunt Carolyn.

As usual, she was wearing bright colors beneath her *Kiss the Queen* apron. Her golden-yellow top paired with white capris and gold flats, along with matching jewelry, looked too classy to be cooking in. Yet, there wasn't a stain to be seen.

Parker returned her smile and met her halfway down the hallway. He didn't know how much she knew about his past, but he always felt she knew something. From day one, she'd treated him like a son, and she might never understand how much her tight hugs meant to him. A hug from her felt like a hug from his mother, and he welcomed it.

"Hi, sweetheart," she said, holding him tightly before pulling back to look at him. "I haven't seen you in weeks and it shows. You're too thin. Food is set out around the house, but make sure you come to the kitchen before everyone gets here. I set a couple of your favorite dishes aside for you."

Parker laughed. Most people had a plate set aside, but she knew that wouldn't be enough for him.

Aunt Carolyn greeted Chelsey and a few other people who walked in behind them before returning to the kitchen. Instead of following her, Parker and Chelsey moved toward the back of the house where a guest bedroom was located, as well as a den and stairs to the walkout basement.

Parker didn't recall seeing Kenton's truck outside, but if he was there, he'd be in the lower level.

"Let's go downstairs and maybe grab a drink. I have a feeling I'm going to need one before I talk to your brother."

Chelsey laughed. "It's not going to be that bad, but to make sure, talk to him while he's holding KJ," she said of Kenton and Egypt's toddler. "He's calmer then."

Parker grinned. "Noted."

He glanced around, surprised no one was in the den watching the eighty-inch flat screen television mounted on the wall. By the sounds of laughter and activity on the second floor, in the basement, and outside, it sounded as if those who had already arrived were spread out.

Good.

Before they made it to the stairs, Parker tugged Chelsey to the side of the landing that was near a secluded corner of the den. A large plant was positioned near a wall that would give them a little privacy.

Chelsey started laughing. "Oooh, what are we doing?" she whispered, a mischievous glint in her pretty brown eyes.

Parker held her against his chest, and her arms went around his neck. "I can show you better than I can tell you," he said, whispering the way she had. He might not get much alone time with her once everyone arrived. So he nibbled on her top lip, then her bottom one while murmuring, "I love you. I love you so damn much."

He had never said those words to another woman, and it was like he couldn't stop saying them to Chelsey. They didn't begin to express how much she meant to him.

"I love you, too," she said.

This time when their lips touched, Parker moved his mouth over hers and poured everything he felt into that kiss. Chelsey knew how important she was to him, but he wanted to make sure she felt how much he adored her. Besides that, Parker was determined to make up for all the months that they'd been apart.

My woman.

My love.

My heart.

Chelsey pressed a hand to the back of his head, deepening their lip-lock. His hands slid to her perfectly round ass, and he cupped her firm butt cheeks as their moans mingled. She felt so good, that if he didn't...

"Son of a..."

Parker startled at the sound of a harsh voice and jerked away from Chelsey, feeling like a high schooler getting caught making out in the hallway. When he glanced over and saw Kenton glaring at him, he groaned.

So much for having a talk with his friend. The man looked as if he was about to murder him.

"What the hell is going on here?" Kenton growled as he inched toward them. "Your ass better tell me why you're kissing my sister."

Before Parker could respond, Chelsey charged toward Kenton and pushed against his chest, barely moving him backward.

"Who I kiss is my business," she said only loud enough for the three of them to hear. "Now, calm the hell down so we can talk."

Parker moved forward and looped his arm around her waist, pulling her back some. This was between him and her brother. It was up to him to calm his friend down and explain the situation.

"Listen, man," Parker started, but Kenton charged forward and swung at him.

Damn.

Parker ducked, barely missing getting struck in the face, but he hadn't been prepared for the punch to his gut.

"Oomph," he gasped, but out of reflex he threw a punch, catching Kenton in the jaw, and hitting him hard enough to stun him.

The big man shuffled back a little, and before Parker could get out of the way, his friend charged at him. It felt like getting run over by a truck as they crashed to the floor while Chelsey cursed and yelled for them to stop. Instead, they rolled around on the hardwood, each trying to get the upper hand while also dodging punches.

A bit more flexible, Parker eventually managed to scurry out of Kenton's reach. He hurried to his feet and got in a fighting stance with his fist raised.

If the guy wanted to fight, fine. They'd fight. Might as well get this over with.

But when Kenton got off the floor, breathing hard, he glared at Parker. "How you gon' be fucking around with my sister?" he barked, then got in Parker's face. "You have lost your damn mind if you think I'm going to—"

"Enough!" Chelsey roared and shoved Kenton, which again was like pushing against a brick wall. Her brother was the tallest and the biggest person on their team, and the man was unmovable when his feet were planted. "Calm down," she ground out.

Parker knew Kenton would be pissed, but he hadn't expected him to go bat-shit crazy and swing at him. When the big man swung again, Parker weaved to the right, and threw a punch of his own, catching Kenton in the chin.

"Daddy! Daddy! Come look! Uncle Parker and Uncle Ken are fighting! They're fighting!" Mason's oldest son yelled, excitement pouring through his words.

Parker hadn't realized the kid was there. He'd come out of nowhere, then disappeared just as quickly, yelling for his dad.

Kenton swung again, this time catching Parker on the side of the head, causing him to stumble back. He shook his head, and when his vision cleared, Mason, London, and Egypt were rushing into the room. There were also footsteps running up from the basement, but before Parker could see who it was, Mason was in his face.

"Are you kidding me?" he ground out and nodded to where the huge plant that was now leaning to the side with a pile of dirt on the hardwood floor. "Look at this mess!"

"He started it," Parker and Chelsey said at the same time while pointing at Kenton, and then they looked at each other.

When London and Egypt burst out laughing, Parker couldn't help but join in. Two overgrown men throwing punches had to look crazy as hell. When Parker glanced at Chelsey, though, she wasn't laughing. She had her hands on her hips while glaring at her brother.

Parker needed to talk fast. "Listen man, Chelsey and I are together. I'm in love with your sister, and you're going to have to deal with it."

Egypt groaned at the same moment Kenton started toward Parker again, but Mason stopped the big man with a hand on his chest.

"Knock it off. Am I going to have to separate you two? You guys already freaked out my kid. Throw another punch, either one of you, and you both will find your asses outside on the front lawn. Now clean up this shit."

"Oooh, Daddy said two bad words," a high-pitched voice squealed from behind them.

They all turned to find Mason's youngest daughter, Miracle, standing there with wide eyes and dressed in a pink princess dress and wearing a tiara. "Mommy, did you hear him? Did you hear what Daddy said?"

"I did, honey, and I'm going to have a long talk with your daddy, but what are you kids doing down here?"

That's when Parker noticed Mason's other kids, as well as Laz's daughter, and Kenton's son. London usually had a couple of nannies helping whenever they hosted parties. Maybe they hadn't arrived yet.

"Come on. Let's get you all back upstairs and settled in before everyone else gets here," London said. She and Egypt ushered all of them back toward the stairs that would take them to the massive playroom.

Standing near the basement stairs were Angelo and Zenobia, each holding one of their twins. And Laz and Journey were huddled next to them.

"Damn, I missed it," Laz murmured before heading back down the stairs.

The others were looking on, curiosity written on their faces before they turned away murmuring something as they followed after Laz.

"Whatever's going on here, fix it *now*," Mason said, then trained his gaze on Parker. "After everyone gets here and has something to eat, I want to talk to you and the guys in my office."

Parker nodded. He had touched base with Mason the night before regarding the best way to pull everyone together. After asking Parker if he was sure about wanting to go after Wolf, and Parker saying yes, Mason agreed to get the guys together later today.

When he walked away, Chelsey reached for Parker's hand and linked her fingers with his. Ready to face off with Kenton, she opened her mouth to speak, but Parker squeezed her hand to keep her silent.

"Ken, man, I'm sorry. I didn't plan to tell you like this, but it is what it is. I'm in love with Chelsey, and I have every intention of spending the rest of my life with her."

Silence pulsed between the three of them until Kenton relaxed his shoulders. "This is who you've been pining over? He's the guy who had you walking around like somebody stole your money?" he asked Chelsey incredulously, then he turned his angry eyes to Parker. "And you... She's the reason you've been acting like a stupid jerk and not hanging out with us?"

Parker huffed out a sigh, not wanting to say too much just yet. "Partly. I get that she's your sister, and I respect that, I really do. But what goes on between me and Chelsey is between us. You don't have to like it, but you—"

"She's my little *sister*, Parker," he spat, looking like he wanted to pummel him. "She's too good for you and every other bastard trying to get with her."

"I know," Parker said. He'd had the same thought more than once. "But that didn't stop me from falling in love with her. She's an amazing woman, and I'm glad she's giving me a chance to prove to her that I'm worthy of her."

"Parker," Chelsey said, seeming surprised by his words, but before she could comment, he kept going.

He turned to face her. "We all know you're out of my league, Chels, and I—"

"I am not!" she snapped. "I don't know where all of this is coming from, but stop it. You are worthy of love just like the rest of us, and that's what you have with me. I'm in love with *you*. No one else, and if my lughead of a brother has a problem with that, then that's his problem. Not yours."

"You know what? Do whatever the hell you guys want to do," Kenton said, some of his anger gone. "But Parker, if you hurt her, you're going to have to deal with me, and next time I *will* beat your ass." With that, he headed down the stairs without a backward glance.

"All righty then... that went well," Parker said, rubbing the side of his head where Kenton had made contact moments ago.

"Yeah, it could've been worse," Chelsey said, and they both laughed.

It felt good to laugh again. The last few months, Parker hadn't had much to laugh or smile about, but that was changing. Everything was about to change for the better, and he was looking forward to what lay ahead for them.

Chapter Seventeen

Chelsey didn't want to leave Parker's side. In her mind, she knew he was fine, but her heart hurt for him. Her brother had been way out of line. First, throwing a punch, but when the jerk told Parker he wasn't good enough for her, she wanted to knock him the hell out. But what really pissed her off was when Parker agreed.

God, Chelsey hoped he didn't really think that and if he did, she was going to have to make sure he knew differently. She didn't know what that would take, but she planned to spend the rest of their lives together showing him that he was worthy of love. That he was worthy of her.

As for her brother, she wasn't sure when or if she'd ever talk to him again. At least that's what she was thinking as she and Egypt strolled out of the main house and headed toward the guest house behind it.

Chelsey had eaten with Parker, but then her sister-in-law dragged her away from him, saying it was time to join the wives. There were drinks and dessert already at the guest house and apparently a sound system. Considering how loud the music was bumping, it was safe to say wives' night was in full effect.

"Sis, I don't know about this. I'm not one of you," Chelsey said as they walked along the cobblestone path, the building several feet away. It might've been a two-bedroom, two-bathroom guest house, but it was bigger than some people's main dwelling.

Egypt glanced over and smiled, and Chelsey couldn't help but return her smile. Her sister-in-law's quiet, calm spirit and kind eyes had the ability to provide immediate comfort in any situation. She was beautiful, both inside and out.

Her brother had really lucked out in the wife department. Egypt had so much going for her, and Chelsey also loved her style. Her micro braids were in an intricate knot on top of her head, and though the sun was starting to set, her smooth dark skin gleamed under the sunlight. The red, gray, and blue African print sundress, with matching red sandals that she was wearing, showcased her sexy-chic style.

Now, if anyone was too good for someone, it was Egypt who was too good for Kenton. But Chelsey would never tell him that.

"You're one of us, even if you don't have the *wife* title yet," Egypt said as they neared the house. "The way Parker was looking at you earlier, and the way he's been acting lately, it's probably only a matter of time."

"*Heyyyy*, that's my song," Chelsey heard someone say as Egypt pushed open the door. They both stopped in the doorway, and Chelsey started laughing.

Geneva Carrington was dancing on the coffee table and singing off-key to Beyoncé's song, "Cuff It." Her dance moves might've been on point, but the only person in the room who should be singing was Zenobia. Married to one of Atlanta's Finest—Angelo Gonzalez—Zen was a famous award-winning singer who sang like an angel, and she currently had her fingers in her ears. Every few seconds, she visibly cringed when Geneva hit certain notes.

"Have you lost your mind? Get your ass off my table!" London yelled from the opening of the kitchen, trying to sound authoritative, but the last word cracked on a laugh.

"What the hell is wrong with you?" Journey roared, stopping next to London to look at her sister as if Geneva had two noses. "You're worse than the kids. Get down from there. I can't take you nowhere."

They all burst out laughing, and Chelsey and Egypt closed the door and moved further into the house.

London carried a large tray of petite desserts and set it on a wood sideboard buffet cabinet. There were wine glasses lined up on the cabinet as well, and Journey set two bottles of wine next to them. Then she turned down the music.

"Chelsey, I wish I could say that my sister is usually on her best behavior during our gatherings, but I'd be lying."

"Whatever," Geneva said, rolling her eyes as she stepped off the table and sat on the sectional sofa. "We can't all be strait-laced and in control like my lawyerly sister. Just once I wished she'd let me have some fun without chastising me."

"Seriously?" Journey swatted Geneva's shoulder, then sat next to her. "You were dancing on a table, and it's not even your table! You would think after having a baby you'd grow the hell up."

As they fussed back and forth good-naturedly, Chelsey sat in one of the recliners. Geneva, a beauty salon owner, was married to Myles Carrington, a former CIA agent and one of the quietest of the Atlanta's Finest team. He and Geneva were opposites in almost every way possible, but they seemed to balance each other.

Chelsey could understand why Myles was drawn to

Geneva. She was fun, vibrant, and had a wicked sense of humor; definitely the life-of-the-party type. The red bodycon sundress fit her spirited personality. She also didn't look like a woman who had just birthed an infant—a baby girl—a few months ago.

"Grab some snacks and something to drink," London announced after returning from the kitchen with a charcuterie board of meat, cheese, and fruit. "If you don't want wine, there's non-alcoholic beverages in the cooler." She pointed to the blue and white chest on the floor next to the cabinet.

There were only six of them in the house. The kids were at the main house either with their fathers or the nannies. Chelsey was still full from dinner, but she placed a lemon bar and some type of chocolate treat on a small plate and poured a glass of wine. On the way back to her seat, she glanced around the cozy space.

She had attended several cookouts and parties hosted by some in the group, but she'd only been to London's home once, and this was her first time in the guest house. The living room was tastefully decorated in bright colors with a tan sectional sofa in front of large windows. A coffee table, two end tables, and two leather recliners rounded out the furniture. The natural stone fireplace in the center of the main wall added to the room's welcoming feel.

Once they were all seated again, Geneva said. "Since Chelsey is new to the group, let's pick on her. Especially since she had grown men fighting like idiots."

Chelsey groaned. *Okay, here we go.*

Egypt chuckled. "Welcome to the Wives' Club, sis. Brace yourself. They're about to be all up in your business."

"Don't be *scurred*," Geneva said and laughed.

"Gen, leave her alone. You're going to scare her away before we get any answers, and I have plenty of questions,"

Journey said, reminding Chelsey that the woman had once been a state prosecutor.

She and Geneva might've been sisters who favored each other, but personality-wise, they were very different. While Geneva was a good-time girl, Journey was more reserved. Even though this was a casual event, she still looked conservative. Her makeup was lightly applied, and she wore her shoulder-length hair in a bob. Everyone else looked as if they were attending a picnic. Not Journey, though. Her short-sleeve, pale pink button-up blouse, paired with tailored cream-colored pants, was cute but she looked as if she might be planning to attend a meeting with a client.

Though she and Geneva were different in some respects, they did have something in common. They were both badasses in their own right. That probably had something to do with their father; a retired cop. They looked like girlie girls, but there was a no-nonsense edge to them both.

"Yeah, welcome to the club," Zenobia said from the recliner next to Chelsey and lifted her bottle of water.

She had that *girl-next-door* vibe and didn't look like what most would expect of a multimillionaire superstar. The T-shirt and denim shorts, along with her hair pulled up in a long ponytail on top of her head, had her looking like a freshman in college.

The front door burst open, and Chelsey and the others startled.

"Wait!" Dakota yelled and was huffing as if she'd been running. "I hope you guys didn't start without me. Let me get some wine before Journey starts interrogating Chelsey. That's assuming she hasn't already."

Everyone laughed, and Chelsey smiled. They clearly knew each other well.

Dakota was Hamilton's wife. The former stuntwoman was

someone Chelsey had looked up to since meeting her years ago. The fearless mother of three was a force to be reckoned with. To look at her, with her short hair slicked back and her cinnamon-toned face free of makeup, she looked to be in her late twenties instead of in her forties. No one would ever guess she was a tae kwon do black belt master and owned a dojo. And thanks to her, *everyone* in the room knew some form of self-defense.

"Dang. I guess Dani isn't here," Dakota said from across the room as she inspected the bottles of wine. "Otherwise, she would've brought the hard liquor."

Dani, who owned a bar that they all frequented, was Ashton Chambers' wife and the only one not in attendance. She was another baddy and had married the former Atlanta PD detective-turned-security-specialist a couple of years ago.

Now that Chelsey thought about it, she was surrounded by badasses; badasses whose lives had been threatened at one time or another, and they survived. There was nothing like being among tough, amazing women.

Wine glass in hand, Dakota grabbed a large floor pillow from the corner of the room and dropped it near the sofa before sitting on it. "Okay, so what I miss?" she asked.

"Journey was getting ready to begin her interrogation," London said, smiling.

Chelsey shook her head and took a swig of her wine.

"Okay, first question," Journey said, and everyone laughed, including Chelsey. "Why did you and Parker keep your relationship a secret? Though Laz wasn't forthcoming," she said of her husband, "I assume you two have been together for a while."

The night before, Chelsey and Parker had decided that she'd share whatever she wanted with the wives, especially since Parker would be talking to their husbands. He was even okay with her telling them a little about his relationship with Wolf as long as they understood the importance of keeping it quiet.

Chelsey wasn't sure what all she'd share, but she did talk about her and Parker's relationship. She explained that they'd dated for months before breaking up and then getting back together. She also told them about her horrible track record with men, which was why she'd wanted to keep the relationship quiet until she knew for sure they'd make it.

"I can't believe Kenton didn't know," Zenobia said, then turned to Egypt. "Did you?"

Egypt smiled. "I had a feeling, but I didn't know for sure until last week."

That surprised Chelsey. Her sister-in-law never said anything.

"What happened last weekend?" Dakota asked, and they all looked at Egypt, including Chelsey. She had no idea what she'd say.

"I saw Parker on video Saturday night storming out of the kitchen at Supreme. That was after he disapproved of the dress Chelsey wore on their assignment and after he said it would kill him if anything ever happened to her."

Those damn cameras.

Chelsey was going to have to remember they were practically everywhere in the building at Supreme.

"But what else is going on with Parker?" Egypt asked. "He's been out of sorts, and I have a feeling it was more than just him having a broken heart."

Without sharing every detail, Chelsey told them about Parker's mother, as well as his attempt to make his father pay for her death. She also gave them an abbreviated version of the beating Parker had taken.

"Oh, my God. I had no idea," London said, her expression

horrified, and the others in the room held similar expressions. "Thank God Mason found him."

"My heart goes out to him. I know what it's like to walk through life constantly looking over your shoulder, unsure if your biggest secret might blow up in your face," Egypt said, and Journey squeezed her hand.

That had been exactly how Egypt had to live after leaving the witness protection program. She was truly a survivor, and thanks to the Kenton and the Atlanta's Finest team, she no longer had to live in fear.

"That's an awful way to live," Dakota agreed. "And I don't blame Parker for wanting to end Wolf once and for all. Though Hamilton would have a fit if I inserted myself into Parker's plans in any way, let me know if there's anything I can do to help."

The others said the same thing, and Chelsey's heart squeezed.

She had already known that these women were amazing. By them offering to help in any way they could only made her love and respect them that much more.

Parker would never involve the wives. He didn't even want to involve their husbands, but he couldn't go after Wolf alone.

The women talked a few minutes longer on the subject, and Chelsey wondered if Parker knew how loved he was by everyone. He wasn't just their husbands' coworker. He was like a brother to them. He was *family*.

A knock sounded at the door before it opened, and Aunt Carolyn strolled in with a birthday cake. "I heard someone is celebrating a birthday." Considering it was decorated with salon equipment on it— scissors, a blow dryer, a comb and brush—there was no doubt who it was for.

"Oh, my goodness!" Geneva shrieked. "That is too cute to eat."

London stood and started them all singing happy birthday to Geneva. Never one to shy away from attention, Gen climbed back on the table and started dancing.

As everyone laughed and the evening progressed, Chelsey marveled at how much fun she was having. She also felt like she was truly one of them.

Hopefully, Parker was experiencing the same love from the guys.

Chapter Eighteen

Parker released a slow breath as the guys of Atlanta's Finest stared at him as if seeing him for the first time.

They were spread out around Mason's home office. Kenton and Angelo lounged on the long sofa, while Laz, Myles, and Hamilton sat at the round table near the desk. Mason sat behind his desk while Parker perched on the corner of it. The only people on the team who weren't in attendance was Ashton, Nelson, and Connor.

"Damn, man. Why didn't you ever say anything?" Angelo asked.

There was no doubt the former DEA undercover officer had heard of Wolf. Criminals like Parker's father were one of many reasons why Angelo had left the agency. No matter how many drug dealers or leaders of organized crime they got off the street, more popped up. The heartless bastards multiplied faster than the DEA could get them and their products off the street.

"Why are you telling us now? Has something happened?"

Myles, who they often referred to as a ghost, asked. The former spy was the quietest of all of them and the most observant. Nothing got past him, and he was like a walking, talking encyclopedia when it came to strategizing. He was one of the biggest assets to their team. Hell, they all were incredible, and Parker was honored to call them friends.

"Nothing's happened yet," Parker said, and then he told them about how the media had gotten a picture of him. Though he probably didn't have to explain, he told them that he feared that Wolf would one day see the photo. Though Parker had some work done on his face, anyone who'd once known him might still recognize him.

"I'm also bringing this up now because I'm planning to go after Wolf. I can't keep looking over my shoulder, hoping he won't discover I'm alive. As long as he thinks I'm dead, I'm fine, but I don't want to keep taking that chance.

"Are you kidding me right now?" Kenton ground out. "You're the son of a gangster who tried to kill you, and you've been hiding from him. Now you're dating my sister, pulling her into your bullshit life. You need to break things off with her... now!"

"That's not going to happen," Parker said. He didn't bother telling Kenton that he had already tried that.

"If you love her—"

"There's no *if* about it!" Parker snapped. "Kenton you might as well get this through your thick skull. I'm in love with your sister. No matter how you try to deny it, it's a fact. She's the main reason I need to deal with Wolf once and for all, because I'm planning to spend the rest of my life with Chelsey."

Kenton balled his hands into fists at his sides, but he didn't move from the sofa. "How can you claim to love her and risk her life like this?" There was so much emotion behind his words, and Parker understood his concern. Hell, he was concerned, too, but he either needed to destroy Wolf, or plan to hide out for the rest of his life.

He looked Kenton in the eyes. "I considered disappearing, but if I do, I'm taking Chelsey with me."

Kenton leaped to his feet. For a big man, he had the agility of a tiger. "The hell you will! No way you're taking her on the run with you. Besides, she'd never go."

"You sure about that?" Parker said calmly. If he raised his voice and argued with Kenton, they might end up back where they were hours ago rolling around on the floor throwing punches.

Breathing hard, Kenton stared him down, and Parker could imagine what the man wanted to do to him. He hoped his and Chelsey's relationship wouldn't ruin his friendship with Kenton, but if he had to choose between being with her or being friends with Kenton, he'd choose his woman every time.

"How can we help?" Hamilton asked, ignoring Parker and Kenton's exchange.

Parker ran a hand down his chin as he organized his thoughts. He'd prefer to go after Wolf alone, but he knew that wasn't realistic. His father wouldn't go down without a fight, and Parker wouldn't fool himself into thinking that he could be successful alone.

"I'd first like to brainstorm ideas on how I can take down Wolf's operations."

Angelo released a long whistle. "I haven't personally dealt with the Kingz, but I know they are formidable adversaries."

Parker nodded. "I know."

"What do you know about Wolf and what he has going on these days?" Myles asked.

"Wolf's territory has tripled since I left California, and he owns several businesses in various sizes. I know of ten of them, but there might be more. I'm not sure if they're all above board, but I'd be surprised if they aren't set up to clean money."

There was no doubt in Parker's mind that his father was involved in money laundering. He'd done it when Parker was a kid. Now, he'd probably taken operations to the next level.

"I also heard he's in the process of partnering with a gun trafficker." Laz had been the one to share that information with him, and Parker knew his friend's contacts were solid.

"To take him down, you're going to have to hit him from all sides at once," Angelo said. "The moment Wolf notices any changes with his products, distribution, or if his businesses are getting unwanted attention, he's going to disappear. Or he's going to come out fighting. And as organized as the Kingz are, I'm sure there's an escape plan."

Parker had thought about all of that; he just hadn't come up with a solid plan to address each area. But as the guys, including Kenton, tossed ideas around, he felt more encouraged. He wasn't in this alone.

"I can't believe I'm going to say this, but I think we should reach out to Rock," Angelo said of his brother-in-law, Monty "Rock" Rockwell.

Zenobia's half-brother was once the biggest drug lord in Miami, and maybe even on the east coast. Supposedly, over the last couple of years, he had cleaned up his act and had gone legit.

Though it wasn't *impossible* to do, Parker would be surprised if everything Rock was involved in was legitimate. These days, many considered him a smart, savvy businessman. No one, specifically law enforcement and maybe even the government, seemed to care that the multimillionaire once made his money illegally.

But who knew? Maybe the guy really was walking on the

right side of the law.

Angelo and Rock had met many years ago before Angelo even knew Zenobia existed. To say this world was small was an understatement. Years ago, while undercover, Angelo had infiltrated Rock's organization. During the op, when Angelo thought he'd finally play a role in taking Rock down, the operation went horribly wrong. Not only did some of Angelo's fellow DEA agents lose their lives, but Angelo almost died, too. The worst part of the situation was that the DEA abandoned him, and he almost spent the rest of his life in prison.

The moment Angelo had been able to clear his name, he left the organization and never looked back. At least not until a couple of years ago when he provided personal security for Zenobia when she had a stalker. Angelo had fallen hard for the pop singer, but then he learned that she was Rock's half-sister. Shit hit the fan, and it had turned into one of the most dangerous assignments for all of them. But in the end, Angelo got the girl, and he and Rock were at least cordial. They would probably never be good friends—too much bad blood—but for Zenobia's sake, they tried not to kill each other.

"What do you think Rock could offer to the situation?" Mason asked, and everyone, except Parker, probably was thinking the same thing.

Parker already knew. That phrase *game recognizes game* would be the best way to explain it. Rock knew the drug game. Hell, he probably invented some of the rules. He'd also dealt with and destroyed plenty of leaders like Wolf.

Though Parker's father was successful in the crime syndicate world, he wasn't at Rock's level and may never be. Zenobia's brother had already been where Wolf was trying to go. The man could cause more damage to Wolf's empire than Parker could ever dream of doing.

Yeah, if he could get Rock's help in this, it would be game over before Wolf even knew what hit him.

As Angelo explained that to the group and what a value Rock could be, Parker wanted Angelo to make the call. They needed all the help they could get—especially Rock's type of help.

"If he says yes, and if our bosses will give me and Parker some time off," Angelo said, glancing at Mason and Hamilton pointedly, a mischievous gleam in his eye, "we can fly to Miami next weekend with Zenobia. She already has plans to visit him for the weekend."

That meant flying on Rock's private jet. He always offered it up to his sister whenever she wanted to visit Miami; or go anywhere, for that matter. Or whenever he wanted to see her, the twins, and his mother who lived with Angelo and Zenobia.

If Parker could get Rock as an ally, there would be no doubt in his mind that they could take Wolf down. Not only that, but they might also be able to do it without Parker having to come face to face with his father.

That was something he'd been thinking about. The anger he had toward Wolf ran deep, and Parker feared that if they ever came face to face, he would kill his father. The bastard had almost killed him, and though he'd moved on with his life, Parker hadn't been able to move past that.

Yeah, more than anything, he hoped Rock would help. But what would it cost Parker if he did? Rock was a businessman, plain and simple, and from what Parker had heard, a shrewd one at that. Would the former gangster be willing to lend a hand for nothing in return?

Only one way to find out.

They met for a few minutes longer and settled on an initial gameplan. When everyone else filed out of the office, Hamilton asked Parker to hang back.

"I forgot to tell you that we got a hit back on the guy from the fundraiser," Hamilton said.

Parker was slipping. With everything else on his mind, he had forgotten that he'd asked them to look into him.

"His name is Sean Thompson. He's originally from Oakland, California, but he's been living in Georgia for the last twenty years. He's an electrician by day and a DJ by night."

"Criminal record?"

"When he was twenty, years before moving here, he was arrested for carrying a concealed weapon. Outside of receiving a fine, he'd gotten off without any jail time since it was a first offense. Other than that, he's clean."

Hamilton handed him an electronic tablet with the man's photo and personal information. Divorced. Two kids. Lives in Loganville, Georgia. Most of his family lived on the West Coast, except for two of his brothers and a couple of cousins. The documentation also included his current employer, job history, and even the man's credit report.

He glanced at the photo again. Nothing stood out. The guy still wasn't familiar.

"Thanks for this," he said and handed the tablet back to Hamilton.

"Any particular reason why you wanted him checked out?" Mason asked.

Parker told them about the exchange at the fundraiser, and how he'd wanted to make sure that he hadn't met the guy before.

The three of them talked for a few minutes longer about how they thought the meeting with Atlanta's Finest went. All agreed it went well, and Parker promised to keep them abreast of everything.

When he finally left Mason's home office, Kenton was waiting for him in the hallway.

"You know you were wrong, right?" Kenton said. He was leaning against a nearby wall, his usual easygoing demeanor back in place. Parker knew what he was referring to.

"I do, and I'm sorry for how you found out about me and Chelsey, but Kenton, man, I love her. I don't know how many times you'll need to hear it. I'll keep saying it over and over again until you understand that she's it for me. Of course, I'd prefer to have your blessings, but if not..." Parker shrugged, "... that won't change my feelings for her. I'm planning to spend the rest of my life with your sister."

Kenton didn't respond, just kept staring at Parker as if trying to determine if he was serious. He'd soon learn that he was dead serious, and not him or anyone else was going to keep him from Chelsey.

When Kenton pushed away from the wall, Parker braced himself. If the man wanted to go another round with him, fine. He wouldn't back down, and he sure as hell wouldn't hold back on his punches this time.

Instead, Kenton stuck out his hand.

Parker stared at it for a second before grabbing hold of it.

"I'm sorry," his friend said. "I was way out of line earlier. I've been my sister's protector since the day my parents brought her home from the hospital. Some habits die hard. You and her together caught me off guard, and I reacted before thinking. All I ask is that you treat her right."

"I will. Chelsey is my heart. So you don't have to worry about that."

They pulled each other in for a handshake-hug, pounding each other on the back in the process.

"Good," Kenton said. "As for the situation with your father, let me know what I can do to help."

"Will do. Thanks, man."

Now that Parker had his guys onboard, all he needed to do

was talk Rock into lending a hand. Hopefully, that meeting would go as easy as this one, but Parker kind of doubted it would.

Still, he had to try.

Chapter Nineteen

"If I help you, what's in it for me?"

And there it was.

Parker stood between Chelsey and Angelo as they faced Rock, who was standing behind his huge oak desk. It was Friday evening, and they'd arrived in Miami a short while ago and were now in Rock's home office.

Parker had known it was only a matter of time before Rock posed that question. Heck, he grew up with a gangster, and they rarely did anything for anyone unless it benefited them in some way. But in all honesty, it was a fair question. He was asking Rock to use his knowledge, resources, and possibly his influence to help him destroy Wolf. There were risks involved. Why shouldn't he get something out of the deal?

"What do you want?" Parker asked.

He folded his arms across his chest and braced himself for whatever was coming next. The thought of selling his soul to a devil to take down another devil didn't appeal to him, but he had to get rid of Wolf.

Slow to respond, Rock readjusted his long dreadlocks that

were bound at the nape of his neck. Mixed-race, African American and Latino, the man was around six feet four and solidly built with two hundred and fifty pounds of muscle. Yet, it wasn't his size that made him look intimidating. No, it was the hardness of his eyes that would keep a lesser man from approaching him.

Casually dressed in white linen pants and a royal-blue button-down shirt with the sleeves rolled up over his tatted forearms, Rock looked like just another wealthy guy in Miami. Except he was no ordinary guy. This man had built a multimillion-dollar empire despite the DEA and other government agencies unsuccessfully trying to take him down. Parker had mad respect for him for that alone.

Still, approaching him for help might not be the best decision, but he didn't have any other viable ideas.

"I always liked you, Parker," Rock said, and a slow grin spread across his mouth as he sat in the leather chair behind his desk. "You remind me a lot of Gavin."

Parker had no clue what that meant as he glanced at Gavin who was standing to the right of the desk like some edgy royal guard. At six feet tall and slim, he might've looked harmless in a navy sports jacket, white T-shirt, and jeans, but like Rock, his eyes told a different story. Gavin wasn't harmless at all. He had seen some shit and had indulged in his share of criminal activity. Otherwise, there was no way he'd still be hooked up with Rock after so many years.

"But now that I know a little more about you," Rock continued, "I have a whole new respect for you."

They didn't really know each other. Parker had only met the guy a couple of times when the man visited Atlanta. So he wasn't sure what Rock was talking about unless Angelo had shared some details about Parker's past with him. Which would make sense. No way would Rock agree to meet with him on this subject otherwise.

But the fact that Rock was comparing him to Gavin should've been a compliment. According to Angelo, his brother-in-law often referred to Gavin as his brother and there was nothing they wouldn't do for each other.

Yet, Parker didn't trust easily and compliment or not, he needed to know up front what Rock's help would cost him.

"What do you want?" Parker asked again. "What's it going to take for you to help us? Or should I say help me?"

Silence fell between them as Rock regarded him. He was impossible to read, and for the first time since Angelo mentioned calling him, Parker was having second thoughts.

"I want you to come work for me."

"*What?*" Parker, Chelsey, and Angelo said in unison.

"You do realize I work for Supreme, right?" Parker asked, though the question was rhetorical. "I'm not leaving them. If that's what you're suggesting, this conversation is over." He owed Mason too much and had too much respect for him to walk away from him for the likes of Rock.

Parker reached for Chelsey's hand and headed for the door. He didn't like games, and clearly that's what this guy was playing.

"Wait." Rock's one word crackled through the quietness of the room. "I'm not done talking to you."

Parker glanced over his shoulder. "You are if you think I'm leaving Supreme."

"Rock, what the hell are you up to?" Angelo snapped. "You're either going to help or you're not. Don't be wasting our time."

"Hey!" Rock slapped his hand on the desk, the sound deep and booming. "You're the one who called me. I'll take as much time as I damn well please! You're all here because you know I can help take Wolf down, maybe even with as little as a few phone calls." His gaze leveled on Parker. "And you and I both come from the streets. Surely, you knew I wouldn't be doing anything to help you without getting something in return."

Still holding Chelsey's hand, Parker returned to the desk. "*Again*, what do you want?" he bit out, his patience dwindling.

"I want you to oversee my security. Not just my personal security but all my security needs. I have some big projects in the works, and I want someone I can trust and depend on to have my back."

Parker stood, dumbfounded. Rock didn't even know him. What made him think he could trust and depend on him?

Granted, it wouldn't be a hardship for Parker to live in a city that averaged over two-hundred-and-forty days of sunshine a year. And the beaches? Yeah, he could live with that, too.

But working for Rock—who may or may not have gone straight —was too much of a risk. There was a strong chance the man still had his hands in illegal activities. That was something Parker wanted no part of, especially since Chelsey was in his life now. No way would he put her in jeopardy any more than he already had.

"What about Gavin?" Parker asked, as if he was seriously entertaining this crazy idea. "Isn't he currently over your security?"

"I look out for my boss, but I have enough on my plate without overseeing all of security. Besides, I agree with Rock. You'd be better suited; for more reasons than one," Gavin said and Rock nodded.

Parker understood exactly what that meant.

Whether Rock had gone legit or not, he'd made a lot of enemies—enemies who might someday try to come for him. Rock could hire anyone to oversee his security, but Parker had something many others didn't. He had law enforcement as well as criminal experience. A valuable combination in Rock's world.

Now Parker was the one studying him. There was nothing more dangerous than a smart criminal, and Rock didn't get to where he was today by being a dummy. No, the man might be ruthless, but he was also good at strategizing.

"Why not hire Supreme Security?" Angelo asked. "You've said more than once that they have the best security model you've seen, and that you're impressed with the organization. Parker doesn't provide personal security outside of Georgia, but there are several guys on staff who do. You'd have your choice of people to be on your detail, and you already know that Mase and Ham hire the best."

"I agree. I'm seriously impressed with what they've built, and I want to create that here...with Parker overseeing it. The main point here is that Parker would head my security. I doubt Mason and Hamilton would let him be here all the time for that. Yes, I'll want personal security, especially since some of my future business deals will be taking me out of town on day trips here and there.

"But the security team I want to build would be much bigger than that. I recently bought a major record label in which I agreed to provide security for certain artists, and I have several other unrelated deals in the works, including building a resort here in Miami and one in Paris. Both, for a *very* high-end clientele. I'm going to need the best security team money can buy, and I want that team based in Miami with *Parker* leading it," he emphasized again.

Well, damn. Now he had Parker curious and if he was honest, a little interested. Yet, his loyalties would always be to Mason.

"Parker, if that's something you think you'll be interested

in, why don't you run it by Mason? I know you're his golden boy so I'm sure he wouldn't let you leave Supreme easily."

Exactly how much had Angelo told his brother-in-law? Probably more than Angelo had wanted to, but at least he'd been able to get them a face-to-face with Rock. Which was more than Parker could have done on his own.

"What if I say no? What would that mean for you helping me with this situation?"

Rock picked up the pack of cigarettes that were on top of his desk and shook one out but didn't light it.

"I think the real question should be—how bad do you want to destroy Wolf and the syndicate?"

That was an easy question, but Parker kept his mouth shut.

Again, he needed to decide if he was willing to sell his soul to one devil to destroy another. Then again, assuming Rock really had gone straight, would being over his security really be a bad thing?

If he'd really gone straight, this could be an opportunity Parker didn't know he wanted.

"Think about it overnight and talk to Mason. Then hook up with me tomorrow evening. In the meantime, I'm going to start looking into a few things."

"What exactly are you looking into?" Parker asked.

Rock chuckled. "And you wonder why I want you as part of my team. Anyone else, out of desperation, would've already agreed to work for me. Not you, though. I like that about you, *Knuckles*. Trying to get as much information out of me before deciding on whether you can trust me. I can respect that."

Parker stiffened at hearing his street name. Damn, this guy really was good. The only person Parker had given that information to was Chelsey, and he knew she hadn't shared it with anyone. He didn't even think Mason knew.

Rock picked up his lighter, but instead of lighting the cigarette, he rolled the gold-plated object between his fingers.

"Are you sure you want to know where I'm planning to start with your father?"

"I want to be in on anything that will take Wolf down once and for all. If you know something that I might be able to use against him, yeah, I want to know."

A slow, ruthless smile kicked up the corners of Rock's mouth.

"If you must know, after Angelo called me about this meeting, I made a few inquiries about Wolf and the Kingz. Your father is in the process of brokering a gun deal with someone who owes me. Depending on what you tell me tomorrow about overseeing my security, I might decide to cash in that debt. Which would mean, my ass would be all up in that deal. If that happens, and everything goes as planned, that would be the first dent *we* put into Wolf's organization."

Angelo stiffened next to Parker. "What happened to you going straight?" he snapped. "Our deal was, if you become a law-abiding citizen, then I'll let you have a relationship with my family."

Angelo hadn't wanted Rock anywhere near Zenobia or their twin infants, but after Rock promised that he and his dealings were legal, Angelo changed his tune.

"Relax, brother-in-law. You're the one who came to me to help your friend here. *Remember?*"

Angelo was slow to respond, and Parker should feel guilty about stirring up a mess in their family. Selfishly, he didn't. If Rock had the means and an idea of how to take Wolf down once and for all, Parker couldn't just walk away.

"I might've called you for help, but I didn't ask you to do anything illegal," Angelo countered, looking as if he wanted to leap across the desk and throat-punch the guy.

Heated seconds ticked by with Rock and Angelo staring each other down. The tension was palpable. Thick enough to cut with a chainsaw, and Parker wasn't sure how to slice through it.

Then Rock broke eye contact. "*Fine*, I won't do anything that could bring heat to any of us, and when *we* do go after Wolf, I'll keep everything aboveboard."

Angelo released a low, menacing growl. "Why don't I believe you?"

"You can believe whatever the hell you want, but I'm serious. I told you, Zen, and my mother that I was cleaning up my act, and I have. Now that I have a niece and a nephew, I want to make sure I'm a part of their lives. Besides, the last thing I need in my life is your former DEA cronies, the Feds, or even ATF breathing down my neck." He shook his head and cringed. "Nope, I don't need that type of shit again."

Parker and Angelo were not just coworkers, they were friends, and Parker didn't want any bad blood between them.

Still, he wanted to be rid of Wolf. If he could ensure that Rock kept everything legal, or if nothing else, maintained several layers of protection between him and his criminal contacts, then Parker wanted to move forward.

But before he made any decisions or promised anything, he needed to have a conversation with Chelsey. She hadn't said much during this meeting, and whatever he decided to do would affect her as well as him.

She was giving him a second chance with her, and there was no way he'd mess that up. Which meant he needed to tread carefully on all fronts, but could he do that *and* be connected to Rock in any way?

Chapter Twenty

Wolf increased the speed on the treadmill as he started to relax into his evening run. Normally he tried to get his workout in first thing in the morning by running outside. It hadn't worked out this morning. He'd been pulled into too many different directions, but it was all good. Business was growing faster than he anticipated, and if it meant more work for him, so be it.

The Kingz had been moving three times as much product over the last six months, which was paying off big. For a couple of months earlier in the year, they'd struggled to keep up with demand. Their supplier had struggled to get product to them in a timely manner, and Wolf had to cut them loose. Now he was with a bigger supplier, and even with the price of product being a little higher, he was still turning a profit.

As his feet pounded on the treadmill in a rhythmic motion, his gaze went beyond the floor-to-ceiling windows. Tension eased from his body as streaks of yellow, orange, and purple painted the sky while the sun slowly made its descent.

Sunsets were one of many reasons why he would never

move from the west coast. Especially considering he'd spent an obscene amount of money for his five-thousand-square-foot penthouse in La Jolla. It was worth every penny, thanks to the La Jolla Cove views that were breathtaking.

Yeah, this was the perfect way to wind down after a busy day.

Forty-minutes later, Wolf started his cool-down and noticed the news was on television. It wouldn't have caught his attention had he not seen the words Lit Crystal at the bottom of the screen. He quickly grabbed the remote from the cupholder and unmuted the television.

Authorities confirm that there have been three more deaths linked to Lit Crystal, the latest drug cocktail that has hit the streets of San Diego. One of those deaths is that of a local drug dealer, Mario Jenson, known on the streets as Polar. He was found dead late last night in an Ocean Beach apartment from a suspected overdose of Lit Crystal. We'll have more on that later, as law enforcement is still investigating.

In other news...

Wolf stopped the treadmill and pulled his cell phone from the other cupholder. As he shot off a quick text to Elder, he was relieved that local law enforcement wouldn't be sniffing around the Kingz. So far, Lit Crystal hadn't been officially linked to them, and Wolf wanted to keep it that way. Now that Polar was dead, authorities would be all over The Titans, the crew that Polar ran with. So far, the attention wasn't on the Kingz.

Before he could set his phone down, Elder entered the home gym.

"That was quick," Wolf said and wiped his face with the towel that was hanging from his shoulder. "I just texted you."

"I had just walked into the apartment," Elder said as he looked at his cell phone screen. "So Polar got a hold of our product, huh? Good riddance. Dude was becoming a menace, and if the drug hadn't taken him out, one of the Kingz would've."

"Yeah, well, we're going to need to get that last batch off the streets and recut it. You should know as well as I do that it's bad business to kill off our clients. We want them high, not dead. Besides, since the authorities don't know where the drug is coming from, we need to keep it that way. Too many deaths might draw attention our way and we can't have that."

"Understood," Elder said, shoving his cell into the front pocket of his jeans. "I stopped by because Slick mentioned that you want us to make the trip with you to San Antonio."

"Yeah, Mando is finally ready to deal. I don't expect any trouble, but I don't know the bastard. He'll only meet in person, and I'm ready to lock him down for a date for our first shipment."

"Probably a good idea. I heard he was a little cagey."

Wolf had heard the same thing. He'd been in contact with another gun supplier, but that deal had fallen through. After receiving a tip on a gun trafficker out of San Antonio, Wolf got in touch. It had taken some time to get Armando "Mando" Torres to agree to a meeting. He was overly cautious, which was understandable. Like drug dealers, gun traffickers couldn't be too careful.

"We'll head out in a couple of days. Once we're in Texas, we'll get more information about where the meetup will be."

Wolf tossed the towel in the wicker hamper on his way out of the gym. He strolled down the short hallway past a guest bedroom and bathroom until he reached the kitchen.

"Want something to drink?" he asked when he opened the refrigerator and pulled out a pitcher of green smoothie.

Elder leaned his back against the breakfast bar and folded his arms across his broad chest. "Nah, I'm good. I'll be heading out in a few minutes, but I wanted to tell you the latest on the guy in Atlanta."

Wolf had been wondering how that was going. Ever since Elder had texted him a copy of the photo, Wolf's curiosity had increased. He had looked at it a couple of times since then, and each time he'd felt a niggling of something down his spine. The man in the photo felt familiar. Too familiar, and it was unsettling.

"His name is Parker Wilcox. He's some type of security guard in Atlanta and works for a place called Supreme Security. Looks like he grew up in Chicago. Only child. Parents are dead. No other family. He was a cop—a SWAT officer, to be more specific—and he left that to work at the security firm in Atlanta."

Wolf started to take another sip of his smoothie but stopped, the straw inches from his mouth. "Are you saying he just up and left Chicago and SWAT to become a lowly security guard?"

"That's what it looks like, but according to Supreme's website, they have security guards and security specialists. I'm not really sure which he is."

Wolf continued drinking his smoothie while listening to Elder explain the difference between the two job titles. He'd never heard of a security specialist, but he liked the concept. If he didn't have his crew around him, he might consider hiring a couple to have his back. Then again, if the specialists were former law enforcement or whatever, he didn't need that type of heat watching his back.

"I don't know, Wolf. This guy's background all seems a little too...too perfect. I know there's some good guys out there, but this dude is squeaky-clean. He's never even had a parking ticket, and everything we dug up on him is, is..."

"Too perfect," Wolf finished for him. "Yeah, I get it."

The guy was probably a nobody, but Wolf couldn't seem to let it go. Occasionally, he got like that, where his gut would tell him to do or not do something. Or to dig deeper in some situations. He'd learned a long time ago not to ignore that feeling.

"I know you haven't admitted to this, but I know you see what I see when you look at the picture."

Wolf stiffened. All he'd said the other night was that the guy looked familiar. He hadn't shared the fact that he hadn't been able to stop thinking about that photo. Nor had he said that the guy looked a little like his dead son—Junior.

"Even though it's impossible that it could be—"

"Junior is dead! You know that, so what the fuck are you getting at?"

Elder lifted his hands out in front of him. "Whoa, man. I know that...but what if you have another kid out there?"

Wolf slammed his drink on the counter, glad the glass hadn't shattered, ignoring the way the liquid spilled onto his hand. "I never cheated on Mina!" he roared. "And I ought to beat your ass for even suggesting it."

"What about *before* Mina? We both know your ass got around. So it's not out of the question. Especially since this guy is a few years older than what Junior would've been today. It's possible that whoever his mother was, you could've known her."

Wolf remained silent as Elder explained that this Parker guy had been raised by a single mother until he was five. Then he was adopted, and those parents died during a fire while he was away at college.

"What if you have another son out there? Wouldn't you want to know?"

Wolf mulled over that question, but he didn't need to know if he had another kid out there. Especially some grown dude. That didn't stop his curiosity, though.

"Send someone to Atlanta. Hell, they can even go to Supreme and pretend they want to hire the guy for security. I want them to—"

"I'll go," Elder volunteered.

"No, you don't have time. We'll be in Texas for the next few days, maybe even a week. After that—"

"After that, I'll head to Atlanta with a couple of guys and dig a little deeper into Parker Wilcox. I just have this feeling..."

Yeah, unfortunately, Wolf had a feeling, too. There was something about the eyes of the guy in that photo. Something Wolf couldn't shake. Even if this Parker guy wasn't his son, it was a little spooky at how much the man favored Junior.

Maybe I should be the one to go to Atlanta.

Chapter Twenty-One

Chelsey stood on the balcony of their hotel suite and allowed the crashing of waves against rocks to lull her into a peaceful state. The sun had set hours ago, and she couldn't wait to see their ocean view in the morning.

As she held onto the wrought iron railing, the gentle breeze blowing her curly hair around, she gazed into the distance, awed at how the moonlight shone brightly and reflected off the water. She basked in its beauty and the calming feeling it presented.

The whole setting was the perfect end to a long day.

Well, maybe not exactly the end. It had been hours since the meeting with Rock, and she and Parker still needed to talk more about it. They'd chatted some over dinner, but the restaurant hadn't been a good place to discuss something that private and serious. They also couldn't say much on the way to the hotel since Rock had offered them a car and a driver during their stay in town.

So now she was waiting for Parker to finish with his phone call to Mason, and then they'd weigh their options.

Chelsey glanced over her shoulder when she heard the sliding door open, and Parker stepped out onto the balcony.

"Hey, sweetheart," he said and moved behind her. When he slid his arms around her waist, Chelsey nestled against him.

"Hey, yourself." She could barely get the words out as he peppered kisses on her bare shoulders, along her collarbone, and worked his way up to nuzzling her neck.

A sweet thrill charged through her body at the contact, and her eyes drifted close. Having him hugged up behind her, along with the alluring scent of his woodsy cologne, had her desire for him stirring. Which wasn't unusual. Parker always had that effect on her and she couldn't wait for them to get naked and crawl into bed, but first, they had things to discuss.

"I guess you talked to Mason," she said as more of a statement than a question.

"I did," he said against her heated skin, still insistent on driving her crazy with his sweet kisses.

When Parker eventually lifted his head, he planted a quick kiss on her cheek and continued to hold her close. Except for the sounds of the ocean, silence surrounded them as they stared out into the deepening darkness.

Chelsey wasn't sure what Parker's silence meant. Maybe it meant that during his conversation with Mason, his mentor had given him even more to think about. Or maybe his silence was due to the long day, and he wasn't ready to make any life-altering decisions.

Fine with her. It felt good to be cocooned in his loving embrace with his strong, protective arms holding her tightly. She had longed for some quiet time with him since they'd stepped off the plane earlier. Just the two of them basking in the love they had for each other and the sound of waves crashing in the background.

They stood that way for several minutes until Parker broke the silence.

"After my mom died, I didn't care about anything, except for getting revenge against Wolf. I wanted him to suffer the way I had, and maybe he did. I don't know. All I knew was that because of him, I no longer had the one person who loved me unconditionally. I spent years hating him and hating everything he stood for. I might have a chance to take him down, but now that you're in my life..."

Chelsey didn't miss the emotion in his tone and the way his voice cracked with some of the words.

She turned within his arms to face him, and didn't miss the love in his dark amber eyes.

"I never thought I could ever have a normal life," he said. "I never imagined I could be anything other than a thug raised by a drug dealer. And I sure as hell never thought a woman like you, one who makes me feel like I can be and accomplish anything, would ever give me the time of day. Chelsey, you have no idea what you've brought to my life. What you mean to me."

Tears pricked the back of her eyes as his words penetrated her heart. She was so grateful that he felt the love she had for him. To know that she had that type of effect on anyone made her heart sing. He meant the world to her, too, and no matter how many times she told him she loved him, it didn't matter unless he felt it.

What made this moment even more special was that he made her feel the same way. Outside of her family, no one had ever loved her as completely as he did. She understood the emotions he was currently experiencing. To be loved for who you were, despite any mistakes of the past, meant everything.

She placed her hands on Parker's hard chest and stared into his eyes. "I'm so glad you're mine. I don't know what Mason said to you, but like I said during dinner, I'm with you, baby. However, you decide to move forward, just know I'll be right there with you."

Whatever decisions they made this weekend would dictate their future together, and Chelsey meant what she said. She was sticking by her man, no matter what.

Parker held her face between his hands. "I love you," he choked out and placed his forehead against hers. "I just...I love you so much, and I don't want to make the wrong decision."

She slid her arms around him and said, "You won't."

They stood there breathing each other in until Parker crushed his mouth over hers. The hunger of his kiss sent spirals of ecstasy racing through Chelsey's body. Desire pounded through her veins, joy leaped from her heart, and her knees trembled.

Goodness. This man's mouth and tongue needed a warning label—*too hot to handle*.

Considering the heat behind his kiss, Chelsey was going to spontaneously combust at any second. Their soul-stirring lip-lock rivaled all the others they'd shared, and every cell in her body was on high alert. As their kiss intensified, Parker's hands roamed along her spine until he cupped her butt, and need shot through her.

She wanted him more than anything. She squeezed her thighs together, moaning as the throbbing pulse between her legs grew more intense.

"Parker," she murmured against his lips and fisted the back of his shirt as she squirmed against him. "I need you."

A few more laps of their tongues tangling, then he ripped his mouth from hers while panting, "Same."

Chelsey squeaked, then laughed when he swung her up into his arms and carried her back inside. He turned with her so she could close and lock the sliding door, then he hauled her across the living space.

The one-bedroom suite was the most luxurious hotel room she'd ever stayed in, but at the moment the space was a blur. Parker was moving quickly, his feet silent against the carpet.

Chelsey nuzzled his neck as they entered the bedroom, and she inhaled his intoxicating scent. This fragrance, a mixture of woodsy and spicy, was different than what he usually wore but still just as potent.

He placed her on her feet next to the bed, and when she reached for him, planning to help him out of his shirt, he brushed her hands away.

She sputtered a laugh. "You're such a control freak."

He chuckled while lifting her shirt over her head and tossing it to the floor. "When it comes to getting you naked, definitely." Seconds later, she was stripped bare.

A shiver ran up Chelsey's spine and goosebumps raced over her skin at the desire radiating in his gorgeous amber eyes.

"I'll never tire of admiring your incredible body," he said, placing a kiss on her shoulder before swinging her up into his arms again and setting her on the bed.

"Don't move," he demanded and hurried across the room to his duffle bag. He removed a strip of condoms, tore a couple off, and dropped them onto the nightstand.

As he started stripping out of his own clothes, Chelsey couldn't look away. Her gaze swept slowly over his sexy body. Though there was a large, ornate cross tattooed in the center of his chest with tribal tattoos intricately entwined with it, nothing detracted from his sculpted physique.

As her eyes took him in, she couldn't help but realize how lucky she was that he was hers. The man was beautifully built without a lick of fat on his dark, sinewy body. His broad shoulders tapered to a narrow waist, and his flat abs with its rippling muscles were downright drool-worthy.

Chelsey's gaze went lower to his impressive penis, and heat pooled between her legs at the way it stood at attention. She couldn't wait to have him.

"I know what you're thinking," he said, and her gaze snapped to his, "but I'm taking care of you first."

Though she wanted nothing more than to suck him into her mouth and bring him pleasure, she'd follow his lead.

Parker climbed onto the bed, and hovered above her before Chelsey wrapped her arms around his neck and pulled him close. She loved the weight of him on top of her and the feel of his thick erection pressing against her core. As their lips connected and their tongues tangled once more, she savored his mouth while also grinding against him.

When he broke off the kiss, she groaned in frustration, but then moaned in delight when his lips grazed a sensitive spot below her ear. He continued lower and sucked on her neck just above her collarbone, no doubt leaving a love-mark.

Her skin was so dark that only he and she would probably notice. Not that Chelsey cared. With the way this man knew how to love on her body, she was okay with the whole world knowing how much he pleased her in the bedroom.

"You smell incredible," Parker murmured while kissing his way lower.

She was fairly sure he hadn't missed an inch of skin from her neck to her belly button. His heated touch was making her crazy as he slowly worked his mouth back up her body.

Chelsey whimpered her pleasure and swallowed hard when his hands connected with her breasts. Her nipples pebbled and turned to hardened peaks as his tongue swirled around one while he tweaked the other between his thumb and forefinger.

"Goodness, Parker," she moaned, squirming beneath him.

This was why she always got impatient with him. Her whole body was wound tight, and her toes curled at the way his masterful tongue teased her. He made her feel so good that all she could think about was having him buried deep inside of her. Or him making her come hard and fast.

Yet, her man took his time loving on one nipple before moving to the other. All the while he gently caressed and squeezed her breasts.

Normally a patient person in other areas in her life, it was impossible for Chelsey to be that way when under Parker's control. He always took his time in loving on her body and pleasing her, even when she wanted to hurry him along.

Chelsey was convinced that he enjoyed torturing her with his sweet kisses, his tender caresses, and a tongue that had the ability to twist her up inside.

Torture. It was pure, delicious torture.

Parker slid his hand between her thighs and caressed the sensitive bundle of nerves, and Chelsey sucked in a breath. She slammed her eyes closed as her breath caught. "Oh, my goodness."

Her heartbeat quickened while his touch sent heat radiating throughout the rest of her body. But when he slipped a finger between her slick folds and then another, she cried out and fisted the sheets on each side of her.

"Parker," she gasped, and her sex clenched as he stroked her, sending heat spreading through her body while he worked his digits in and out of her.

"I love it when you're so wet for me," he mumbled.

But when he lowered his head and his tongue replaced his fingers, Chelsey would've bucked off the bed had he not had a hand on her stomach. She released several unsteady breaths while his face was buried between her thighs and his mouth pleasured her.

Ohhhhh....

A whirlwind of sensations swirled inside of her. His tongue and his thumb on her clit worked in tandem and were almost too much to handle.

"Parker," she whined, and her trembling thighs clamped shut on their own accord. Parker gripped her legs, pushed them apart and continued his sweet torture.

She might like sex fast and hard, but she also wanted incredible moments like this, where he made her feel so good, to last forever. Even if they did this long into the night, Chelsey still wanted it to last longer than a few...

"I'm going to..." she gasped, her body tightening and convulsing as she frantically gripped the back of his head.

Her orgasm punched through her like a powerful force, sending her body spiraling out of control. The pleasure, pure and explosive, rocked her to her core, and left her breathless as her body lay limp against the mattress.

"I know I say it all the time, but *damn,* I'll never get enough of watching you lose control," Parker said as he tenderly kissed his way back up her body. "As a matter of fact, we're going to do this over and over again tonight until neither of us can walk straight.

Chelsey sputtered a laugh. "Well, we're off to a good start, because I don't think I can move."

Parker chuckled and snatched a condom from the nightstand and sheathed himself. Within seconds, his large body was positioned between her thighs, and he wasted no time in entering her.

When he started rocking his hips, stirring flames of passion within her, Chelsey lifted her hips, meeting him with every stroke as he drove into her. The deeper and harder he went, the tighter her body got as they moved in perfect sync.

Her heart was bursting with love and desire, as heat rippled beneath her skin. The man felt so damn good inside of her, and with each thrust, she drew closer to another release.

As Parker continued driving into her, he shifted slightly and rubbed his thumb rhythmically over her clit. At first, he stroked her tenderly, but as he picked up speed, his touch became more demanding.

Her mind was a garbled mess as her inner walls tightened around his penis, and pleasure shot to every cell in her body. Chelsey whimpered. Her moves grew jerkier as she chased an orgasm.

"Par—Parker. Ohhhh, Parker!" she screamed his name and surrendered to another explosive release.

Parker didn't stop moving. He continued plunging into her, thrusting harder and faster. He cursed under his breath and gripped the headboard but didn't stop his pace. His other hand went to her right hip, his fingers digging into her skin until a savage growl ripped through him. His body stiffened, then trembled while he growled her name.

When he collapsed on top of her, Chelsey wrapped her arms around his neck and held him close as they both gasped for air.

"Don't move," she panted when he tried to lift off her.

Chelsey loved the feel of his body on top of hers. They stayed that way for a few minutes longer until he rolled onto his back, taking her with him.

As she lay sprawled against his chest, her eyes drifted closed and the last thing she remembered was Parker whispering, *I love you.*

Chapter Twenty-Two

"I love your version of a midnight snack."

Parker glanced up to find Chelsey standing in the bedroom's doorway. It didn't matter that her curly hair was piled on top of her head in a messy ponytail and her face was scrubbed free of makeup. Nor did it matter that she was wearing the hotel's white terry cloth robe that was too big. She was still the sexiest woman he'd ever laid eyes on.

He smiled as she walked toward him. "Hey, sleepyhead. Hungry?"

Her timing was perfect. He had ordered room service and a few additional items that were delivered a few minutes ago. He hadn't been sure if she'd sleep through the night but just in case, Parker had wanted to have food for them.

"This all looks delicious." She bent down and kissed him before dropping onto the sofa next to him. "Wait. You got me flowers? How?" She leaned forward, burying her nose into the two-dozen pink and red roses, and inhaled deeply.

Chelsey loved fresh flowers, and since they'd started dating, Parker tried to surprise her with some at least once or twice a month. Considering how she was gushing over these, maybe he should consider giving her some more often.

"Instead of the red wine we picked up earlier, I ordered a bottle of Jack Daniels, and it was delivered right after the food arrived. It's amazing how helpful a concierge can be."

Parker had set everything out on the cocktail table in front of the sofa. Their choices included a charcuterie board loaded with cheeses, crackers, meat, strawberries, and chocolate.

"I'm clearly in love with a romantic," Chelsey said as she munched on a strawberry. She picked up another one and held it to his lips.

Parker met her gaze and when she smiled, he couldn't help but smile back. As he stared into her eyes, he opened his mouth and let her feed him. When he bit into the red, juicy fruit, a little juice drizzled along the corner of his mouth. But before he could wipe it away, Chelsey leaned forward and ran her tongue across his lower lip, effectively lapping up the excess. Then she lovingly kissed him.

This woman...

This incredibly beautiful woman was all his, and she was like a balm to his weather-beaten spirit. Since they'd started dating, Chelsey had breathed life into him. He'd been living a lonely existence, going to work, hanging with the guys and their families, and then spending way too much time by himself at home.

But Chelsey...

She had become the light to his darkness, bringing sunshine, humor, and joy to his world. Telling her he loved her wasn't adequate enough to express what he truly felt. She would never fully understand how depressing and lacking his life had been after his mother passed. Each time he thought back on those dark years, he was glad he hadn't given up.

Otherwise, he would've missed out on the best thing that ever happened to him.

When the kiss ended and they came up for air, Parker gave her another quick peck before he removed the silver domes from the other dishes. There were three types of wings and an order of potato skins.

"I've decided that whenever we travel, we're staying at hotels with concierges and twenty-four-hour room service."

"Agreed," Chelsey said as she fixed a plate. "But if we keep eating like this, I'm going to have to double the miles that I run every day. Otherwise, I won't be able to burn up all these calories I keep taking in."

Parker wrapped his arm around her shoulders, tugged her close, and kissed the side of her head. "I can help with burning the calories while also keeping your muscles loose and limber," he said suggestively and nuzzled her scented neck. She smelled like vanilla and lavender and good enough to eat.

Chelsey laughed. "I know you can, and I like your form of working out even better than running."

As they talked, laughed, and munched on the snacks, it was the most relaxed Parker had felt since arriving in town. Sitting and chatting with Chelsey was one of his favorite pastimes, and this was what he wanted every day.

"Are you ready to tell me what you and Mason talked about?" she asked.

"Sure. The conversation surprised me. Mason and Hamilton have been thinking about opening a Supreme satellite office in Miami. He also said he wasn't surprised by Rock's request, and he agreed that I'd be great as head of security."

"Really? Wow, that's high praise coming from Mason."

"I know, right? It kind of caught me off guard."

She glanced at him with her eyebrows pinched together. "Why is that? We all know that you're a leader. It's not a stretch for you to lead a group of security specialists, even with all Rock has going on. You've been taught by the best. I have no doubt that if you take Rock up on his proposal, you'll exceed his expectations."

Parker's heart thumped a little harder at her words and confidence in him. He believed he could handle the job, but hearing how those who meant the most to him also believed, made his chest tighten.

"Does Mason think you should accept the job? Or does he want you to run Supreme's Miami office?"

"He told me the decision is mine, but he reminded me that if I decide to accept Rock's help with Wolf, I need to make sure everything is done legit. For me, that's a no-brainer. Not only that, but if I accept his proposal, I'll want everything in writing."

No way would he take a job with the man unless everything was on the up-and-up and in writing. No contract. No deal.

"*Sooo*, what are you going to do?"

"I want to know what you think, because I'd only consider his proposal if you'll be with me."

She turned slightly to better face him and gave him a smile before gazing down at her almost empty plate.

If Parker said yes to Rock's proposal, and Chelsey agreed to follow him to Miami, she'd be giving up a lot. Even if her sisters, their families, and her father no longer lived in Atlanta, Kenton and his family did. Despite their recent disagreement, she and her brother were very close. Would she leave them behind?

Chelsey set her plate on the table and her gaze met his again. "I never imagined leaving Atlanta, but I wouldn't rule it out. I'm behind you one hundred percent, Parker, and I want to be wherever you are."

"And I *want* you to be wherever I am. I know asking you to leave the life you've built in Atlanta is asking a lot, but I'm seriously considering saying yes to Rock. I just need you to think about what you're agreeing to."

Parker removed his arm from around her shoulders and dug into the front pocket of his jeans.

"While you're thinking about that, think about this, too." He got down on one knee next to the sofa. "Think about marrying me."

Chelsey looked at him, her head slightly tilted as she frowned. When he pulled the black velvet box from behind his back and opened the lid, her eyes went wide.

He had purchased the ring earlier in the year, because he knew he'd one day ask her to be his wife. He just hadn't planned on proposing like this.

Actually he had no idea when or how he'd propose. He just knew that she was the one he wanted to spend the rest of his life with.

"Oh. My. God," she said, her eyes as round as dinner plates. "Is that...are you... Oh. My. God."

Parker couldn't help but laugh at her reaction. Rarely was she at a loss for words, and he was glad he could catch her off guard.

"I have never loved a woman the way I love you, Chelsey. And when I think about my future, I see you all up in it. Your sass, your wit, your take-no-bullshit attitude, your big heart, and your ability to make me want to be a better man, is what I want in my life. You're my best friend. My heart. My love. Sweetheart, I don't want to walk through life without you by my side.

"I guess what I'm trying to say is, will you spend the rest of your life with me? Will you marry me and be my wife?"

Tears trekked slowly down her cheeks and her hand covered her mouth as she nodded.

Parker grinned. "I need a yes or a no, sweetheart."

"Yes," she whispered and started crying outright. "Yes, baby, I'll marry you. Oh my goodness. I can't believe this."

She lurched forward and threw herself into his arms, but it caught Parker off guard. He held on tight to her as he fell backward with her on top of him.

They both laughed and again, where she was concerned, Parker felt like the luckiest man in the world. He wrapped his arms around her and kissed the side of her head then rocked back and forth with her. His heart was so full, it felt as if it would burst right out of his chest.

Still laying on his back with Chelsey on top of him, he patted his hand around on the floor for the ring box that he had dropped. When he found it, he pulled out the ring.

"So that we can make this official, give me your left hand." When she did, he slid it onto her finger.

Chelsey sat up and straddled him. With her arm stretched out in front of her, she gazed at the ring and smiled. "It's absolutely stunning." She bent down and pressed her lips to his in a slow, drugging kiss. "I can't wait to be your wife," she whispered.

"Same, sweetheart. Just so you know, the ring has been outfitted with a tracking device."

Chelsey nodded as she stared down at the jewelry. He assured her that he wouldn't be tracking her. She knew all the wives of Atlanta's Finest had jewelry with tracking devices. Most of them had received theirs because of trouble that they'd had, like kidnappings or attempted kidnappings. Parker only got Chelsey's ring outfitted with the chip as a precaution.

"Thank you," she said. "Even though you know I can take care of myself, it does feel good to know that if ever anything happened to me, you'd find me."

"Always," he said and kissed her again.

When they made it back up to the sofa, Parker picked up where they left off in their earlier conversation. "I don't think I can take Wolf down without Rock's help. As long as you're on board, I'm thinking about accepting his proposal, but with a few tweaks.

"Even though Mason told me that I don't owe him anything, I'm not ready to completely walk away from Supreme. He might not be old enough to be my father, but Mason has been a father figure for almost half my life. I can't just walk away. I'm going to suggest to Rock that we set up some type of partnership with Supreme. Or work with them in some way."

"I love that idea. Even though Mason and the guys will always only be a phone call away, a partnership of sorts will keep you close to them."

Parker nodded. That was exactly what he was thinking. He was also thinking that he'd want to build his team from people from Supreme. He wasn't sure what that would look like yet, but it would be the start of negotiations.

The more he and Chelsey talked, the better he felt about moving forward with Rock. He just hoped his decision didn't come back to bite him in the ass.

Chapter Twenty-Three

With a hand at the small of her back, Parker guided Chelsey into the ten-story office building that Rock owned. Once they were inside the lobby, they spotted Angelo near a long receptionist desk, talking to the security guard.

"Oh, good. I'm glad he's here early," Parker said. "This will give me a chance to talk to him before we all meet with Rock."

Chelsey nodded. "Great idea."

Parker wanted to tell his friend that he was accepting Rock's proposal. He also wanted to see if Angelo would consider moving to Miami and joining Parker's security team if everything panned out with Rock.

"I'll wait for you guys near the elevators. Just meet me over there."

Parker gave her a quick kiss on the lips. "Will do. See you in a minute."

She watched as he strolled away, her gaze automatically going to his perfect ass encased in dark blue dress pants. The man looked good coming and going, and he was all hers.

195

That thought made her smile, and she discreetly lifted her hand out in front of her as she strolled across the lobby. It had been fifteen hours since Parker had proposed marriage, and she still couldn't believe it. The three-stone diamond engagement ring with blue sapphires on each side of a central diamond was absolutely stunning.

To say that she'd been surprised by the proposal would be an understatement, even though they'd discussed marriage often. Last night, Parker had told her that he'd gotten the ring earlier in the year, debating on when best to ask her to be his wife.

The timing now, with plans to take down Wolf, hadn't been ideal, but he'd wanted her to know how serious he was about spending the rest of his life with her. Asking her to marry him was definitely one way to do that.

Her gaze went back to the ring, and giddiness bubbled inside of her.

I'm getting married!

She was marrying the man of her dreams, and she couldn't wait. Neither of them wanted a long engagement, but they both agreed that they'd make wedding plans after Wolf was dealt with.

In the meantime, Chelsey would enjoy her engagement to the sexiest man alive.

She and Parker had spent much of the day enjoying the sites. They'd started with lounging and walking along the beach near their hotel. After that, they hung out in South Beach, ate lunch, and did some shopping.

Living in South Florida with its gorgeous beaches was going to be a heck of a difference than living in the Atlanta with its lush greenery, massive trees, and rolling hills. Moving to the Sunshine State, assuming all went as planned, would be a big adjustment. It would also be the first time she had ever lived outside Georgia, but Chelsey was looking forward to the change—as well as the challenges that might come with it.

She glanced up to find Parker and Angelo strolling toward her.

Chelsey was curious about what Angelo would say. She thought it a good idea since he and Zen loved Miami and visited a couple of times a month.

What she found interesting, though, was that Rock hadn't asked his brother-in-law to head up his security. Maybe their past issues were too deep.

Either way, she hoped Angelo would consider Parker's request. With him on the team, that would be a great way to make sure Rock stayed out of illegal trouble. That was a big concern of Chelsey's. Only time would tell whether the guy could be trusted.

The lobby of the ten-story modern building was busy for a Saturday. On the ground level were a few restaurants, a bakery, and according to the directory, the other floors housed various businesses; everything from a law firm to a financial consulting company, and even a dentist office were building tenants.

"Hey, Chelsey," Angelo said, giving her a hug.

"Hey, yourself. You guys ready to head up?"

Parker slipped his arm around her waist. "Let's do this."

As they rode up the elevator, several people got on and off on the way to the top floor. She, Parker, and Angelo were the only ones to exit on the tenth floor where Rock's offices were. When they stepped off the elevator, Angelo walked ahead while she and Parker slowed.

He squeezed her hand and leaned close to her ear. "You ready for this?"

Chelsey nodded. "What about you?" she asked, her voice matching his whispered words. "This could be the beginning of a totally new life for you...for us."

Not only would he be rid of Wolf, but he'd also be able to stop looking over his shoulder for the first time in his adult life. She wanted that for him so much, that she was willing to do anything to help make it a reality.

Before they started walking toward the reception area, Parker brought her hand to his lips and kissed the back of it.

"Like I said, as long as I have you by my side, I'm ready for anything."

Chelsey grinned up at him. She loved when he talked like that, and she couldn't be happier about their engagement. The first thing she'd wanted to do this morning was call and tell India and her family the news.

Instead, she decided to wait. After this meeting, there might be more news to share.

Like the fact that she was moving to Miami.

She sucked in a breath at that realization. This whole situation was wild. Never in a million years did she expect their trip to turn into a job offer to Parker, a marriage proposal, and the possibility of relocating to Miami. In a matter of minutes, their whole life could change.

As the three of them entered the office, Rock stood from behind the desk. While Gavin stood next to the desk, much like he had in Rock's home office the night before.

Rock gestured to the two chairs in front of his desk. "Come on in. Have a seat."

Gavin grabbed another chair from the table in the corner for Angelo, and once they were all settled, Rock began.

"What's it going to be?"

No small talk was needed. The sooner they came to an agreement, the sooner they could handle Wolf and the Kingz. Or, if Rock had a problem with whatever Parker requested of him, then there wouldn't be much of a conversation. They'd head back to Atlanta and come up with a different plan.

"Just so we're clear on the objective, I want to take Wolf and the Kingz down at the same time. I want to hit them from every direction all at once. So, if you help me accomplish that—*legally*—then we have a deal. But," Parker hurried to say when Rock started to speak, "as head of your security, I'm going to want Supreme involved in some capacity."

Rock nodded, looking pleased. "As head of my security, you can do whatever the hell you think is best."

He stood, and so did Parker, and they shook hands.

"I know you don't trust me," Rock said as they reclaimed their seats. "And I understand why, but I give you my word that I'm on the right side of the law."

Parker studied him as if trying to decide if the guy was being honest. "Okay. Then we have a deal."

"To also prove that I can be trusted, I'm going to help you nail Wolf, and then after that, you and I can discuss the security position, draw up a contract, and make everything official."

"That works for me. When do we get started?" Parker asked.

"We've already started." Rock leaned back in his leather chair and steepled his fingers. "I theoretically put myself in Wolf's shoes, tried to think like he'd think, and made a list of everything I would have in place as the leader of the Kingz. I can assure you he has an exit plan if shit ever hit the fan."

"I'm sure he does," Parker agreed. "Which is why we have to attack every aspect of his life all at once."

"Exactly. Okay, so like you," Rock continued, "I don't trust easily, and I want to assure you that those who I've identified to help us will be discreet and trustworthy. We, like you, will have roles to play in taking your father down, and while we're setting everything up, he won't know what's happening until it's too late."

"Good, and thanks for pulling a team together. Actually, I

appreciate you being willing to stick your neck out for me like this, and I'll make sure I do my part," Parker said, and pulled up something on his phone. "I also put together a list of areas I want to make sure we hit as it relates to Wolf. I'm thinking maybe we can compare notes, create a timeline, and decide who does what over the next couple of weeks."

Rock nodded, his gaze steady on Parker. "Okay. I think with all of us working together, we can end Wolf and the Kingz sooner than later."

"As I mentioned," Angelo jumped in, "I have a DEA contact, who I'd trust with my life, who would be more than interested to get in on this. Quietly, of course. In order to shut the Kingz down, we're going to have to have help from the DEA, ATF, and maybe even the FBI, depending on what all we find on Wolf," Angelo said.

Parker reached for Chelsey's hand. He'd always been touchy-feely with her, but she wondered if he was nervous. This was it. He was finally going to get the closure he desperately wanted.

She squeezed his hand without looking at him, wanting him to know that she was right there with him. That they all were. He wouldn't be alone in this like he'd been when he tried taking Wolf down years ago.

"We also have a secret weapon who I believe you know," Rock said to Parker, and for whatever reason, Parker stiffened.

"Who? Because I'm fairly sure you and I don't know many of the same people. More than that—"

"Relax, man. Remember, we're a team now. So your best interest is my best interest." He pushed a button on his desk phone.

"Yes?" the person on the other end said.

"Can you come to my office and bring that file on Wolf with you?"

"Be right there."

Minutes later, there was a quick knock before the door swung open. "Rock, I got some more information that might... Oh, I didn't realize you had company."

Parker leaped from his seat and turned toward the door. Chelsey watched as he and the woman stared at each other in shock.

Who the hell was she? And why did Parker look as if he was going to pass out.

Chapter Twenty-Four

Parker couldn't believe his eyes. He had to be seeing things.

The moment he heard the voice, he knew it was her, but how was that possible? How had she gotten out of San Diego without his help?

Hell, how had she survived the fallout of a plan that had gone horribly wrong?

As his gaze took her in, memories of their last day together swarmed his mind. Gone was the scared, quiet sixteen-year-old girl who he had vowed to help get out of California.

In her place was a well put-together woman dressed in an expensive-looking floral blouse and white skirt. The makeup on her tawny-brown face was flawless, and her long micro braids hung loose down to her waist.

If it weren't for her grayish-brown eyes, Parker wouldn't be a hundred percent sure it was her—the girl he'd met in high school. The girl who he had befriended despite the hatred between the people they associated with. And the girl who worked with him to set up the war between the Disciples and the Kingz.

"Elena?" Her name came out as a whisper while he tried to make sense of this.

Stunning, narrowed eyes stared back at him. "Knuckles?" she finally said and moved closer but stopped a few feet away. "Oh my... *You're alive?* I thought—"

He wasn't sure who moved first, but before Parker realized it, they were in each other's arms. He hugged her fiercely and was glad she made it out of California alive.

When they finally released each other, he said, "I can't believe it's you."

"You two care to fill us in on what's happening here?" Chelsey asked, and her words snapped Parker out of his temporary fog.

Shit.

She was probably thinking more was going on here than it actually was. He and Elena had never been anything more than friends. Two kids who had plotted and had been willing to risk their lives to get out of bad situations at home.

He moved back to the chair he had vacated and reached for Chelsey's hand to pull her into a standing position.

"Sweetheart, this is Elena. I...she...we..."

He stopped and sighed, struggling to get his thoughts and words to cooperate. Shock had rattled his brain, because he still couldn't believe she was standing in front of him.

Parker turned his attention to Chelsey. "Elena helped me start the war between the Kingz and the Disciples. Her brother, Calvin, was the leader of the Disciples."

When Parker looked at the woman again, she was still staring at him as if he were a ghost. "Elena, this is my fiancée, Chelsey."

"*Fiancée?*" Rock said, surprise in his voice. "When did that happen?"

"Last night," Angelo responded before Parker or Chelsey could answer.

Everyone, including Elena, congratulated them, and Parker barely registered Chelsey showing everyone her ring. He still couldn't get over seeing little Elena and her transformation. He had so many questions, but if she was like him, she didn't want to remember the past. Still...

"Elena," he said.

"Kamora," Elena corrected with a gentle smile. "My name is Kamora. Like you, needing a new start, I changed my identity. The other day, when Rock mentioned *Parker,* Parker Wilcox, I had no idea he was talking about you."

It was interesting that Rock hadn't enlightened either of them about the other. How long had he known that they once knew each other? When Parker had more time, he'd try to unpack what that meant. For now, though, he was just glad to see her.

"You look different...yet the same," Kamora said, shock still marring her face.

That had been Parker's main concern when that photo of him and Journey showed up on TV and the internet months ago. Anyone who knew him as Junior or Knuckles from back in the day would probably do a double take. He'd had minor work done to his face, but he still looked like Junior. Yet, most would believe Junior was dead. Or at least he was supposed to be.

"I can't believe it. You're alive," Kamora said in awe.

"Funny, I was thinking the same about you." Parker wanted more than anything to know what happened that day in San Diego and how she got to Miami. "What are you doing here?" he asked instead of voicing all the other questions floating through his mind.

"Okay, I'm still a little lost here," Angelo said, looking from one person to the other.

Hearing Angelo's confusion reminded Parker that Rock knew all along his connection to Kamora. He wondered what else the former drug lord knew.

After introducing Kamora to Angelo, Parker gave an abbreviated version of their past. He made it clear that he and Kamora had never been a couple. They'd just been two people who had befriended each other and realized they had a lot in common.

"We attended the same high school and had a few classes together. During a conversation, I realized she was indirectly connected to the Euclid Disciples, the Kingz' biggest competitor."

"Despite that, we formed a friendship of sorts," Kamora added. "Then one day, I showed up at school with bruised ribs, and Parker asked what happened. My brother had used me as a punching bag the night before, and I was ready to get away from him but didn't know how I could."

Parker was glad she hadn't mentioned that he had offered to take her brother out. She hadn't wanted him to get involved for fear Calvin, who was ten years older and just as ruthless as Wolf, would try to kill him. With her brother being her guardian, Kamora hadn't wanted to make him mad because she had no one else. Their parents had died, and she'd been left with her drug lord brother.

"When we planned to start a war, Knuckles and I... Sorry, I mean Parker and I had a meetup location planned for that night. The plan was to leave California together, and then eventually go our separate ways.

"When you didn't show," she said, looking at Parker, "I knew I had to come up with a backup plan. So I reached out to

205

a cousin in LA and paid him to give me a ride to Vegas. I figured I could get lost there for a while.

"He was the only one who knew where I was, and he thought I was visiting a friend. He had no clue I had run away from my brother. Nor did he know anything about me setting the Disciples up for war.

"When Calvin put the word out that I was missing, my cousin told him where I was."

Parker already knew this story was going to get worse before it got better. When Kamora stopped speaking and shook her head, his gut clenched.

If only he could've helped get her out of San Diego as planned. What she must have gone through...

He didn't want to think about it. When searching for her, he had learned that her brother was dead. He hadn't known when or how, but..."

"This is where I came in at."

Parker's attention jerked to Gavin, who had been quiet up to this point. Actually, neither he nor Rock had said anything for the last few minutes.

"Rock and I were in Vegas on business. Let's just say we found Kamora in an alley before that piece-of-shit brother of hers could do even more damage to her."

Kamora snorted. "He's being modest. They saved my life."

As she recounted how Calvin and his friends beat on her, Parker was taken back to that night with Wolf in the warehouse. He wouldn't wish that type of bodily punishment on anyone. Especially not a woman; or in her case, a young lady.

A stab of guilt pierced Parker in the gut. He had failed her. She had only been sixteen and so desperate to be free of her brother. She had gone along with his war idea probably without considering all the ramifications.

"I'm just glad he'll never be able to hurt anyone else," Kamora said. "Gavin took care of that."

Parker glanced at Gavin who seemed to only have eyes for Kamora. Interesting. There was at least a ten-year age difference between the two, but it was clear there was more than just friendly interest in Gavin's eyes.

Parker was getting ready to ask her more questions—like what role did she play in Rock's organization—but Rock cleared his throat.

"Maybe you two can catch up later. For now, Kamora, what did you find out about Wolf's assets?" Rock asked.

"Right." Kamora carried the file folder as well as a laptop over to the table in the corner, and everyone followed. She spread the contents of the file across the table and logged into the computer. There were photos of homes, cars, offshore accounts information, stash houses, and a host of other documents.

Unease swept through Parker. How had she gotten all this information? Had it been legally attained? Instead of asking, he listened as she gave details about where Wolf's personal homes were located. Anger rolled through Parker when he realized two homes were in his mother's name. One in Puerto Vallarta and another in Cancun.

As Kamora continued filling them in on everything, he faced the fact that he had clearly underestimated his father. Parker had managed to dig up some of this information over the last few months, but there'd been so much he hadn't found.

Concern crept in. Would they be able to take Wolf and the Kingz down without ending up in jail?

Or worse...ending up dead?

As if reading his mind, Angelo said, "Remember, we agreed to do this legally. We all have contacts we can reach out to, but we must ensure they operate aboveboard." He looked pointedly at Rock.

"Man, how many times are you going to remind us?" Rock said, irritation in his tone.

"As many times as it takes," Angelo responded without missing a beat.

For the next couple of hours, they scoured over the information, and they all compared notes.

"We have an undercover ATF contact," Kamora said, referring to the Alcohol, Tobacco, and Firearms agency. "Rock has heard of a possible gun deal that Wolf is involved in, but instead of him...interfering," she glanced between Rock and Angelo, "we'll reach out to our ATF contact and see if he'd be able to somehow broker that deal. Then, if all goes well, they can arrest Wolf."

"Okay, but before we do that, I'll need to reach out to the gun trafficker Wolf is expecting to meet with. The guy who owes me a favor," Rock said, his gaze darting to Angelo as if expecting him to say something.

When he didn't, Rock continued. "I'll talk him into stalling the meetup before eventually canceling it. That'll give the ATF guy a chance for him and his people to set up a fake deal with Wolf, and then they can arrest him."

"Good idea, but we need ATF to wait until everything else is in place before they take Wolf in," Parker added. "Otherwise, Elder, Wolf's second-in-command, will pick up where Wolf left off. And I want Elder and the Kingz shut down right along with Wolf."

The more they talked, the more Parker realized how hard it was going to be to hit Wolf from all sides at the same time. But together, he believed they could do it.

Parker had already been in touch with Luis, the only one in

Wolf's crew who he trusted. Luis was ready to cut ties with the Kingz, and normally, the only way to do that was by death.

Parker was offering him another way out. Along with the help of Angelo and his DEA contact, Luis would help the agency and Parker get as much insight into the drug side of the Kingz business. With that knowledge, they would know how to attack and destroy it.

Then Parker and Rock would help Luis and his family disappear.

Hours later, after narrowing down a plan of action and who would handle what, it became even more paramount that they strike every aspect of Wolf and the Kingz's operations at once.

Hopefully, the Kingz wouldn't catch on until it was too late.

This had to work.

His future with Chelsey and his plans of running Rock's security depended on it.

Chapter Twenty-Five

Chelsey pulled into one of the parking spaces at Brook Run Park and glanced around the area for her friend. She and India were planning to go for a run on one of the trails and had decided to meet up near the basketball courts.

Chelsey couldn't wait for them to catch up on all that had happened over the last couple of weeks. They'd both been out of town at the same time, but while Chelsey and Parker returned to Atlanta a week ago, India had just returned from Spain yesterday morning. She'd had a business trip to Madrid, and Chelsey was looking forward to hearing all the details.

They had a lot to discuss, including Chelsey's big news—her engagement.

Her gaze immediately went to her left hand, and she smiled. Morning, noon, and night, she couldn't stop looking at the ring. Parker asking her to marry him still felt like a dream. A dream that had become a reality.

To say their family and friends had been surprised by the

news would be an understatement. Egypt had wanted to throw an engagement party on the spot. Stunned by her engagement, Chelsey's sisters were asking if she had lost her mind. They didn't know that she and Parker had dated for months and because of that, they thought the proposal was too soon.

Chelsey didn't bother explaining that she had fallen in love with Parker within weeks of them going on their first date. Their bond and sexual chemistry had been almost immediate, but they'd both still had wanted to keep their union quiet at the time.

That seemed like so long ago, and now they were tossing around wedding dates and ideas. They hadn't nailed down any solid plans, although Chelsey would be okay with going to the courthouse. All she wanted was to spend her life with Parker. In her mind and heart, a wedding was secondary. However, when she suggested the courthouse idea to him, he'd nixed it.

She smiled at the memory. Chelsey was pretty sure she had fallen more in love with him that day. Parker had said he couldn't do that to her father; strip him of the opportunity to walk his baby girl down the aisle.

Sure, he'd love to walk her down the aisle, but her dad wasn't like that. As long as she was happy, he'd go along with any decision she made. Unlike her siblings, her father had been thrilled by the news of their engagement and gave his blessings wholeheartedly. That probably had a lot to do with knowing Parker was a part of Atlanta's Finest. Her dad thought the group could walk on water and were the finest people on this side of heaven.

When her cell phone rang, interrupting her musings, Chelsey assumed it was India calling. But when she pulled her phone out of the pocket of her running shorts, she saw that it wasn't.

"Gwen," Chelsey said by way of greeting when she answered the call. "How are you?"

She and her former parolee had been keeping in touch. Gwen was doing great and moving along in getting her life on track. With each call, she gushed about her daughters and filled Chelsey in on how well work and her support group was going.

"I'm wonderful," Gwen said, a smile in her voice.

"What have you been up to?" Chelsey asked.

Small talk flowed between them, and warmth spread through Chelsey as she heard the excitement in Gwen's voice. The woman had every reason to give up on life, but she hadn't. She was excelling, and Chelsey couldn't be more excited for her.

"Okay, let me stop going on and on about myself," Gwen said on a laugh. "That's not why I called you. When I was leaving the meeting with my parole officer this morning, I walked by the receptionist desk on my way out. I overheard a conversation with a guy who was asking about you."

"Really? Who was he?"

"He told the receptionist he was a good friend of yours but had lost contact. She told him you no longer worked out of that office, but I don't think she gave him your contact information."

"Good. Can you describe the guy?"

Chelsey had no clue on who would've been looking for her. Anyone who was important to her would call her directly. Or they'd already know she worked at Supreme now.

"I only glanced at him. He was tall, good-looking with medium-brown skin."

Gwen rattled off more details of what she remembered, and the person she described could've been Terrance. Not many people knew where she used to work, but he did. Only because she'd had him pick her up from there once.

"The only reason I'm calling to let you know is because he sounded like he was desperate to talk to you."

"I think I know who it might've been. Thanks for letting me know." Chelsey wasn't sure what she was going to do with the information, though. Probably nothing since she was done with Terrance.

After she finished talking to Gwen, Chelsey spotted India and climbed out of her vehicle. She headed to where her friend stood on the edge of the basketball court.

"Welcome back," Chelsey squealed. "How was Madrid?"

"Don't even try that small-talk mess. I have barely been gone two weeks, and I return to find you engaged and maybe moving to Miami!" India screeched and flung her arms around Chelsey's shoulders for a hug.

Chelsey laughed and ignored the attention they were getting from a few people strolling through the park.

"I know. I'm still pinching myself. I can't believe it either." Chelsey held her hand up and wiggled her fingers to bring attention to her ring.

India grabbed her hand. "Damn, girl, I'mma need my sunglasses, because you have some serious bling going on here. Chelsey, it's beautiful! I'm so happy for you and Parker, and I hope you know that I'm taking full credit for you guys getting back together."

Chelsey grinned. "Why am I not surprised?"

"Because it's true, and my man has good taste. That ring is stunning," she said as they started walking toward the trail that they'd run on.

"*Your* man?" Chelsey said on a laugh. "Don't you mean *my* man?"

"I said what I said. Remember, I was the one who was rooting for Parker even when he broke my best friend's heart."

Chelsey nodded. "True. You never gave up on him."

"Nope, I didn't. He's the only man you've ever dated who I would've broken the girl code for."

They both laughed and started their run in a slow jog before picking up speed.

For the next hour, they chatted nonstop about Madrid, India's clients, Miami, and Parker's new job offer. Chelsey hadn't told her friend about Parker's past and the revenge he was planning. She didn't even go into details about Rock's past, basically glazing over everything regarding the trip to Miami. Still, they had plenty to discuss during their run.

Once they made it back to their starting point, they were both winded.

"Whew, that was a good run," India said, and they slowed to a walk. "I needed this."

"I know, right? Me too. I have to work tonight, so I'm glad we were able to meet up in the middle of the day."

They chatted about their work plans for the rest of the day, and Chelsey was even more thankful they'd been able to hook up. Seemed they both were busy these days, and anytime they could get together was precious.

"Are you walking home or do you want me to..." Chelsey's words trailed off when she saw the person leaning against her car.

"What is it?" India said, following Chelsey's line of sight. "Who is that?"

"Terrance." They were at least fifty yards from him, and he hadn't seen them yet. Chelsey pulled India behind a tree and near some bushes. Where they were standing, she could still see him, but he couldn't see them.

"Terrance the Loser? *That Terrance?*" India asked, glancing at him again. "What is he, like, stalking you or something? How'd he know you were here?"

"Good question, but it's probably because I don't change up my routine enough," Chelsey mumbled.

She used to have Fridays off, and instead of running in the mornings, she'd run in the middle of the day depending on the weather. All he'd had to do was drive by, and he'd easily see her car since she always parked in the same lot.

"I was going to offer to drop you off at home," Chelsey said, "but I think it would be better if you weren't seen with me. I don't trust this guy. I don't want him to know who my friends are or anything else about me. So to be on the safe side, you go and head home. I'm going to talk to him."

"Not by yourself," India said. "If you're concerned about my safety, then you should be concerned about yours, too. Either we go together, or you call the cops to get rid of him."

Chelsey pinched the bridge of her nose. "India, I can handle him. He's not a criminal. He's just a low-down-dirty-liar, and the less he knows about who I hang out with, the better. Now go. If I don't text you in ten minutes to let you know all is well, then call the cops."

"Or maybe I should call Parker. I doubt if he'll want you meeting with this guy alone."

Chelsey sighed. "Please don't and besides, he's on an assignment. I promise you nothing is going to happen with Terrance. Just go. I'll text you soon."

After a slight hesitation, India relented. "Fine, I'll go, but I'm not going far. I'll be out of sight, but in shouting distance. So go before I change my mind and call Parker anyway. You've got ten minutes. Starting now."

Chelsey growled under her breath. India was one of the most stubborn people she knew. It would be a waste of time arguing with her.

Chelsey jogged in place while glaring at her friend. "You get on my nerves."

India flashed her a saucy smile. "Yeah, I love you too, Mrs. Wilcox. Now, go handle the loser, 'cause I got things to do. *Chop. Chop.*"

Chelsey sputtered a laugh, then took off at a jog.

Mrs. Wilcox. It had a nice ring to it.

As she neared the parking lot, Terrance spotted her and straightened.

She had only seen him for their dates, and during those times he was nicely dressed. Today, though, he looked like any other guy hanging out near the basketball courts wearing a T-shirt and basketball shorts.

She never would've pegged him for the tattooed type, though. He had a sleeve tattoo on both arms, which was something she hadn't been privy to when they'd gone out. Each of those times, he'd been fairly buttoned up, looking like the professional she thought he was.

Barely winded, she stopped a couple of feet from him. "What are you doing here?"

"I came here to play a pickup game of basketball. When I saw your car, I figured you were running one of the trails. So I waited for you. I've missed our talks, and I was hoping we could hook up. Why haven't you returned my phone calls?"

Seriously?

There was definitely something wrong with this man if he thought she'd ever want to be anywhere near him. Surely, he hadn't expected to ever hear from her after the stunt he'd pulled.

Then again, considering how expectantly he was watching her, maybe he had.

She planted her hands on her hips. "Why should I have called you back, Terrance?"

He gritted his teeth. "Because it's common courtesy to return people's calls."

Chelsey's mouth dropped open, but she quickly closed it. Apparently, he was an idiot.

"It's also common courtesy not to lie to someone about who you are, but that didn't stop you, now did it?" *Bastard*, she wanted to say but kept the term of endearment to herself.

"Come on, Chelsey. I made a mistake. I should've been honest, but since me and my ex weren't together any longer, I figured I didn't need to mention her."

There was no way she'd ever believe him over Parker. If Parker said Terrance was still with the woman, she believed him, but this was a non-issue. She was engaged to the man she loved, and Terrance was just one of many mistakes of her past.

"Get away from my car, Terrance, and lose my damn number."

He charged toward her, but she wasn't sure what he saw on her face, because he suddenly stopped less than a foot from her. She was ready for him. All she needed was an excuse to knock him the hell out.

Breathing hard as if he'd been the one to have just run four miles, he pointed a finger at her. "You ain't all that!" he snapped.

"No? Then why are you here whining about me not calling you?" she retorted.

He growled under his breath and shoved his hands into the front pockets of his basketball shorts. "I haven't forgotten that you sicced some dude on me."

"I don't know what you're talking about," she lied. "But I do know I didn't *sic* anyone on you. Maybe that's your guilty conscious messing with you since you tried to play me. Did you honestly think that I wouldn't eventually find out what type of loser you were?"

"You better hope I don't find out who that guy was who

217

pulled a gun on me," he said, ignoring her question. "Because when I do, it won't end well for him."

Chelsey chuckled, unable to help it. Parker was the last person this jerk wanted to fool with. "Actually, *you're* the one who'd better hope you don't run into him. I told you he was crazy, and I wasn't kidding. Now, get away from my car before I call the cops and tell them you've been stalking me."

Surprise registered in his eyes before they returned to the stoney glare he'd been giving her. "You wouldn't."

She pulled her phone from the side pocket of her running shorts. "Try me."

Chelsey didn't bother asking if he'd gone to her old job. At this point it didn't matter. She just wanted to be done with him. Hopefully, the threat of calling the police would make him think twice before calling her again or showing up out of the blue.

Instead of him saying anything else, Terrance stormed away. Considering he'd claimed to be there to play basketball, he instead headed to his car.

Good. She hadn't been kidding about calling the cops, though she hadn't wanted to.

Climbing into her vehicle, Chelsey glanced over at the tree where she and India had been hiding and spotted her. Then she texted her.

Chelsey: *Want a ride home?*

India: *Thanks, but I'll walk. Need to work off the chocolate cake I ate last night. Talk later. I'mma want details.*

"Of course you do," Chelsey mumbled and laughed as she started the car.

When she backed out of the parking space, she noticed

Terrance was still sitting in his car. When he saw her vehicle, he scowled and pointed a finger at her.

Chelsey shook her head.

Dude had issues.

Well, as long as he left her alone, they wouldn't have a problem.

Let him come near her again, and he was going to regret the day he ever met her.

Chapter Twenty-Six

Chelsey needed to hurry. She had overslept, thanks to fooling around with Parker late into the night. No complaints, though. Considering his long work hours lately, and his work on the *Destroy Wolf* project, they were lucky to get any time together.

It had been weeks since his meeting with Rock, and he and everyone else were getting closer to having everything in place. She and Parker were also growing closer. They hadn't moved in together, but they spent every night together at one of their homes. Once Wolf was taken care of, their lives would settle down and they could start planning for their future.

As she stepped out of her shower, she grabbed her towel and started drying off while thinking about work. Egypt had her doing everything from admin work to providing security for some of their clients. Since it looked like she and Parker would be moving to Miami soon, she hadn't settled into just one job at Supreme. She loved every assignment they gave her, but hopefully, she'd feel the same by the end of the day.

Even though she wasn't officially a security specialist,

today she'd be working the front desk—the one area of the company most of Atlanta's Finest hated to work, but it was required. There had to be armed security on duty 24/7, no exceptions. Most of the guys claimed it was boring and made for a long day, but Chelsey was looking forward to a little downtime.

After drying off, she tossed the towel into the hamper before leaving the bathroom in search of underwear. She rummaged through the top drawer of her dresser and pulled out a purple lace panty set, then hurried into them.

Now for the rest of my clothes.

She went to the closet to finish dressing but paused at the foot of the bed to stare at Parker's sleeping form. He was laying on his stomach with his face buried in the pillow, and his strong, muscular back, as well as his firm bare ass was on full display. The firm ass that she wanted to palm and squeeze.

Pervert, she thought, then grinned.

Who could blame her? The man's whole body was a work of art, and she wasn't just referring to his tattoos. At the moment, she didn't care that it was almost eight and she needed to be at Supreme by nine. No. All she could think about was how much she wanted to climb back into bed and have her way with her man.

No time, she reminded herself. She still needed to...

"Chels," Parker murmured and turned onto his back.

Her favorite part of his body was on full display though he wasn't at the ready like usual, but that was all right. They didn't have time for a quickie, even though it wouldn't take long to get him ready.

"Hey, I thought you were asleep," she said when she moved closer but frowned when realizing his eyes were still closed. Maybe he'd been talking in his...

"Chelsey!" he screamed, startling her, and she froze.

Panic clawed through her body when he kept screaming her name as he thrashed back and forth in the bed.

Whoa!

"Parker, baby wake up." she said again as she tried to shake him awake. Normally, he was a light sleeper, but whatever he was dreaming had him deep in...

"Chelsey!" he cried out, and her heart leaped into her throat when he bolted upright in bed.

He barely missed from slamming his head into hers and was looking around frantically. Eventually he zoned in on her, and his whiskey-colored eyes met hers. They were red-rimmed, and she didn't miss the fear she saw in them.

"Chels. Oh, thank God." His frantic gaze traveled over her before he pulled her roughly into his arms, holding her tight enough to crack her ribs.

"Parker, you're scaring me. Are you okay?"

She wrapped her arms around him and his body trembled against hers. His breathing was ragged, and whatever he'd been dreaming about had clearly freaked him out.

"It was just a dream," she said, rubbing his back, hoping to help settle him. "Do you want to talk about it?" That had been more than a dream. It had been more like a nightmare.

When he didn't respond, just continued holding her close, she kept quiet. Minutes ticked by before his breathing eventually began to slow, and he loosened his hold.

He cupped her face between his large hands and kissed her lips. "Come back to bed," he said, and kissed her again, while ignoring her question about the dream.

"I'd love to, but I need to get to work."

She glanced at the bedside table, noting the time. It was ten after eight. Thankfully she only lived twelve minutes from Supreme, which was a miracle within itself. It was almost impossible to get anywhere around Atlanta in that short amount of time, but she had lucked out by living so close.

"Talk to me," she whispered, caressing his stubbled cheek with the pad of her thumb. "Tell me about the dream."

Parker dropped back down on the pillow and reached for her hand as if afraid she'd move away from him.

"It was nothing. Just a reoccurring dream of when my mother died."

He positioned his other arm over his eyes, which wasn't unusual since it was often how he fell asleep. She thought about what he'd said; that the dream had been about his mother, but he'd been screaming her name.

Knowing it was a bad idea she readjusted her position on the bed and pulled the sheet up over his lower body. Then she stretched out next to him and rested a hand on his flat abs.

"Parker, you screamed my name several times in your sleep."

He lifted his arm from his eyes and sat up slightly to look at her. "I said your name?"

"Yeah, multiple times." She propped up on her elbow. "Tell me about the dream. Something terrified you and it had to do with me."

He shook his head. It took Parker so long to respond, she thought he wouldn't tell her, but then he said, "Instead of me holding my mother in my arms while she was bleeding and me begging her to wake up...it's you in my arms."

Yikes. No wonder he'd been shaken up. "Have you had the dream before?" she asked.

"Yeah, the first time was the night I pulled the gun on Terrance at your place. The dream freaked me out, but I haven't had it since. Not until now."

"What do you think it—"

"Chels, can we not do this? I don't want to talk anymore

about the dream or what it means. I'd rather make love to my sexy fiancée."

Before she could respond, he had her flat on her back. His hard body covered hers and was raring to go if his thick erection pressing against her was any indication. How this man's body could go from zero to sixty in a heartbeat was mind-blowing, but damn if he didn't feel good on top of her.

"I hate it when you distract me like this," she moaned as he sprinkled kisses along her neck.

"How about we table the dream, and instead have a quickie before you have to leave?" He unsnapped the front of her bra and moved the lacy material aside. "Easy access. My favorite."

When he sucked one of her nipples into his mouth, her thoughts scattered. That always happened when his mouth or hands made contact with her breasts. She couldn't think straight. All she could do was feel, and her body craved his touch and sweet kisses.

Okay. Maybe there was time for a quickie.

Parker raised up on his knees and helped her discard the bra. Then he reached for the waistband of her panties. He started sliding the lacy material down her legs, and when he got them to her ankles, Chelsey kicked them the rest of the way off.

"Damn, baby," he said, his heated gaze taking in her nakedness as he lifted her left leg and placed a kiss near her ankle.

As he worked his way up her leg, peppering kisses along the way, Chelsey moaned. With each brush of his lips, her skin tingled and her nerves went on high alert.

God, this man and his wicked mouth sent warmth spreading through her body. When he reached the middle of her thigh and stopped, Chelsey's gaze shot to his.

"What? Why'd you stop."

He lowered her leg. "On your knees," he said gruffly.

His extraordinary eyes held an intensity that promised

pleasure, and a slow smile spread across Chelsey's mouth. She did as she was told and got on all fours. As her anticipation of what was coming next grew, her heart pounded a little faster.

Parker sidled up behind her, and one of his hands cupped her breast, while the other gripped the headboard. And as he squeezed and fondled her, he kissed along her spine. Each touch of his lips on her heated skin sent her heart rate into overdrive, and the throbbing pulse between her thighs intensified as her arousal steadily grew.

Yeah, this was definitely going to be quick, because she was so turned on, it wasn't going to take much for her to come.

Parker's arm snaked around her, and he reached between her thighs, his large hand settling over her sex. When his finger slipped into her, she sucked in a breath.

"Good, you're wet for me," he said, stroking her as he used his legs to nudge her thighs further apart.

Seconds later, the head of his dick bumping against her sex, had Chelsey squeezing the pillow that her hands were propped on. Parker thrust into her from behind and filled her completely.

Oh yes...

After getting engaged, they'd decided that since she was on birth control and they were both clean, that they'd forego condoms. Chelsey was glad they had. Pleasure soared through her body as his thick length glided in and out of her. Each stroke was like that of a masterful violinist, using his bow to stroke smoothly across violin strings.

She felt every inch of Parker's dick as he filled her to the hilt, and he felt incredible.

And when he suddenly pulled out, then just as quickly drove into her again, Chelsey gasped. Her hand shot out to grip the headboard as he put more power behind each thrust. Her breasts jiggled with the moves and her inner walls squeezed around his thick erection.

"Chels..." He groaned her name while picking up speed. "Damn, baby."

This was one of her favorite positions, him behind her, driving into her hard and fast like he couldn't get enough of her. With each thrust, the erratic beat of her heart kicked up and pressure, like an $EF4$ tornado, built inside of her.

"P—Pa—Parker," she panted, her breaths coming in short spurts. "I'm close. I'm—"

"I know. I know," he rasped out, then cursed as his moves grew jerkier. "Come...come with me, Chels!"

As if his words held the power to control her body, an orgasm ripped through Chelsey so violently, she saw stars behind her eyelids as she cried out his name. Parker came just as hard, his body vibrating before he collapsed against her, sending them both crumbling onto the mattress.

Chelsey couldn't help but laugh while gasping for air. "Whew!" she breathed, her body like a limp rag tangled with his.

When they eventually caught their breaths, Parker wrapped her into his arms, holding her tighter than necessary. It wasn't until Chelsey felt him tremble that she tried to pull away, but he didn't loosen his hold.

"If anything ever happened to you," he said into her hair, emotion clogging his voice, "I don't know what I'd do. You're mine...you're my heart and I—"

"Ahh, baby. Stop worrying. It was a dream," Chelsey insisted, and eventually eased out of his hold so that she could look him in the eyes. "It was just a very bad dream. Nothing's going to happen to me. I promise."

Chapter Twenty-Seven

Later, at Supreme, Chelsey might've been monitoring the front desk, but her mind was still on Parker. They had a lot going on these days and it all played on loop through her brain, forcing her to think about everything but work.

This morning had been interesting, to say the least. The sex was amazing as usual, but there were moments since leaving home that Parker's nightmare overshadowed those memories. Did it mean anything that the dream had recurred? Maybe all the work he'd been doing on the *Destroy Wolf* project was starting to get to him.

The last few weeks, Parker had been busy at Supreme while also working with Rock, Angelo, and Kamora to make sure everything was on schedule in taking down Wolf. His days started early, and they sometimes ran late into the night. Was it all stressing him out? Or had something happened to trigger the dream?

Chelsey wasn't sure, but she was worried. Mainly because of how the nightmare was making him behave. Parker was normally the most laid-back, fearless person she knew, but he told her he was afraid that something would happen to her. As if the dream would come true.

Before leaving home, she tried telling him that it was just his subconscious messing with him, but he didn't believe her. He'd even had the nerve to tell her that he wanted to put security on her.

That still pissed her off, and she shot that idea down. How crazy would it look for her—a person providing others with protection—to have a security detail on her?

Nope. She could take care of herself, and that's what she told him. But what started as a simple conversation had turned into a major disagreement.

"What's on your mind?" Kenton asked, interrupting her thoughts. He was sitting next to her at the front desk. "You've been spacing out for the last ten minutes."

"I'm still mad at you," she said, though she was over his freak-out weeks ago regarding her and Parker's relationship.

Kenton shrugged. "It's not the first time, and I'm sure it won't be the last. It comes with the territory as a big brother. So what did Parker do to piss you off?"

She narrowed her eyes at him. "What are you talking about? He hasn't done anything."

"Oh, I figured your brooding had something to do with him."

Chelsey debated on whether to tell him about Parker's dream. Kenton could be a pain, but he was a good listener. Still, she didn't like the idea of discussing her and Parker's personal business.

Then again, her brother had experienced his share of nightmares. They'd started after one of his FBI assignments ended with the death of his confidential informant, as well as his partner. Kenton had almost died that day, too, and it took years of therapy for him to get his life back on track. He'd probably understand Parker's frame of mind better than anyone. Maybe...

Her cell phone, that was sitting on the long receptionist desk vibrated, and she glanced at the screen. It was a text message.

Parker: I'm sorry, baby. I worry about you, but I know you can take care of yourself.

Chelsey placed her hand on her chest. God, she loved this man. Even though he was afraid for her life, he was trusting that she knew what was best for herself.

She sent back a quick text.

Chelsey: I forgive you, and I love you.

Parker: I love you more. TTYL

She grinned at the five heart-eyes emojis he added on the end of the message. Her big strong, manly-man sending emojis was too cute. Especially because he only sent them because she loved stuff like that.

"I guess you two made up," Kenton said dryly as he rocked in his chair next to her.

Chelsey laughed. "Whatever." She shoved her phone into her pants pocket.

"But seriously, despite how I acted, I'm happy for you and Parker. He's one of the good ones, and I know he'll treat you right."

Chelsey's heart melted at her brother's kind words, and she hugged him. "Thanks, bro. That means a lot coming from you."

In their family she and Kenton were the closest in age. Growing up, he'd been her best friend, her confidant, and her protector. So his opinion meant everything to her.

"That doesn't mean that I won't kick his ass if he hurts you."

Chelsey laughed and playfully punched him in the arm. "See, you had to go and mess up a beautiful moment with threats. But just so you know, if you lay a hand on him again, you'll have to deal with me."

"*Ohhh*, I'm so scared." He mock-shivered. "You always did think you were all that and could beat up somebody."

A loud beeping sounded interrupted their banter.

"Is that a camera sensor?"

"Yep." Kenton rolled his chair forward to look at the large monitor.

It showed six different areas of the exterior of the building. A man and a woman stood outside at the main entrance, appearing to be arguing. When Kenton pressed a couple of keys on the keyboard, he activated the camera's audio.

"Are you sure about this?" the woman asked. "What if they think I don't need security?"

"Well, you do, and we need to convince them to take your case. So come on," the man snapped.

"We like to get a good look at people before we let them in," Kenton said. "We normally keep the volume off during the day because it picks up traffic and people walking by."

Supreme was located on a side street, and the building and parking lot took up the block. The only other structure was the huge warehouse across the street that was being renovated.

The guy outside reached for the handle and tried to push the door open, only to realize it was locked. "What the hell? They're supposed to be open."

"We never unlock the door until they push the buzzer. I'm sure they'll notice it in a minute," Kenton said. "That gives us a chance to take still shots of people who look suspicious."

Chelsey nodded. "That's not a bad idea."

"Just an extra safety precaution. We might provide personal security, but the well-being of our people come first.

Which is why Egypt and Hamilton are so thorough with vetting potential clients. We might agree to take on those who come to us for help, but not without knowing what we're getting ourselves into."

Though it was mentioned in the training Chelsey had gone through, Kenton went on to tell her that there were times when a simple protection assignment could turn into so much more.

Through offering security to clients, Supreme had assisted law enforcement numerous times with catching criminals; everything from stalkers to drug dealers and a host of other miscreants. Supreme provided way more than just basic security.

"I'd say that guy looks suspicious wearing long sleeves, jeans, and combat boots when it's ninety degrees outside," Chelsey said.

Tattoos traveled up the side of the man's neck but were mostly covered by his collar, and Chelsey didn't miss the tats on the knuckles of his fingers. One was a black dot which usually meant he served time in prison, but there were other tats that she didn't recognize.

The high-definition quality of Supreme's cameras was impressive, so much so that she could almost count the number of freckles on the woman's fair skin. As the lady paced in front of the building, Chelsey took in her short sundress and sandals, which were more fitting for the hot weather than the guy's attire.

"She looks anxious," Chelsey said, but that could easily be caused by whatever situation she was in. "If we're suspicious of them, do we still let them in?"

"Yep, because one or both could be in trouble and really need our services. I already took a couple of pictures of them, and emailed them to Egypt."

"And this is why Hamilton insist that armed security

monitor the front desk," she muttered it more to herself, but Kenton confirmed it.

They both stood before he unlocked the door and let them in.

When the couple stepped in, Chelsey said, "Welcome to Supreme Security. Can we help you?"

"Yes. My sister needs protection," the guy said as they slowly approached the desk. They didn't look related, but there were plenty of siblings in the world who didn't look alike.

The man glanced around, seeming to take in every inch of the large open space. To the right was a waiting room of sorts that held sofas and upholstered chairs. A comfortable area that wasn't often used, except for by employees.

Previously, the main floor was an open space. Visitors used to be able to see down the long hallway behind the main desk. But recently, a wall and a locked door had been added to keep the reception area confined.

The main hallway, behind the wall, included several conference rooms, bathrooms, as well as the kitchen that was toward the back of the building. Though there had never been a problem with anyone trying to force their way into Supreme, the wall was an extra precaution.

"Your names?" Kenton asked.

"I'm James White and she's Debby."

"All right, Mr. and Miss White. I'm Kenton and this is Chelsey. Do you have an appointment?"

"No," James said. "Does she need an appointment to get protection?"

Kenton explained Supreme's process, including the fact that an appointment was preferred, but under emergency circumstances they accepted walk-ins.

Chelsey watched their two visitors carefully. James carried himself confidently. As for Debby, the way she wrung her hands together and shuffled from one foot to the other, her nerves were getting the best of her. Chelsey wasn't sure why she was this anxious or why she needed security, but her brother seemed more than capable of protecting her. By the looks of him, he could handle himself and wouldn't take shit from anyone.

Though she didn't like to judge, he looked a bit thuggish.

Maybe a gang member?

During her time as a cop, she'd encountered plenty of them, enough to recognize their edginess, their cockiness, their energy. She had also learned to identify gang tattoos, but because this guy's body was covered by his clothing, there weren't any visible signs of an affiliation.

Still, she wondered.

"Why are you staring at us like that?" the woman snapped as she narrowed her eyes at Chelsey.

"Like what?" Chelsey asked calmly.

"Like you don't believe I need protection!"

Though surprised by the woman's outburst, Chelsey remained calm. "What do you mean, I don't believe you? I have no idea what threat there is to you, because you haven't given details of why you're here."

"Debby," her brother said, a warning note in his tone.

His sister straightened. "I'm sorry. I'm—I'm on edge," she sputtered, her words tumbling over each other. "My ex threatened to kill me."

"I understand," Chelsey replied.

Deep down, she sensed these two were up to something. *But what?*

She grabbed the electronic tablet from the desk to gather information from them. "We don't take threats lightly. Have you gone to the police and reported him?"

"They're not going to do anything. That's why we came

here," James said. "I want someone watching her back whenever I can't."

Chelsey nodded. "Okay, Debby, I'll need some information from you. Then I'll set you up with an appointment to meet with an intake specialist."

While she talked with Debby, Kenton chatted with James.

"How'd you hear about Supreme?" Chelsey heard Kenton ask.

"My cousin, Sean, recommended you guys. He said y'all do good work, and he said to request Parker Wilcox."

Every cell inside of Chelsey went on high alert. Not because it wasn't uncommon for people to request a particular security specialist, but because of *who* they requested.

"We appreciate when other clients refer our services. When did your cousin use Supreme?" Kenton asked.

"Actually, he didn't use y'all. Someone he knows used the service. I don't know the guy's name."

"When you get a chance, check with Sean to get the name," Kenton said, then turned his attention to Debby. She looked even more nervous than she had when they first arrived. "We offer a discount to clients who refer us to their friends, and you'd also get a discount if we take on your case."

"*If?* What do you mean, if?" James snapped. "If someone is threatening her, I'd think you'd automatically offer her protection."

"Not automatically," Kenton said as he moved from around the desk, towering over both visitors. It was a power move since the guy was getting a bit testy. "Our intake person will get some details about your sister, about the threat, and then they'll decide if her case is one we can take on."

James shook his head. "Nah, nah. She can just talk to Parker Wilcox since he'd be the one protecting her."

"It doesn't work like that," Chelsey chimed in. "Based on

234

what comes of the interview with Debby, our intake person will determine what type of protection she needs and what security specialist to assign to her. That will be dependent on the threat, as well as who Supreme has available for the assignment."

James glanced at Debby, who was looking at him and nibbling on her lower lip. It was as if they were having some private conversation with their eyes. Neither said a word, which only made Chelsey more suspicious of their motives.

"If you guys want to set up an appointment, I can do that, but first I'll need to see your IDs," she said.

"You know what? I don't want to do this," Debby said, backing away. Her movements abrupt, she turned and rushed toward the door.

"Debby, wait!" James called out. When his sister left without stopping, he turned to Kenton. "Let me talk to her. She's just scared."

Yeah, she's scared of something...but what? Chelsey thought.

James backed his way to the door, while saying, "If we decide to move forward, we'll be in touch."

"No problem," Kenton said, and they watched the two leave.

Chelsey folded her arms across her chest. "Was that normal?" she asked, already knowing the answer.

"Nope, and I'm glad we have photos of them." Kenton moved back around the desk. "We'll check out the information you gathered from *Debby*, if that's even her name. If she doesn't check out, we'll run facial recognition on the two of them."

"Good." Chelsey tapped her fingers on the desk as thoughts and various scenarios ran rapid through her mind. "There was something about them... The way they were behaving had my bullshit meter going crazy. I also didn't like the way they dropped Parker's name."

"Yeah, I noticed that, too. We get referrals all the time, and occasionally people request a specific person. However, that's usually *after* a security member has been on their detail."

Chelsey nodded. "I want to know who they are and why they were really here."

More importantly, she needed to know what they wanted with Parker.

Chapter Twenty-Eight

Wolf gritted his teeth and squeezed his cell phone tightly in his hand as he paced the length of his office, struggling to keep himself from throwing the device across the room. What was wrong with this world? Couldn't anyone do anything right?

There'd been one issue after another today, and the people he had in place to handle such issues acted as if they couldn't remember how to take care of anything. Like they couldn't do their jobs—jobs that they'd overseen for years. Now all of a sudden, they'd been calling him for every damn thing, and he was sick of it.

First it was the computer system at his pizzeria that had malfunctioned first thing that morning. Thankfully, the manager eventually got it back up and running before the start of business. Hours after that, he'd been informed that some kids had broken into the office at one of his car washes. So far, his people couldn't tell what, if anything, had been taken. Then he'd gotten a call from the site manager of his largest liquor store. The building alarm kept going off even though the system was disarmed during business hours.

What. The. Actual. Hell.

Was there some stupid dark cloud hovering over him and his operations? That had to be it. That had to be why he was about ready to say *to hell with it all.*

He stopped in front of the large window that overlooked a courtyard with a water fountain flanked by flowers and palm trees and peered out. As usual, there wasn't a cloud in the sky. So his theory about a dark cloud hovering above him was definitely metaphorical.

"Hello? Wolf, are you still there?"

He had temporarily forgotten that he was talking to the manager of his cell phone store, the one in Chula Vista. He'd been on the phone with her for the last fifteen minutes, with her doing most of the talking.

That store was one of several front businesses Wolf owned to conceal some of his illegal activities. That one, along with his car washes and beauty salons, were set up perfectly for laundering money.

"Wolf?"

"Yes, Maxine," he said as he rubbed his temple, feeling a headache coming on.

"We're going to need a new computer. This is the second day this week that it just shut down on me. I reached out to Elder, but he isn't answering his phone."

"Yeah, he's in LA taking care of personal business," Wolf lied. Whenever either of them left town, they rarely gave anyone their location. Not even to people in their crew. It was safer that way, in case they had traitors in their midst.

"Oh, okay. Well, anyway, the other day he said you haven't approved new technology for our location."

Wolf listened as the talkative woman went on and on. Yes,

Elder had mentioned they needed to update the computer systems in several of their businesses, but Wolf kept putting it off. He didn't know a damn thing about the devices. If it was up to him, he'd run all their businesses with pen and paper, like they used to do back in the day. In his opinion, modern technology was highly overrated. Everything ran by some form of it and made their companies too vulnerable to outside sources.

"Call the tech guy you used a couple of months ago," he finally said. "Find out what it would cost to overhaul the whole system."

"Great! Thanks. I'll contact him today."

Wolf disconnected the call and sighed in relief. He had too much on his mind to be dealing with minor issues. He needed to get ready for the gun deal that was going down in three days. Mando, the dealer out of San Antonio who Wolf had been in communications with, had finally come through.

The man had postponed meetings twice in a matter of weeks, but Wolf's patience had paid off. Not only was the guy coming to Southern California to meet, he was also sending a small shipment of guns. Wolf would be able to look them over before deciding to buy.

So, the day hadn't been all bad. This could be the beginning of another good connection.

Mando was rumored to have the best variety of weapons at the most affordable prices. Whether that was true or not was yet to be seen, but he'd heard the man was in the process of moving his operations to Southern California. This could end up being a win-win situation for all involved.

Wolf had just sat at his desk when his cell phone rang again, and he groaned. Maybe he should turn the damn thing off. Instead, a quick glance at the screen showed it was Elder.

"What do you want?" Wolf snapped. "And if you're about to give me some bad news, save it. I've had enough for one day."

Elder chuckled. "So, I guess you're getting a taste of what I have to deal with when you're chilling out doing nothing in your penthouse. *Good.* Now you know how valuable I am."

Wolf heard rustling over the phoneline and then what sounded like wind blowing. "Where are you?"

"I'm climbing out of the car and getting ready to go into the house I rented here in Atlanta. We had to pick up some groceries. Looks like we'll be here a while longer."

He and two members of their crew had flown to Atlanta a couple of days ago. The plan was to meet Parker Wilcox and ask a few questions. Personal questions to determine if him and Wolf were related somehow.

"What did you find out?"

"Not much yet. My nephew, James, said the place is locked down tighter than Fort Knox. Getting to this guy Parker isn't going to be easy," Elder explained. "I just want to see him face to face. Get a read on him. But the plan we'd had in place fell apart."

Elder told him how James and some woman made a visit to Supreme, acting like one of them needed protection.

"Supposedly, there's a mandatory interview process potential clients have to go through before the firm will agree to take them on as clients."

Wolf frowned and shrugged as if Elder could see him. "Well, have them go through the damn interview. How hard can it be? They answer a few questions, pay the folks, and then get Parker as their bodyguard."

"It's harder than you'd think. They don't take on just *anyone* as clients, and once they asked for ID, Jame's friend got nervous."

Wolf sighed. They didn't have time for this nonsense. He didn't have any kids out there, and letting Elder talk him into going to Atlanta was probably a fool's errand. But his friend could be convincing when he wanted to be, and if Wolf was honest, his own curiosity was still getting the best of him.

"You know, if this guy really is Junior, and I'm not saying that he is," Wolf hurried to say, "But *if* he is, that means we have some traitors in our crew. When we left Junior in that warehouse bleeding out..."

Wolf shook his head. There was no way. He had killed Junior with his own hands. He saw him take his last breath. It wasn't possible that...

Wait.

"Who were the cleaners that night?" he asked, his mind spinning at the route his thoughts were going. When they beat someone to death, certain crew members were responsible for making the body disappear, and then cleaning the facility where the murder took place. By the time they were done, the body should be disposed of and the place spotless.

"Man, that was like a hundred years ago. I can't remember."

Yeah, it was a long time ago, and they'd been in the middle of a gang war. They also hadn't had that many cleaners.

"It might've been Shred and Luis, but—"

"I think you're right," Wolf said.

Unease simmered just below the surface as he thought about what this all could mean. Had he failed to kill Junior? And if he did, who helped keep him alive?

"Okay, stay in Atlanta and see what you can find out," Wolf conceded. "Get Thomas or whoever to go back to Supreme and hire—"

"I have a better idea. Something I should've done in the first place. Something that will be easier to get us the answers we want. Did Junior have any identifying marks on his body? Like scars or birthmarks?"

Wolf thought back. "He had a two-inch scar on the right side of his neck shortly before he died." Some kid had cut him with a broken beer bottle, but Wolf didn't know if it had left a permanent scar. "He also had a birthmark, a half-moon, on his side. Wait, it was more on his upper hip. I think the left one."

He shook his head and pinched the bridge of his nose. This was ridiculous. There was no way Junior was alive. His son was dead.

"Elder, on second thought, we don't have time for this shit. You and the others get back here so we can—"

"We're already here. We might as well see what we can find out. Besides, I have a plan, and I know it's going to work."

Wolf started to ask for details, but he trusted Elder. He and his friend were tighter than most brothers and had known each other since they were kids. Elder knew how he thought. Hell, they were mentally wired the same.

Even though Wolf knew there was no way that man in Atlanta could be Junior, he was still curious. Whatever Elder had planned would get the answers they wanted.

Then they could get back to business.

Chapter Twenty-Nine

It's time to make the call.

A nervous energy surrounded Parker as he entered his second bedroom that doubled as an office. He'd been counting down the days of when he'd finally be able to make the call to Luis and tell him that it was time to disappear.

Though they hadn't talked much over the years, they'd communicated more these last several weeks than they had since they were kids. Parker wanted his friend to escape the wrath that was about to swallow up Wolf and the Kingz. So, he'd put him on notice that he should get ready to run.

This was it.

Parker was finally going to get the closure he'd been wanting for years.

He unlocked his desk and pulled out a brand-new burner phone from the stash in the bottom desk drawer. He never used his personal phone when reaching out to Luis. It wasn't that he didn't trust his friend. It was mainly for Luis's protection. The less contact he had with Parker, the better for him and his family if Wolf found out.

Sitting back in his seat, Parker first sent Luis a coded message of letters and numbers that only they'd understand. Once Luis responded back with an agreed-upon code, then Parker would know it was him and that it was a good time to call.

Seconds ticked by with no response, and just when he started rocking back and forth in his chair, a text came through.

Luis: Clear.

Good.

Parker wanted to talk to him before Chelsey walked in. She was cleaning up the kitchen, but they both had a conference call with Rock in a few minutes. Reaching out to Luis needed to be done now.

He dialed his friend, and Luis picked up on the first ring.

"What's up, man?" his friend said.

Hearing Luis's slightly accented voice, a mixture of his Mexican and Black heritage, made Parker smile and brought back memories of the past. The good and bad times, but mostly good. They'd had some fun growing up despite their circumstances.

"It's time to make a move," Parker said. "Disappear within the next twenty-four hours or if possible, sooner."

"Will do. We're ready," Luis confirmed.

Parker had sent enough cash for him and his family to live on for six months. Even longer if they left the US and found a cheaper country to live in. There were five people planning to travel with him, and Rock had managed to get them all passports under a new identity.

How? That's what Parker had wanted to know, especially considering how quickly he'd been able to get it done.

The less you know on the subject, the better, was all that Rock had said.

Of course, that didn't sit well with Parker, but he kept his mouth shut. He wanted to do everything he could to help Luis start a new life. It was the least he could do for the guy who'd helped save his.

"Wolf's been a little irritable," Luis said, "because of computers going haywire, a break-in at one of the businesses, and a few other issues."

With Luis's help, Parker and Rock's tech guy had been able to hack into all of Wolf's computer systems. It helped that the tech people Parker's father used could be bought off easily.

Thanks to Luis, they'd also gotten addresses to all the Kingz stash houses, including the ones in LA. The DEA had initially been concerned that they didn't have enough people who could move in on all the buildings at the same time, but Parker would find out this evening if they worked it out.

More importantly, Wolf wouldn't know what was happening until it was too late.

"Normally, Elder or Slick handled the day-to-day operations, but Elder is out of town," Luis said. "Supposedly he's in LA, but you know what that means."

It meant that Elder could be anywhere in the world. Wolf and his right-hand man had always been secretive about their travel locations. Some things never changed.

Parker wasn't concerned, but he'd see if Rock's tech guy could find out Elder's location. Normally, he'd reach out to Wiz, but Parker was trying not to use much of Supreme's resources in this case, even if Mason had okayed it.

As for Elder, Parker wanted to make sure that when they took Wolf down, they took him down, too. Elder didn't have control of every aspect of the Kingz organization, but he had enough authority to do damage.

The authorities wanted them behind bars, but if it was up to Parker, they'd both die a painful death.

"Luis, thanks for everything you've done to help. Be safe.

Remember, keep your family close, and leave all old electronics behind. Only use the new phones and laptops I sent you. At least until Wolf and the Kingz have been disbanded. It's safer that way."

They talked a few minutes longer before disconnecting. Though the burner couldn't be traced, Parker wasn't taking any chances. He removed the SIM card and cut it up with a pair of pruning shears, then tossed the phone.

He just hoped his friend didn't do something stupid like double-cross him. Of course, Parker and Rock had a fail-safe in place in case Luis or his family betrayed them. There were trackers installed in all the new devices Parker had sent him.

So, if Luis lost his mind, and decided to deceive him in any way, Parker would hunt his ass down and take out him and his family. Unfortunately, that attitude was something he had inherited from his father—that *vengeance is mine* mentality when it came to people who betrayed him.

Hopefully, Luis wouldn't let him down, but if he did...all hell was going to break loose.

* * *

"What are you going to do about James and Debby, the people who came to Supreme yesterday?" Chelsey asked as she sauntered into the room looking like a delicious snack.

Her fitted T-shirt hugged her upper body and put her full breasts and perky nipples on display. The ripped, skintight jeans? Hell, they wrapped around her curvy hips, molded over her shapely thighs, and made him want to strip her out of them and bury himself balls deep inside of her.

A wicked smile kicked up the left corner of her luscious mouth, and Parker groaned when her tongue made an appearance. She moistened her tempting lips, and his dick twitched behind his zipper.

"We only have five minutes before the conference call. So whatever you're thinking—forget it."

Parker laughed and discreetly adjusted himself while trying to get his body under control. She was right. They only had a few minutes before they were scheduled to meet with Rock and Kamora via a Zoom call.

When Chelsey rounded the desk, Parker pushed his office chair back and reached for her, guiding her onto his lap.

"You think you know me, huh?" he said, inhaling her sweet scent.

She looped her arm around his neck and leaned against his chest. That put her lips inches from his.

"I do, and I love what I know about you," she said and nibbled on his top lip, then his lower one before kissing him.

What started as a sweet kiss of their tongues teasing one another, quickly turned into a fiery connection. Especially when Chelsey slipped her hand between their bodies and cupped his dick.

A moan slipped from him as he ground against her hand. He already couldn't control himself when it came to her, but when she caressed him like this, even through his pants, he felt as if he'd explode.

"Baby," he groaned against her mouth and reached for his belt buckle, then his zipper. But before he could take things further, his cell phone alarm went off.

"Dammit," he growled, then grumbled and dropped his forehead to her shoulder. "You're always starting something."

Chelsey giggled and moved to get up, but Parker stopped her with a hand on her hip.

"You can sit on my lap during the meeting. I'll keep the camera off."

She tsked. "Dude, and have you poking me in the butt with that stiff rod in your pants? I don't think so."

Parker laughed at the truth of that statement. His dick was still hard just thinking about being pressed against her sweet ass. That's the type of effect she had on him. It didn't matter the time, the day, or the place, his body responded whenever she was near.

"Oh, and don't think I didn't notice that you distracted me," Chelsey said as she stood. She adjusted her shirt and leaned against the credenza that was behind his desk. "We need to dig further into James and Debby. I don't know what they were up to, but they were up to something."

"I agree," Parker said. After pulling himself together, he began logging into the meeting.

He had watched the video footage of them at Supreme several times, but the only thing that gave him pause was their mention of *Sean*. It was too much of a coincident that they dropped the same name as the guy at the fundraiser. The guy who thought he'd looked familiar.

It was possible that Sean had witnessed the altercation with Troy and saw what went down when they'd been on Jeff's detail. Still, that didn't explain why James asked for him, especially when Laz had been lead on that assignment. If Jeff had been the client they were referring to, Laz would've been the person that James would've mention. Or at the least, Chelsey.

Out of curiosity, Egypt had put a call into Jeff. They were just waiting to hear back from him.

But whoever James and Debby were, and whatever they were up to, Parker would deal with them after he took care of Wolf. Right now, that was his top priority, and the takedown date was getting close. Very close.

Tonight, he'd find out when the DEA, ATF, and the Feds—

or as Rock called them, the alphabets—would be ready to move in on Wolf and his operation. He hoped everything would go as smooth as they all planned, but he was cautiously optimistic. Trying to hit Wolf from all sides at the same time was risky and almost impossible. Still, they were going to give it a try.

A few minutes later, Rock, Kamora, and the tech guy, Logic, showed up on the large computer monitor.

"Hey, you guys," Parker said and rocked back in his seat. He automatically found Chelsey's leg, and he rested his hand on her thigh, but then she linked her fingers with his.

It was like he had to touch her, and he was glad she never seemed to mind. It didn't matter where they were, whether sitting on the sofa, riding in the car, or lying in bed, if she was within reach, his hands sought her out. The touch of her was like a calming elixir, bringing him comfort like nothing else.

"Three days," Rock said by way of greeting. "The alphabets will be ready to move in then."

"Assets will be frozen, stash houses will be raided, and Wolf and his crew will be arrested," Logic added.

He rarely said much during their meetings, but when it came to looks, he fit the tech *geek* profile. Each time they met online, Logic, had on a checkered shirt with a print tie. Rarely did one match the other. Then there was his wire-rim glasses that were square in shape and could be considered fashionable by some. His huge afro always looked unkempt but that could be because he ran his hand over it or his fingers through it every fifteen minutes, leaving it standing on end.

But Parker wouldn't be surprised if there was more to the guy than his online persona. He was learning that anyone who worked for Rock had a story. He just didn't know Logic's. At least not yet. They'd get to know each other once Parker made the move to Miami.

He listened as Kamora filled them all in on a few more details regarding the takedown and what would happen after everyone was in cuffs. He didn't know how she'd developed relationships with the alphabets, but she talked about them as if they were friends.

Had she been a confidential informant at some point in her life?

He wasn't sure, but she was another person on Rock's team who Parker was looking forward to getting to know better.

"There's no way they can gather the whole crew up at once," Parker said to Kamora. "Have your contacts considered that?"

"They'll get as many as they can," she said. "The information you gave us about the walk-up apartment complex Wolf owns will be helpful. And it was confirmed that several crew members live in some of the units."

Luis had been helpful with that information, along with everything else that he'd shared. That apartment complex hadn't showed up on the information that Kamora had gathered. Parker wondered if they were missing anything else.

"There's no guarantee that we'll get everything Wolf owns, and the alphabets might not be able to scoop everyone up," Rock said as if reading Parker's mind. "But you know how the authorities are. They care about locking down the leaders of crime syndicates. If they can cut them off from the top, they have a better chance of dismantling the rest of the operation."

That was why Rock was still walking around a free man. The alphabets were never able to get to him. Sure, they got some of his crew, some who were still locked up, but they'd never been able to capture Rock. And according to Angelo, Rock's crew was loyal. When they were arrested, they kept their mouths shut and not one tried to make a deal.

"Are you ready for this?" Rock asked.

Even if Parker wasn't, it was too late. There were too many people and organizations involved now to turn back.

"I'm ready. I'm ready to take Wolf and the Kingz down once and for all."

He only wished he could be in San Diego to watch it all play out.

Chapter Thirty

P arker stood outside the restaurant where he and Chelsey were supposed to meet, but he didn't see her anywhere.

"Excuse us," someone said next to him, and he jerked, realizing he was in the middle of the walkway to the entrance.

"Oh, sorry about that." He moved to the side to let the group by, and his gaze continued traveling over the parking lot, but he didn't see Chelsey.

Where are you?

He pulled out his cell phone to call her, hoping she was okay. It wasn't like her to be late for anything, especially when she'd been looking forward to their date.

Her phone rang twice before she picked up. "Parker, baby, I'm so sorry," she said in a rush. "Time got away from me and India, and I just got home. Let me change clothes really quick, and I'll be right there."

Relief flooded through him. "Are you sure you don't want to do something different?" Parker asked. "I can pick food up for dinner or we can..."

"No way. You promised me a night out on the town with dinner and dancing and that's what I want."

Parker frowned. He didn't remember anything about them going dancing. Then again, considering how she'd been putting up with him the last few weeks, there wasn't anything he wouldn't do for her.

Two more days.

In two days, when Wolf was out of the picture, Parker could get his head back on straight. Right now, he had a one-track mind. He couldn't seem to think of anything else but the fact that his father was going down.

"Oh, crap," Chelsey grumbled. "I need to charge my phone before it dies. I'll meet you in front of the restaurant in fifteen min..."

When she didn't continue, Parker glanced at his phone screen. The call had dropped and he chuckled.

"Alrighty then." He guessed she really did need to charge her phone.

The good thing was, it never took her long to get dressed, and she only lived five or ten minutes from the restaurant. Yet, Parker doubted she could get to him as quickly as she was thinking.

Instead of returning to his truck to wait, he moved further away from the busy entrance. No sense in sitting in his vehicle when it was a beautiful evening. The weather was gradually changing into autumn with warm days and cool nights. As the sun slowly started its descent, a gentle breeze made it comfortable enough to stand outside.

While he waited, he called Angelo. They'd been playing phone tag for most of the day, and he was looking forward to talking to his buddy.

"Hello," Angelo answered.

"Hey, man. What's going on? Are you in town?" Parker

leaned against a thick wood pillar while keeping his attention on the parking lot for Chelsey.

"Nope, still in Miami. You know how much Zenobia loves the beaches, but I called to check on you. The big day is almost here. How you holding up?"

"Anxious," Parker said on a nervous laugh.

Most of his Atlanta's Finest team were being kept abreast of everything regarding Wolf, especially Angelo. He'd been instrumental in getting the DEA and a few others involved.

"I'm glad it's almost over. I can't wait to be rid of Wolf."

"I hear you, but keep in mind, the best-laid plans don't always work, especially with drug dealers. This I know," Angelo said. His time working undercover for the DEA had left a black mark on his soul. "I can give you fifty horror stories about how bad raids went or how we'd have everything planned to a second and then, poof. One small twist of fate and months of planning flies out the window."

Parker rubbed the back of his neck. "Yeah, I know you're right." Still, he was trying to think positive. He wanted a life where he wasn't always looking over his shoulder. That could only happen if Wolf and the Kingz weren't in the picture.

"However," Angelo continued, "I think we have a good plan with some amazing people working together. It'll happen, one way or another. You'll get your freedom. In the meantime, I wanted to let you know that I made a decision about joining your security team in Miami. Count me in, bro."

"Yes!"

Parker couldn't stop the grin that spread across his face. Angelo would be the second person on his security team. Chelsey would be first. He had already told Rock that he'd asked Angelo to join him. Rock was cool with it and said he had a lot of respect for his brother-in-law, even though he'd never tell him.

"That's awesome, man. I'm glad you're in. So I guess Zen is okay with moving to Miami?"

Angelo snorted. "Are you kidding me? Why do you think we're always here? She and her Mamita have been hinting around about us making this leap for some time now. So, yeah, they're excited, but with all of my family in Atlanta, I hadn't been ready to make a move this big until now."

As they talked, Parker glanced around. Despite the number of people coming and going from the restaurant, he zoned in on two guys. Dressed in T-shirts and jeans, they were making their way from the parking lot.

What snagged his attention was how they moved, how they carried themselves in an arrogant type of way. He recognized the walk. Hell, he had *mastered* the walk.

They also had their heads on a swivel as if they were up to something or expecting trouble.

More importantly, they kept glancing at him.

Okay...what's going on here? Or was he being paranoid?

"Lo," Parker said slowly, using the nickname that they sometimes called Angelo. He lowered his voice. "Umm, let me call you back." He disconnected the call before giving his friend time to respond.

The guys, still glancing around as they moved in his direction, split up, coming toward him from different sides. That was, assuming he was their target. He still wasn't sure since he was standing outside of a busy restaurant minding his own damn business.

He wanted his hands free—just in case. Slipping the phone into his pocket, Parker thought about his options. His 9mm was in his glove compartment, but he had a small Glock in his ankle holster. Or he could just fistfight his way out of whatever was happening here.

"Parker Wilcox," the first guy said when they were a couple of feet away. "Need to talk to you?"

"Do I know you?" he asked, trying to buy some time while taking in the situation.

He gave them both a quick once-over. One was tall, around his height, but not as big. The other might've been about five feet ten, with some extra weight on him—weight that wasn't muscle.

Parker could take them.

When his attention returned to the talker, the tall guy, he noticed the full sleeve of tattoos on his left arm, and his breath stalled in his throat.

Oh, shit. Shit. Shit. Shit.

He looked away. He didn't want to bring attention to the fact that he'd spotted a six-point crown tattoo with flames shooting out of the center point on the inside of the man's left wrist.

The Kingz.

The other, who had managed to move closer when Parker wasn't paying attention, didn't look like a banger, but...

Parker felt the muzzle of a gun in his ribs, and he gritted his teeth. He could disarm the asshole, break his hand, and put a bullet in the other dude before they knew what happened.

He wouldn't.

Not yet.

Not before he got some answers.

"Don't make a scene and no one gets hurt," the guy with the gun said close to his ear.

"If you don't want a scene, get that damn gun out of my back." Parker might've sounded calm, but inside he was fuming.

"Can't do that. You being former SWAT, you probably have a few tricks up your sleeve."

256

Someone did their homework, but the tall guy had called him Parker. Not *Junior.*

Parker suddenly had a bad feeling that whatever was going on here had something to do with the two visitors at Supreme the other day.

"Just want to talk."

"Then talk," Parker snapped.

"Not here."

"I don't know who you are or what this is about. I'm not going anywhere with you."

"See that little girl right there?" the other guy said of an adorable grade-schooler who was skipping toward the entrance of the restaurant with her parents strolling behind her.

"You either take a walk with us or I'm gonna shoot her. I won't kill her. I'll just maim her, then I'll do the same to her parents."

The last thing Parker wanted was for innocent bystanders to get hurt, but...

Ah, hell. *Chelsey.*

Dammit!

She was in the parking lot walking toward the restaurant. On any given day, he'd be able to spot her anywhere, even if he wasn't looking for her. But today, the yellow blouse she was wearing was like a blinking neon sign that screamed: *look at me.*

He needed her to get out of here. Or maybe he could go with these guys, and at least get them away from the restaurant.

Parker snuck another look at Chelsey, and she looked directly at him and smiled. But just as quickly, her smile dropped. They had a special connection, and Parker prayed to God that she could somehow read his mind.

Don't come any closer. Get out of here. Go! Now!

She froze.

Yes. That's it, sweetheart. Turn around and get out of here.

When she eased back, partially hidden behind a minivan, Parker released the breath he hadn't realized he'd been holding. He didn't want Chelsey anywhere near him. In case whatever he decided to do next with these guys went sideways, he didn't want her to get hurt.

Knowing her, she'd be able to read the situation and call the cops. Or better yet, maybe she'd send out a 311 alert to Atlanta's Finest. The code meant that one of them was in trouble, and the calvary would show up within minutes.

Right now, Parker needed to figure out how to deal with these bastards.

And how the hell did they find me?

"Let's go," the guy with the gun said.

Yeah. Let's.

Chapter Thirty-One

Chelsey's pulse pounded loudly in her ears as she ducked behind a minivan while keeping her attention on Parker.

What the hell was happening here? Who are those guys?

One thing had been clear, Parker hadn't wanted her to approach. Even from a distance, she'd been able to read it in his eyes. Then there was that slight shake of his head, and the firm set of his mouth, that told her to back up.

But what was going on? At first glance, it looked like three buddies in a quiet discussion. Yet, after a closer look, she could tell right away something was off. She didn't recognize either of them. And no way would Parker let anyone but her stand that close to him the way the men were doing. Which meant they probably had a gun on him.

And how was it that, with all the people milling about, no one seem to notice something was up with those guys?

Chelsey's heart was beating so hard, she was sure it would leave an imprint on the inside of her chest. As a former cop, she'd been in her share of uncomfortable situations that made her palms sweat and her pulse beat erratically.

Yet, this was different. This was Parker.

She needed to call for help.

Kenton. She'd call him.

She dug into the back pocket of her jeans for her phone, but it wasn't there. Hell, it wasn't in either pocket. A growl rumbled through her body as she unzipped her small crossbody bag, frantically looking through it. Her cell wasn't in the compartment where she normally kept it.

Oh no! *No. No. No!* Had she left it on the charger at home?

God! Please let it be in the car.

A peek back at Parker, and her heart sank. They were on the move. He was going with them. Why? He wouldn't walk away with them on his own accord, especially knowing she was there.

They were heading up an aisle, a few rows over, and Chelsey moved with them, careful to stay low in case someone else was watching. It helped that the sun had practically disappeared, and the parking lot lights, as well as twilight cast a subtle glow. She could track them while also staying in the shadows.

Nothing was making sense. Even if they had a gun on Parker, he could easily disarm two guys without breaking a sweat. No way would he let them lead him away...unless...

Had they seen her? Were they threatening to do something to her if he didn't cooperate?

Chelsey wasn't sure, but she needed to take action. Her car was only a few parking spots away. She could get it, but then what? She had to keep eyes on them. They were moving a little faster and seemed to be heading to a huge black SUV with dark tinted windows.

When they were a few feet away from it, Parker whirled around, catching the two men and Chelsey off guard.

Yes! Handle them, baby, she thought as she inched toward them, still staying low. Parker drew his arm back and slammed his fist into the tall guy's jaw, successfully knocking him to the ground.

Surely someone would call the cops if they were witnessing this, but no one was in the vicinity.

Parker swung at the other guy, but the man was ready. He punched Parker in the chin, sending his head snapping back, but Parker managed to land a few punches.

Chelsey didn't want to do anything that would distract him, but she had to help.

As she moved closer, the back door of the SUV burst open. She gasped quietly and ducked. She could still hear Parker and one of the thugs scuffling, and when she peeked around an old Buick, she saw a big guy leap out of the SUV.

She almost screamed Parker's name, but he saw the guy. Still, it was too late. With the help of the first thug, they grabbed him.

"Hey! What's going on over there?" she yelled in her deepest voice while staying out of sight, hoping to distract them. But when she looked over the hood of a car, they had managed to get him into the SUV.

Oh, damn!

Chelsey sprinted to her car, still trying to stay out of sight. She barely got in and started it when the SUV took off toward the exit. Thankfully, there were cars lined up in front of them. That gave her time.

She pulled out of her parking spot and headed for the same exit, glad another car was between her and the SUV.

While she waited, she checked her cupholder, the passenger seat, between the seats, and even the floor, for her cell phone. Nothing. She wanted to scream, but she didn't have time to freak out. She had to keep her shit together and keep an eye on that SUV.

They pulled out into traffic, and she was careful to keep a couple of cars between them. Slapping a hand to her chest, she willed her heartbeat to stop racing.

Breathe, girl. Breathe.

She couldn't ever remember being as scared as she was in this moment.

"What am I going to do?" she whispered.

Even if she followed them to wherever they were taking Parker, then what?

She didn't have her cell phone, she didn't have time to stop somewhere to find a phone, and she had no clue who she was dealing with.

But at least she had her gun and a switchblade in her glove compartment.

Still, it would help if she knew who the guys were and what they wanted with Parker.

No soon as the thought entered her mind, a sinking feeling engulfed her.

James and Debby—they had to be connected somehow. Or had Wolf found him? Had he somehow found out about the raids that were being set up to take down his empire?

Chelsey needed answers, and the only way that was going to happen was if she kept up with the guys who had kidnapped Parker.

When the SUV pulled onto the Downtown Connector in Atlanta, Chelsey slammed her hand against the steering wheel and cursed whoever was driving that SUV. Of course, they had to get on the most congested highway in the country. *Damn them!*

It didn't matter the time of day; traffic was always ridicu-

262

lous along that stretch of highway. And now it was dark as hell outside as she merged into the bumper-to-bumper traffic. At least the driver probably wouldn't notice her following them.

Now...all she had to do was stay calm so she could be a help to Parker.

Hang on, baby. I'm right behind you.

* * *

Wolf had just gotten home and poured himself a glass of whiskey when he heard his phone ringing in the living room. Instead of rushing to it, he leaned against the kitchen counter and sipped his drink.

It had been another chaotic day, and for the first time in a long time, he was exhausted. Mentally and physically, he didn't want to do another thing today. He especially didn't want to talk to anyone.

Pushing away from the counter, he carried his drink into the living room and settled into his leather recliner.

Peace.

Calm.

Silence.

This was exactly what he needed to get his mind to settle down.

He took another sip of his drink before setting it on the table next to him. When he leaned his head back, he closed his eyes and reflected on the day.

Life had gone fairly easy for him over the last few years. Business was great. He'd made some powerful connections having a few politicians and cops on his payroll. He also had more money than he could spend in a lifetime.

But over the last month, business had been kicking his ass. It wasn't all bad, but it was getting harder to keep up.

Sure, after gliding through life, it was probably his turn to experience some chaos. That was the best way he could describe all that had been going on lately. He lifted his glass for another sip but stopped when his phone rang again.

When he didn't pick it up, it signaled that he had a text message.

It could be important, he thought and stood to grab it from the coffee table. When he saw he'd missed several calls, a voice message, and a text from Elder, he called him back.

"Man, where the hell have you been?" Elder barked. "I've been trying to reach you."

"I've been busy," he said returning to his recliner. "What's so important?"

"We have Parker Wilcox. We got him over an hour ago."

"Okayyy," Wolf said slowly. "Exactly what do you mean you *have* him? What have you done?"

"We snatched him up," Elder said. "I have him in an abandoned warehouse, bound, and—"

"Have you lost your damn mind?" Wolf roared. "You kidnapped some guy who you *think* looks like my *dead* son? At least tell me you idiots had your faces covered."

Silence filled the line, and Wolf wanted to throw his glass across the room. Elder was smarter than this. Or at least he should've been, but apparently not.

"By your silence I'm assuming that's a *no*. So let me make sure I have this right." Wolf stood and started pacing. "You flew to Atlanta because of a *feeling* that some guy was Junior. You snatch him off the street and tied him up so you could question him.

"What's the plan for when you find out he's not Junior? I shouldn't have ever agreed to any of this nonsense. What are you going to do with him, seeing that he can identify you stupid jerks? What? You're planning to kill an innocent man? We don't need this type of bullshit right now!"

"It's him," Elder shouted. "I'm telling you he's alive."

"But he isn't! You stupid—"

"Be careful, man," Elder growled. "I just told your ass that your son is alive. Listen. To. Me. Junior is alive."

Wolf stopped in the middle of the floor. His mind was going a million miles a minute as he tried to process what he was hearing.

"He's alive," Elder said again.

Wolf staggered and gripped the arm of the chair before sitting back down, shock radiating through his body. "How's that possible?"

"I don't know, but I think it has something to do with Luis. After you and I talked, I called him and Shred, but I only heard back from Shred. He said that night, he left Junior's *dead* body with Luis for him to take care of."

"*What?*" Wolf growled.

"Yeah, he said he got sick and was throwing up, and Luis told him to go home. That Junior was a lightweight, and that he'd be able to lift him into the incinerator. He said he'd handle it. Shred assumed he did."

"But he wasn't dead," Wolf said more to himself, shocked by that revelation. "It's been over fifteen years. If Shred is telling the truth, Luis had to know Junior was...is...alive."

"Yeah, if only we could find him. He's not answering his phone, and no one has seen him today. Also, no one is at his house. It's like he's disappeared. But we're going to have to think about that later. I need to know what you want me to do about Junior. At some point, people around here are going to start looking for him. How do you want to handle this?"

Wolf stood and placed his hand on his chest. His heart was beating so hard, like it was trying to leap from his body. Still shocked, he tried to wrap his brain around the news. He believed Elder, but he wouldn't fully believe him until he was able to look this Parker Wilcox in the eyes.

"Don't touch him," he said and headed down the hallway to his bedroom. "He's mine."

He had a plane and a pilot at his disposal, but it was going to take at least four hours to fly to Atlanta. That would put him there around two or three in the morning.

"In the meantime," he said to Elder, "I'm going to need you to gather up supplies for me. The usual."

And by the usual, he meant torture equipment.

The timing was perfect. Wolf would be able to take out his frustrations on this guy by beating the shit out of him.

Not just any guy. His son.

Junior was alive.

"I'll have everything here when you arrive," Elder said.

"Good. Also, while I'm in Atlanta, have Slick find Luis. I want him hanging from the rafters by his wrists when I return to San Diego."

Luis was a dead man.

Chapter Thirty-Two

Parker's head was swimming as he slowly regained consciousness. Feeling like shit, he kept his eyes closed while trying to pull himself together. Whatever the hell those bastards had in that syringe had knocked him out immediately.

Elder.

Parker was almost positive he'd seen Elder in the SUV before everything went black.

Everything happened so fast. One minute Parker was throwing punches, and the next he was being shoved into the vehicle. He didn't remember anything after that.

Eyes still closed, he focused on his other senses. The air was damp and cold, and the space smelled a little like rubber and...cardboard. Maybe he was in a warehouse.

The only sounds were of traffic in the distance and several people talking quietly. He couldn't make out what they were saying, but there were at least two different voices. Maybe three.

He slowly opened his eyes, happy it didn't make his head

hurt worse. Glancing around through half-opened lids, he confirmed that he was in a warehouse. The space around him was empty, except for stacks of wood pallets to his right. Against a far wall, old tires were strewn everywhere.

He also didn't know how much time had passed. They had removed his watch, and by the feel of it, his phone and wallet weren't in his pockets. His gun was also missing.

He had to get his hands free. Which he was trying to do now. They must've used a whole roll of duct tape around his wrist and ankles. He could barely move.

When he heard someone approaching, he stiffened.

"Oh, good. You're awake. Parker Wilcox," he said the name as if testing it out on his tongue. "I had only planned to knock you out long enough to calm you down, but I guess I got carried away with the sedative."

Parker stared at a man who he'd known all his life. *Elder.* The person he hated almost as much as his father. Elder was probably the only other person who'd known that Wolf had killed Parker's mother. Yet, he did nothing except say—*sorry about your mom.*

But what had Parker expected? The man worshipped Wolf and did anything he told him to do. No way would he go to the authorities to report a murder, especially when the murderer was his oldest friend.

"Who are you? What is this about?" Parker asked.

He didn't know for sure, but he had a feeling that whatever was at play here had nothing to do with the havoc they were planning to release on Wolf and the Kingz. Something else was going on, and the only way he'd get any answers would be by acting clueless.

Hell, at the moment, he was clueless. No way they could know he was Junior.

Could they?

But if Elder was in town, Wolf might be, too. That meant they knew about him, or suspected he was Junior.

Did they also know about the takedown? That the Kingz would be dismantled in a matter of days? Well, hopefully in a matter of days. With whatever was happening here, all the plans he'd made might be ruined.

"Do you know why you're here?"

"No clue. I just know I was kidnapped."

"I wanted to talk...face to face," Elder said. "I didn't want to drug you or have you bound."

"Yet, here I am with shit running through my veins, and my wrist and ankles bound."

"That's your fault. You almost broke one of my guy's jaw. Of course I had to restrain you."

"You're telling me that if two people you didn't know held you at gunpoint, threatening to shoot folks, and then tried to get you to go somewhere with them, you wouldn't have tried to get away?"

Elder shrugged. "Fair point, but you didn't give us a chance to explain what this was all about."

"Cut the shit and this duct tape, then you can explain all you want," Parker snapped.

His patience was shot, and the moment he was able to get free, he was killing everyone involved.

That thought made him think of Chelsey. Since he was still with Elder and his goons, it was safe to say she hadn't called the cops. Then again, maybe a plan was being drafted to get him out of there. Because once Mason and the guys realized he was missing, they'd come for him.

"When my nephew Sean sent me a photo of you, claiming you looked like a friend of mine. I laughed it off, because there was no way you could be who you looked like."

Oh, shit. That was the connection. The guy at the fundraiser, Sean, must have snapped a picture of him.

"Does the name Maverick or Wolf sound familiar to you?" Elder asked, watching him closely as if thinking that if he stared Parker down, he'd crack.

"No. Should it?" Parker asked, his words slurring a bit, but at least he could keep his head straight. He stared right back at his father's longtime friend.

It was paramount that he didn't show fear and didn't break eye contact. For this guy to find him, he must know a lot about him. Or at least a lot about the persona that had been created for Parker Wilcox. If he said the wrong thing or made a wrong move, Parker could get himself killed.

No, actually, Elder wouldn't kill him. He'd take him, or try to take him, to Wolf, because there's no way Wolf wouldn't want the pleasure of killing him...again.

Elder folded his arms across his chest. "Either you're a hell of an actor, or you suffered some type of brain injury and don't realize you're Maverick Farron Jr."

Stay cool, Parker told himself. He had to keep this charade going as long as possible.

Parker frowned. "I don't know what you're talking about, but *clearly* you have the wrong person. Just let me go."

"Not yet. You're going to be my guest here for at least another couple of hours."

"For God's sake, you kidnapped the wrong person! I'm not who you think I am!"

"Yeah, and if you're not, then I'll apologize. For right now, sit tight. It's going to be a while."

The moment Elder walked out of the room with his cell phone plastered to his ear, Parker tugged on the restraints. They were tight, but if he pulled on them enough, they'd eventually get loose.

They had to. His life depended on it.

* * *

Impatience clawed through Chelsey as she rubbed her hands together while staring out the window. She'd been hiding outside of the abandoned warehouse in her car forever, but she couldn't leave. Not when they still had Parker. She was afraid to go in search of a phone or for help. Afraid she'd leave and return to find the thugs and Parker gone.

The industrial area was in the middle of nowhere, and it was scary dark where she was hiding. When she had first arrived, she hadn't been able to follow close behind in her car, but she'd been able to see what building they entered.

She was currently across the parking lot, partially shielded by another warehouse. Ideally, she'd prefer to be closer, but at least she had eyes on the SUV. Every few minutes, she left her vehicle and ran across the lot to peek through a window.

Parker was alive. From what she could see, they had him bound to a chair on the far side of the building. All she had to do was slip in, get him out of the restraints, and get them the hell out of here.

Shouldn't be hard at all, she thought sarcastically.

Slipping back into the black hoodie that she'd had in her trunk, she made sure her gun was on her, then climbed out of the car. It was time to get closer to the building. Maybe she'd get an opportunity to slip inside.

When she was out there, she'd been alternating between the front and the back of the building, watching and hoping for a break. The SUV was parked on the side near one of the entrances, and so far, all three men were still inside.

She had to do something. She needed to get them out of the

building. Maybe if she created a diversion outside, they'd come out and investigate, then she could slip in. But then what?

Noise from the side where the SUV was parked caught her attention, and she crept to the corner of the building and peered around it. Two of the men walked out and opened the doors of the SUV, while the third guy stood in the doorway. Chelsey couldn't see him well. Yet, she did pick up a little of the conversation.

"One of my nephews, not James, but the one you met yesterday will be here soon with a toolbox and some supplies," the guy who seemed like he was in charge said. "We should be back soon with the boss."

"Will do," the guy in the doorway said.

The boss? Who was their boss?

He said something else before climbing into the driver's seat, but Chelsey couldn't hear him.

Yes! This was the break she needed. She could handle one guy. All she had to do was figure out how to get in and out quickly with Parker. And she needed to do it before anybody else showed up.

When the guy went back inside and closed the door, Chelsey started checking doors and windows. Earlier she had found several entrances, but she hadn't tugged on them for fear they'd hear the noise inside. She could do that now, though. Find the weakest door or window that she could penetrate.

After going around the entire exterior of the warehouse, she decided to return to one of the back doors. It was on the opposite side of where the SUV had been parked. When she reached the corner of the building, the skunky, pungent scent of weed permeated the air, and she peered around the edge. The guy who had been left behind was standing near the door she wanted to enter, smoking a joint.

Oh, it cannot be this easy.

But thank goodness. This might be the only break she got.

Chelsey tiptoed back the way she came, looking on the ground for a weapon. She didn't want to shoot anyone unless she absolutely had to, but she definitely needed something to knock this bastard out.

She found a 2x4, picked it up, and crept along the side of the building again. Another quick look at the guy, and this time his back was to her, and she soon realized why. *Ugh!* His nasty ass was peeing up against the building.

Perfect. Now she had to try not to get pissed on.

She tiptoed her way closer, and as he zipped up his pants, she said, "Excuse me."

He startled. "What the fuck!"

When he started to glance over his shoulder, Chelsey swung as hard as she could and the 2x4 connected with the side of his head with a loud *thunk*. Without a word, he crumbled to the ground and didn't move.

Chelsey didn't wait. She dropped the 2x4 and rushed into the building. She was fairly sure there were no other guys besides Parker inside. But she took out her gun and kept it at her side as she moved through the space. Making sure no one else was inside took longer than she expected, but she was glad she didn't run across anyone.

"Parker," she whispered-shouted as she ran to him.

"Dammit, Chels, what are you doing here?" he said, surprise in his tone, but then he went back to tugging on the bindings that were on his wrist.

Feeling emotional at the sight of him, she threw her arms around his neck and held him tightly. "God, I was so worried," she said, and planted kisses near his ear, his cheek, and then on his lips even though they didn't have much time.

"It's good to see you too, but sweetheart, you shouldn't be here," he said in a rush, still tugging on the duct tape.

"I had to follow you, especially since I couldn't call anyone. I accidentally left my phone on the charger at home," she whispered while trying to pull the duct tape off one of his wrists. Those assholes had wrapped it tightly. That's when she remembered the switchblade in her back pocket.

"Come on, sweetheart. We have to hurry. Start with the tape on my right wrist, then my right ankle. Actually, don't cut it all the way through. Just slice it somewhere it's not noticeable. Enough to where I can break free with a good tug."

"Why?" she asked as she did what he said. Except she did both wrists before going to his ankles.

"If they come back before I get loose, I don't want them to be able to tell that the tape has been cut.

Chelsey stopped and looked at him when she realized some of his words were slurred. She set down the knife and held his face between her hands as she gazed into his eyes. They were glossy and a little red.

"Those motherfuckers drugged you?" she ground out, suddenly wanting to kill all of them.

"Yeah, whatever they used knocked me out and left me with a pounding headache. Not sure what it was, but my stomach's a little queasy too."

He looked exhausted, which was expected. She needed to get him out of there and checked out at a hospital.

"Are you hurt anywhere? Can you walk?" she asked, and went back to working on the duct tape around his right ankle.

"I'm fine, but we need to hurry. They'll be back soon."

"Who are they? What do they want?"

"The Kingz. They found me."

Chelsey's hands froze. *Oh, damn.* She had feared Wolf and his crew might be responsible for this, but she'd hoped she was wrong.

He quickly told her about the conversation with Elder, but

he wasn't sure if his act was believable. He feared they knew he was Junior.

"Do the left ankle, and then I want you to get the hell out of here. I'll take care of the rest. Go out the way you came in, and I'll be right behind you."

"No way. We're going together."

Maybe if there weren't drugs in his system, she'd let him dictate their next move. But he didn't look good, and he'd been sitting tied up for over an hour. She wasn't sure if he could run or even walk for that matter.

"Hurry," he said in a rush. "I need you to get out of here. They'll be back soon."

"I know, but I'm not leaving without you."

"Where's the other guy?" he asked.

"Outside, I knocked him out."

As soon as the words left her mouth, she heard the side door open. The one where the SUV had been parked. Chelsey froze for a second, and then looked at Parker.

"Give me the knife and go," he whispered, and she did. "Go! *Now*."

She squeezed his hand and ran toward a stack of pallets that would keep her hidden while she raced for the door she'd entered. But when she thought she was in the clear someone came from behind the pallets, and she gasped. A gun was pointed at her forehead. She cursed under her breath.

"You should've killed me when you had a chance," the guy from outside said. His eyes were narrowed, as if struggling to see her. No doubt his head was feeling like it would explode. But he waved the gun in front of her, gesturing for her to walk back the way she'd come.

Before she made it back to Parker, Chelsey heard footsteps and something banging against something. When she got into the clearing, a man stood holding a large, red toolbox, rope, and a tarp.

"Aw, hell," she murmured when their gazes met.

"*Chelsey?* What the fuck are you doing here?"

"*Terrence,*" she said through gritted teeth as disgust clawed through her body. "I guess I could ask you the same question."

Chapter Thirty-Three

Mason hurried down the hallway of Supreme, hoping everyone he'd contacted was in the conference room. Getting a call in the middle of the night was never a good thing, especially when it was about one of his people. *Parker*.

When he received the call from Angelo, saying that Elder and Wolf were in town or at least heading into Atlanta, it shook him. The first thing he did after that conversation was call Parker—several times with no luck. Then he called an emergency meeting with the Atlanta's Finest team.

The moment he walked into the conference room, Mason was bombarded with questions. Of course, he was since he hadn't given much information over the phone. He thought it best to talk to everyone in person at the same time.

"No Kenton or Laz yet?" he asked more to himself than to the others.

He assumed they were still handling the tasks that he'd given when he called them earlier—find Parker and Chelsey.

277

Since neither was answering their phones, he assumed they might be together.

"So, what's going on?" Myles asked. "Your message was a bit cryptic."

The former CIA spy didn't say much on any given day. Mason was surprised he was asking a question. Myles' motto was that it was best to not be seen or heard. Most of the time, he was so quiet, it was easy to forget he was in the room.

"Parker and Chelsey might be missing," Mason said.

"Are we sure they didn't elope?" Ashton asked.

It would be great if that was the case, but Mason didn't think so. Parker would've given him a heads-up even if they didn't tell anyone else.

"Not sure, but I don't think so. Angelo called from Miami," Mason said as he stood at the head of the table, leaning on the back of a chair. "According to Rock's tech guy, Logic, some of the Kingz are in town. Elder has been here for a few days, and a couple of hours ago, Logic was alerted that Wolf had chartered a plane. If he's not in Atlanta yet, he'll be here soon."

Mason told them he had Kenton and Laz doing an initial search for Parker and Chelsey. He explained that he was assuming they were somewhere together, but they didn't know for sure.

He had sent Laz to Parker's house since he was the only person, outside of Mason, who had a key and the security code. He also sent Kenton to Chelsey's place.

While driving to Supreme, Mason had heard from both of them, letting him know they hadn't found either. Kenton did, however, find Chelsey's cell phone at the house which was why she hadn't been answering.

"Are we assuming that Wolf and Elder might have them?" Ashton asked.

"And how did Logic find out the Kingz were in town?" Hamilton asked.

"I don't want to assume anything, but it's too much of a coincidence that we find out the leaders of the Kingz are here and no one knows where Parker is.

"As for how Logic found out, a couple of days ago, he began monitoring the men's whereabouts. This was started after Elder was already in town, but since then, he knows the guy rented a car at Atlanta's Hartsfield airport a few days ago. As well as a house near Midtown. He had Angelo to call us, to give a heads-up, when he received an alert a couple hours ago about Wolf chartering a plane."

"Do we know where the Kingz are?" Myles asked.

Before he could answer, Kenton and Laz walked into the room.

"Anything?" Mason asked as the two men sat in a couple of empty chairs at the end of the table.

"I called India to see if she'd heard from her or seen Chelsey," Kenton said. "She said Chelsey and Parker were meeting for dinner around eight. Over five hours ago."

"They weren't at Parker's place," Laz said. "And after Kenton told me which restaurant they were planning to go for dinner, I went there, but they were closed. I was hoping to see if I could look at their security footage. Maybe I'd see Parker arrive or leave, or something.

"I do know he was there, because his truck is in their parking lot. But there were no signs of either of them."

"Egypt called Wiz to see if there's a way he can tap into security feeds from city street cameras or neighboring businesses near the restaurant," Kenton said. "He's working on that."

Mason nodded. "That's a good plan."

"How does Wolf being here affect the raids that are taking place in a couple of days?" Ashton asked. "Will the FBI be able to regroup and take them down here in town?"

The former police detective still had connections with Atlanta PD. Mason just hoped they didn't have to get them involved.

"Good question. Rock and Angelo are flying in. They should be here soon, and maybe they'll have more information on that front. I do know Rock's assistant, Kamora, has put the agencies involved on notice. Letting them know Wolf and Elder's whereabouts and that there might be a problem. This whole set up is a little dicey because they don't know about Parker's past."

"How's that possible? I thought that's why they were working with him, because of what happen when he was a kid," Ashton said.

Mason shook his head. "Nope. He and Kamora, as far as I know, haven't shared information about the gang war from years ago, or anything real personal. The Feds know Wolf is Parker's biological father and the two don't have a relationship, but that's all they know.

"They're under the impression that Parker is helping them get inside the Kingz organization. Angelo and Kamora are the ones who sounded the alarm bells with information that convinced the DEA and others to set up a sting operation. They want Wolf and the Kingz off the streets, and they jumped at the opportunity to be involved in a takedown.

"I guess Kamora used to be an FBI informant or something. She has a contact in the agency."

"Question is, do they realize that these weeks of them planning a takedown might've been a waste of time?" Kenton asked.

"They are aware of a possible problem and are standing by until they hear from Angelo or Kamora."

"In the meantime, any other ideas on how to find Parker and Chelsey? We also need to figure out where Wolf and Elder are. Any confidential informants that might know something?"

He posed that last question to Laz. The former police detective still had his ears to the ground and kept in touch with his old CIs.

"I'll make some calls." He stood with his phone in his hands and headed for the door. "Maybe the Kingz have some other business here."

That would surprise Mason, but anything was possible.

"We're going to need to tap into every connection we have in the city and find them," he said, recognizing the urgency in his own voice. "All of them."

A cell phone rang. It was Hamilton's, and he grabbed it from on top of the conference table.

"It's Egypt," he said and answered. He nodded and listened for a few minutes before slapping his hand on the table. "I can't believe I didn't think about that. Thanks." He disconnected the call and stood. "We have a way to find Chelsey, assuming she has on her engagement ring. I forgot Parker requested one of our GPS trackers for it."

"That's right," Mason said.

The software was on Hamilton's computer, and with a simple login, it would give them access to Chelsey's GPS location.

Wiz and Laz had both experienced their women being kidnapped. When they came up with the plan to put trackers in Olivia and Journey's jewelry, Mason had loved the idea. Now, all the wives had them, and after this with Parker, he was thinking they should do the same for the guys.

"Gear up! We're hitting the streets," Mason said, and they all filed out of the conference room.

They needed to find Parker as quick as possible. If he and

his father came face-to-face, it wasn't going to end well. Maybe not for either of them.

Parker hated the man so much, there was no telling what he'd do to Wolf if he ever saw him again.

Chapter Thirty-Four

"Why is she here?" Terrance asked. He set the toolbox and supplies down. "Don't you know she's a cop?"

"Wait. What?" the guy with the gun, the one Parker thought of as Asshole #2, lowered the weapon and backed up. "I didn't know she was a cop."

"Well, she used to be."

Terrance moved closer to Chelsey, close enough to kiss her, and Parker growled under his breath. She was always telling him she could take care of herself, and she'd proven it plenty of times. Currently, she was the epitome of calm. Yet, he wanted to leap out of that chair and beat Terrence with it.

But he had to stay cool and wait. He couldn't let them know he'd gotten loose. Not while he was coming up with a plan for when Elder returned with Wolf.

That's who Parker wanted.

That's who he wanted to confront, because he was done hiding. He was done looking over his shoulder, and he was done living like a fugitive.

It was time for him to deal with his father once and for all. He had hoped to let the Feds handle him, but those plans might be shot. And since Wolf was coming to him, it was going to be up to Parker to take away everything the man cared about—the syndicate, his money, and his power.

"She came here trying to free her boyfriend, but I caught her just in time," Asshole #2 said, and went back to holding the gun on Chelsey.

"Her *boyfriend*?" Terrance turned to Parker and looked at him as if he'd just noticed him sitting there.

He really was a stupid bastard. Parker still couldn't believe Chelsey had gone out with the guy more than once. What the hell had she seen in him?

Terrance stood in front of Parker, and the hatred in his eyes was palpable. "You're the one who pulled the gun on me that night at her place," he said, getting in striking distance. "I guess you ain't so tough without your weapon now, huh?"

"Actually, I am," Parker said before he could stop himself. "I can beat your ass with my eyes closed."

He felt, more than saw, Chelsey ease closer. She must've been inching toward him the whole time. Instead of being four or five feet away, she was now within two feet of him. The others didn't seem to notice.

"Your uncle said don't touch him. His boss has plans for him," Asshole #2 said to Terrance.

"My Uncle E ain't here," Terrance said, nudging Parker hard with his foot.

He's related to Elder?

"Touch him again, and I'll kill you."

Everyone turned to Chelsey, including Parker. There was so much venom in her voice and loathing in her eyes, Terrance should be afraid. Instead, he laughed. He laughed so hard one would think she was Eddie Murphy telling jokes.

"*You?* You honestly think you can take me?" He rushed toward her, and Parker stiffened when the idiot grabbed the front of her hoodie.

She can take care of herself, Parker reminded himself seconds before Chelsey throat-punched Terrance.

Then with the quickness of a ninja, she kicked his legs from under him, sending him crashing to the floor face first. Nobody saw it coming, especially Terrance who was laid out gasping for air and holding his face.

"Get away from him!" Asshole #2 yelled, aiming the gun at her.

"*Maaaan,*" Parker growled, his hands balled into fists while he struggled to stay seated.

He had to stick to his plan. Sit tight until Wolf arrived. But that was hard to do while watching this shit. Chelsey might've been well trained, but guns could accidentally go off.

"Get the gun out of my face," she said calmly.

"Not until you get the fuck away from him!"

She struck. Grabbed the barrel of the gun, twisted it back toward the man until he couldn't hold onto it. Then she pointed it at him.

"Now, get on your knees!" When he didn't move, Chelsey cocked the gun, and he hurried to his knees with his hands up.

"*Damn, woman.*" The words slipped from Parker before he could stop them. "I think I just fell more in love with you."

She grinned. "Baby, you ain't seen nothing yet. Wait until I hogtie them and put them out by the dumpster."

Parker couldn't stay seated any longer. He stood to help her but stumbled when his legs gave out. Catching himself, he stood still until he got his footing.

"You okay?" Chelsey asked. She kept the gun trained on the guys while she rustled through the toolbox.

"Yeah, I'm fine." When she pulled a roll of tape from the

box and handed it to him, he almost laughed. "Great, more duct tape."

They made quick work of slapping tape over the guys' mouths, and then dragged them out back. Tying them up with the rope Terrance had brought with him was tricky, but they got it done.

"How do you want to handle this?" Chelsey asked once they were back inside.

After shoving Asshole #2's gun into the back of his waistband, hidden under his shirt, Parker retook his seat. Chelsey placed the tape back around his wrists and ankles, but in a way he could easily break free.

"I'd prefer we get out of here and let the authorities deal with Wolf and Elder, but I need to confront him. I just don't like the idea of you being here, but I know I'll be wasting my time asking you to leave."

She placed a lingering kiss on his lips. "You know me so well."

"I do, and if you don't leave, at least stay out of sight. Once Wolf gets over the initial shock of seeing me alive, he's going to want to inflict his own level of punishment. I'll be able to handle him as long as I know you're safe."

Chelsey shook her head. "I don't like this. What about the others?"

"Wolf won't let them touch me."

"Maybe we should stick to the original plan of letting the authorities..." Chelsey's words trailed off when they heard a door open, and voices filtered in.

Parker didn't have to tell her to get lost. She squeezed his arm and ran to the back wall where tons of tires and pallets were located. He hoped they were enough to keep her hidden.

Two men came into view. One was Asshole #1—the guy

who had first approached Parker at the restaurant. The other man walking beside him—Wolf.

But where was Elder?

As Wolf talked to the guy, asking him where the men who were supposed to be watching "Junior" were, all Parker could do was stare.

All thoughts of anything else flew from his brain as his past life flashed through his mind like a black-and-white film. *Gangs. Drugs. His mother's death.*

Asshole #1 stood back while Wolf approached, walking slowly as if approaching a dead body in a casket.

Parker never imagined he'd see his father again. Dressed in a jogging suit, something he usually didn't wear, he looked fit. He looked healthy. He hadn't changed much. Older, with a little gray around the temples, but what hadn't changed was the evil in his eyes.

"How are you still alive?" Wolf asked, looking as if he was seeing a ghost. He stood before Parker with his hands tucked into his pockets as silence surrounded them.

Parker wasn't sure what he expected to feel if they ever saw each other again, but he felt nothing. No love. No hate. Nothing. This man was dead to him, and he wished he had closed this chapter of his life a long time ago.

"Elder thought you had some type of amnesia and didn't know who you were, but that's not the case, is it? No sense in denying it. I can see it in your cold, lifeless eyes." He shook his head, looking at Parker with disgust. "You could've been leader of the Kingz. You had the brains and the balls for it. Yet, you turned out to be my biggest disappointment. What a waste."

Wolf glanced over his shoulder at Asshole #1. "Find out where everyone is. Probably outside somewhere smoking."

The guy hesitated. "Are you sure you want me to leave you wi—"

"Go!" Wolf barked, and the guy walked out the way he'd come in.

If he went to the back of the building, it wouldn't take long for him to find the guys that were tied up.

"How'd you do it?" Wolf asked, still standing several feet away. "How'd you live? I bet you feel pretty good about yourself thinking you'd gotten over on me, huh? *Fifteen years.* All this time I thought your traitorous ass was dead. You should've been burned to ashes, but no. Here you are."

Parker said nothing. Hell, he didn't know what to say. He could threaten the guy, tell him he was going to hell, or he could warn him that he was about to lose everything he'd worked so hard for.

But he said nothing.

His father pulled his hands from his pockets, and Parker zoned in on the brass knuckles that were slid onto his fingers.

Damn, that would hurt if the man tagged him.

When Parker met Wolf's ruthless gaze, the man smiled, and anger stirred within Parker.

"I'm not that punk kid who you beat to a pulp fifteen years ago," he said. "I'm a man who will fight you until there's no more breath in your body. But unlike you, I won't stop until I know you're dead."

Wolf's rusty laughter filled the space. "And you're planning to do some damage to me while you're bound to a chair? Really?"

"Get off me!" Chelsey growled, and Parker stiffened. "Let me go!"

"Ouch! Bitch!"

A slap reverberated through the air and when Chelsey cried out, Parker almost lost his shit. But his woman must've started fighting back, because Elder howled as if she had him by the balls.

Parker didn't wait. He leaped from the chair and crashed into Wolf, knocking him to the concrete floor. The move stunned him at first, but his father started swinging. Parker got tagged by the brass knuckles, but he kept throwing punches.

All the hatred Parker had carried over the years came out each time he slammed his fist into his father's face, his neck, his head. Then he wrapped his hands around the man's neck and squeezed.

Die! The word roared through his mind.

He ignored the way Wolf pounded against his arms. He clawed. Punched. Slapped at his arms, but Parker didn't loosen his grip.

Not until Wolf landed a blow to his temple.

Pain burst through his skull.

Stars floated in front of his eyes.

Bile rose to his throat.

He lost his grip on Wolf, and his father took advantage, throwing Parker off him while grabbing the gun from the back of Parker's waist band.

They both were panting, and Parker tried not to make a sudden move. It wasn't the first time someone held a gun to his face.

His father's eyes held so much malice, Parker felt it deep in his soul.

"You should know better than to start a fight with the devil," Wolf said, lethalness dangling from each word. "It'll never end well for..."

Parker grabbed the barrel of the gun as red-hot fury charged through his veins. Their bodies slammed against the floor. Wrestling back and forth for control in a tangle of arms and legs. Each struggling for the upper hand.

The gun went off. Two shots. The sound like an explosion in Parker's brain.

His mind swirled. His eyes blurred. His ears rang.

And Wolf went limp.

Dark, thick blood oozed from the bullet hole in the side of his father's face, and the air left Parker's lungs. He collapsed to the floor next to Wolf, unable to move a muscle.

He's gone.

It's over.

Numbness turned to relief, and Parker closed his eyes, struggling to keep his shit together. He had just killed his father, and the weight of that knowledge almost crushed him.

No, he had no regrets, but still, this moment was...a lot.

Parker startled when he felt a hand on his shoulder, and his eyes flew open. That's when he heard Chelsey screaming his name. Her fear was coming through loud and clear. Seconds later, her gorgeous face came into focus.

"Oh, thank God! Are you hit? Talk to me."

Her words came in rapid-fire succession while her hands slid up and down his body as if searching for a wound. He didn't have the energy to tell her he hadn't been hit. All he could do was stare at the gray concrete ceiling.

Commotion all around him met his ears, that were still ringing a little.

"Is he okay?"

"Are you okay?"

"Do we need an ambulance?"

Everyone talked at once. *His team.* Atlanta's Finest had arrived.

"Parker? Come on, baby. I need you to say something." The pleading in Chelsey's voice snapped him to attention.

He wasn't sure how long he'd laid there, but he forced himself into a sitting position. God, he was tired. Every muscle in his body, as well as his mind, was weary, and he could barely move.

Chelsey's arms were around him, and she planted kisses on his face. He could feel her trembling against him. "Please tell me you're okay," she said, tears staining her cheeks.

"Yeah, sweetheart. *You?*"

She nodded.

Parker glanced beyond her and saw Atlanta's Finest standing around, some of them gripping the arms of Elder, Terrence, and the thugs who had kidnapped him.

Parker had never been so happy to see a group of people in his life. "What the hell took y'all so long to get here?" he asked, and the laughter that flowed around the space soothed his tattered spirit.

His friends. His family.

Rock seemed to come out of nowhere. He strolled over to where Wolf lay and stared down at the lifeless body. Then he met Parker's gaze.

"Well, I guess this is one way of getting rid of the slimy motherfucker."

"Seriously, Rock?" Angelo said from somewhere nearby, and that started a swell of loud talking around the warehouse.

Parker tuned out everyone and gave Chelsey, who still had her arms around him, his full attention. He wanted to touch her, hold her, but he didn't want his bloody hands on her body.

Instead, he buried his face into her neck and soaked up her warmth.

"It's over," he whispered, struggling to keep his emotions at bay. "It's finally over."

Epilogue

Chelsey's heart was so full as she glanced around the ballroom where her family and friends were eating, talking, and laughing. The beautiful wedding reception, that doubled as a going away party, had been a surprise from her sisters, as well as Egypt and India. Chelsey couldn't stop smiling as joy swirled inside of her.

Since she and Parker had enough excitement in their life to last a lifetime, neither of them had wanted a wedding. They'd flown to Vegas last weekend and eloped, and those seven days away, basking in each other's love, had been just what they needed. Time to rest and relax as they mentally prepared for their move to Miami.

Four months ago, after the kidnapping and Wolf's death, she feared they'd never get any peace. That they'd never be able to bounce back. It had been emotionally draining going through debriefings, interviews, and reliving that horrible time in their life. But they survived, and Parker got the closure he'd needed.

They had also heard from Luis recently, who had settled

and was doing well in Spain with his family. Parker had shared the news about the Kingz being disbanded, and how Elder, along with most of their crew, were behind bars.

By the time the Feds were done with their investigation, tons of drugs, millions in cash, and Wolf's assets had been seized. Though the syndicate had been dissolved, there was always a possibility that they could reorganize, but they'd never be what they once were.

Chelsey looked up to see Parker heading in her direction, and butterflies fluttered in her stomach. Sometimes it was hard to believe she was married. That she had fallen in love with an amazing man who made her feel cherished and protected. Parker was more than she thought she'd ever have in a mate, and she felt like the luckiest woman alive.

"What are you doing over here by yourself? Is everything okay?" he asked, and pulled her into his strong arms, then kissed her lips.

"Everything is wonderful." She melted against his hard body. "What about you? Are you enjoying yourself?"

"I am. At first, it all felt a bit overwhelming, because this is goodbye in a sense. I'm leaving behind some of my friends, people who have become my family. Part of me is still processing that, even though I know Mason and the others are only a phone call away, I won't see them every day. It's hard, you know?"

Chelsey smiled up at him. "Yeah, I know. I'm going to miss them too. The good thing is, once we get settled, I have a feeling we're going to have more visitors than we can handle. Egypt already created a spreadsheet with dates of who's planning to use the guesthouse and when."

Parker grinned. "Maybe we shouldn't have showed them pictures of the property. I still can't believe Rock included that house in the signing bonus. It's way more than I expected and more than what we need."

"I agree, but I'm going to love every minute of decorating it." Chelsey tightened her arms around her husband's waist and stared into his handsome face. "Are you ready for this new chapter in our lives?"

He lowered his head and nibbled on her top lip before kissing her sweetly. When the kiss ended, he said, "Sweetheart, as long as this new chapter includes you, I'm ready for anything it entails."

Before you go...

Thank you for reading PROTECTED! I hope you enjoyed Parker and Chelsey's story. If you haven't read the rest of the Atlanta's Finest series, be sure to check it out on my website - www.sharoncooper.net

Also, if you enjoyed PROTECTED consider leaving a review on review sites or social media outlets. Thanks!

To get sneak peeks of upcoming stories and to hear about giveaways that are exclusive to my newsletter subscribers, visit https://sharoncooper.net/newsletter to join my mailing list.

Acknowledgments

I didn't realize, until a super fan (smile) told me, that it was TWO years between the last Atlanta's Finest story and Parker's story. Yikes! Well, I'm so glad I was finally able to get Parker's story into the hands of those of you who have been patiently waiting. However, I couldn't have done it without some help.

Huge shout out to my amazing husband, Al, who showers me with unconditional love and support! I love you, my dear!

I also want to thank Author Sheryl Lister for the gentle nudging (hahaha), and author Fiona Zedde for her unwavering encouragement and the much-needed laughs. Also, to more of my favorite peeps—Brenda S., Carolyn J., Claire F., and MidnightAce—thanks for only being a phone call away! Whew! I appreciate each one of you! Much love to you all!

And as always, I LOVE, love, love my readers! You guys are the reason I keep writing. Thank you for your continued support!

Other Titles By Sharon

Atlanta's Finest Series
Vindicated (book 1)
Indebted (book 2)
Accused (book 3)
Betrayed (book 4)
Hunted (book 5)
Tempted (book 6)
Committed (book 7)

**Jenkins & Sons Construction Series
(Contemporary Romance)**
Love Under Contract (book 1)
Proposal for Love (book 2)
A Lesson on Love (book 3)
Unplanned Love (book 4)
Bid on Love (book 5)
The Cost of Love (book 6)

Jenkins Family Series (Contemporary Romance)
Best Woman for the Job (Short Story Prequel)
Still the Best Woman for the Job (book 1)
All You'll Ever Need (book 2)
Tempting the Artist (book 3)
Negotiating for Love (book 4)
Seducing the Boss Lady (book 5)
Love at Last (Holiday Novella)
When Love Calls (Novella)
More Than Love (Novella)

Reunited Series (Romantic Suspense)
Blue Roses (book 1)
Secret Rendezvous (Prequel to Rendezvous with Danger)
Rendezvous with Danger (book 2)
Truth or Consequences (book 3)
Operation Midnight (book 4)
Casino Heat (book 5)

Finding Love Series
Legal Seduction (Contemporary Romance)
A Dose of Passion (Contemporary Romance)
Model Attraction (Contemporary Romance)

Stand Alones
Something New ("Edgy" Sweet Romance)
Sin City Temptation (Contemporary Romance)
A Passionate Kiss (Contemporary Romance)
Soul's Desire (Unparalleled Love series)
Show Me (Irresistible Husband series)
His to Protect (Harlequin Romantic Suspense)
His to Defend (Harlequin Romantic Suspense)

Sharon C. Cooper

Business Not As Usual (Romantic Comedy)
In It to Win It (Romantic Comedy)
Kiss Me (Irresistible Husband – Contemporary Romance)
Mr. One and Only (Baes of Juneteenth)
Fiancé for Hire (Men for Hire)

About the Author

USA Today bestselling author Sharon C. Cooper loves anything involving romance with a happily-ever-after, whether in books, movies, or real life. She writes contemporary romance, as well as romantic suspense and enjoys rainy days, carpet picnics, and peanut butter and jelly sandwiches. Her stories have won numerous awards over the years, and when Sharon isn't writing, she's hanging out with her amazing husband, doing volunteer work, or reading a good book (a romance of course). To read more about Sharon and her novels, visit www.sharoncooper.net